The Mark

Alexander Lycur

To those that persevere...

CHAPTER ONE

It was supposed to be a simple operation, or so we were told at the briefing. We're hunkered down on the rooftop of the Hilton in the dead of night, binoculars in hands, tracking a presidential candidate through the expansive windows of his five-star hotel room across the street. The general is splendid in his uniform. He has so many medals and ribbons pinned to his chest that were it not for an enormous paunch created from dietary excesses for the impeccably shined decorations to rest on, he would probably topple over. Cigar smoke fills the room by him and his aides, despite a no-smoking sign on the wall beside the entrance door. Earlier, we witnessed the smoke alarm in the room have its batteries removed shortly after a hotel employee received a dressing down for protesting. A small compromise had been reached with a balcony door wedged ajar for the billows of smoke to gradually drift out into the Central American air.

Who could smoke in this weather? The musty, unmatched humidity in forsaken equatorial countries make us constantly drip beads of perspiration. Agent Fitzgerald and I know why this presidential candidate is about to find out he will be out of the race to lead his country. I only need to zoom in on the large cigar to find the Montecristo ring, still snugly fitted around the base of the torpedo he is holding. There's more than one general running for the presidency, and almost all have hard right-wing tendencies. General Luis Lopez is the exception. He holds a strong authoritarian bent on politics but he's no nationalist. Most of his allies and financial support come from other spheres of influence around the peninsula. The cigar ring and its insignia tell me more about the fate of this man than the dossier we received on our way to the airport.

But we have bigger problems to worry about.

Two men. That's all the government was prepared to send. What a joke. Fitzgerald and I were handed our orders and told specifically not to talk to each other about our past: our careers, where we're from, or even about any girls. Nothing. This is a standard operating procedure that everyone breaks, and how can you expect not to? You're placing your life in someone else's hands and vice versa, so of course you want to know everything about the guy next to you. But this time we were unusually warned that doing so could have a grave negative impact on operational effectiveness. The point was hammered home to me in a private briefing with my colonel. I could expect a court-martial if I didn't comply. The powers-that-be probably didn't want us to cross-pollinate our disdain for this mission and work out whose boss was responsible. Then there's the usual defence that if we're caught, we have no real knowledge of each other, so it's harder to use this as leverage to confess to our captors.

Before the first briefing, I had never seen Fitzgerald before and to be honest, I suspect he is out of his depth. So then why the fuck are we here? Couldn't this be done by some right-wing militia who rules every city in this country but this communist stronghold? Fair enough our top brass were 'off-the-record' completely against our nation's policies of helping rebellious, uncontrollable factions instead of vicious dictatorships, but that would've been more effective than sending two of their own to do their job instead. We should've consulted on this and left.

I was so close to protesting. I had planned my walkout in the briefing room and was about to tell my commanding officer to go and fuck himself. I wasn't even told our extraction plan due to 'operational sensitivity.' Maybe my superiors know I'm at breaking point. I have had enough. For too many years, I was an unquestioning sycophant to the cause following stupid orders from stupider men who thought it would be a great idea to manipulate someone else's country for their gain. I've seen more than my fair share of soldiers die in jungles, deserts, cities, and towns to know I can't bear to see any more die on a whim.

But something stopped me at the last second and I don't know what. Did I realise it was no use? What was it? A complete de-sensitivity to violence and bloodshed? Or that I had nowhere else to go?

I should've seen an independent psychiatrist a long time ago. I can't trust the military's 'mental health officer' for the same reason I can't trust the military: there's no chance of impartiality. Last time I saw him, I was cleared for service within forty-five minutes.

I know why we are here. The official line: 'No chances of blowbacks, no use of private sector forces.' It's the motto around the barracks and the go-to excuse for why we are mobilised so often for overseas operations. The defence department and foreign intelligence services came to the conclusion that they should learn from their mistakes and keep everything in-house. No point in teaching people ways to eliminate the opposition, unless you want your operatives to be in the crosshairs of an enemy sniper's scope one day.

While we wait, I play a game trying to guess where Fitzgerald is from. I know he's not army intelligence. He's not even military. He's with an intelligence agency and was given operational superiority, which is farcical. I drew the conclusion on the chopper out here that my colonel rolled over for a general's star and to play politics while I'm offered as a sacrifice and stuck here taking orders from this greenhorn. It's a joke given the work will come from my right index finger and nobody else's. Fitzgerald can't even handle his sidearm, a lazy Colt Mark IV Series 70 Government. Earlier, he clumsily loaded the magazine and almost stowed it away in his shoulder holster with the safety off.

What shortfalls he has with weapons, though, he makes up for as a decent spotter.

'When are we going to take him out? It wasn't in my brief,' I ask.

'Relax, Buddy,' Fitzgerald assures me. He grins and his pockmarked cheeks lift and splay from his face. 'How many operations like this have you been in?'

'We're not supposed to talk about that,' I say. 'Enough is as good an answer as I'm prepared to give.'

'Oh shit. There's no need to toe the company line. Whatever company that may be.'

He snorts in laughter. Well thank God he's not some stiff. It relaxes me slightly. His jovial belly, pale skin, and receding hairline make him stick out like a sore thumb here. But then again, he'd stick out in any country.

'Been working jobs like this for about six years,' I say.

'That's good enough for me, Buddy. The only thing I hate about countries like this one is the shitty food and malaria-infested water you wouldn't use on your garden.'

'What about the language barrier?'

He snorts again. 'Does it look like I can't speak the language?'

'Well…Yes, it does.'

'*Lo Siento*,' he replies with perfect pronunciation. 'Buddy, you are the muscle in the operation; I am the intelligence. Despite my appearance, I can assure you I have gone through rigorous testing and, of course, I am bilingual. How did you expect to survive in a foreign country without me?' More snorting. 'I'll give you a little tip. Most of the training I've had prior to this operation means next to nothing when it comes down to the crunch. Instinct was instilled on us at the very start of the program. *Instincts* are what get you out of sticky situations. The only advantage I have over you is being able to read common signs when it comes time to run for our lives. Ain't that right, Buddy?'

'Then why are you here?'

'For the odd event that you'll need me to read those signs. You are a protected species in our parts. In these days of increasing humanitarianism, it's hard to find good help around here. That and I need to confirm your kill. This guy is very important to us.' A tiny snort follows.

'And how many of these missions have you been on?'

'This isn't really my specialty.'

'What the fuck? So *none*?'

'There's always a first for everything.'

'Then I better shoot straight.'

'I hope so, Buddy. Because if you don't, I'll have to follow through and make sure. Then we'll both be in shit.'

I chuckle a little. He couldn't hit the building with his pistol, and he knows it. But fucking hell, his first mission! This is bordering on insanity. This isn't the time for amateur hour with lives at risk.

'What's your speciality?'

'Interception and translation.'

We are even more fucked. I take a few calming breaths and try to meditate blinding rage out of me. When I get back to base, someone will be getting knocked out. I compartmentalise this feeling and save it for later. There's nothing that can be done now. We are here, right in front of our target and can get the job done. If I walked away now, I would have to go into hiding for the rest of my life for desertion of duty.

We are dependent on each other more than we'd like. Fitzgerald is surprisingly far from nervous. It's as if he is just going through the motions.

We share an ominous few minutes of quiet as we sense our time for action is approaching. Fitzgerald signals me and I reach down, pull out a Dragunov SVD sniper rifle from behind the ledge, and concentrate down its scope. The bulky frame of the mammoth rifle contradicts its relatively featherlike weight.

'To tell you the truth, Fitzgerald, I'm a little pissed off that I didn't get a rifle with a suppressor.'

'Can you figure out why that is? Do you also know why you're holding a Soviet issue sniper rifle there, Buddy?'

'Yes, I do. To blame the general's left-wing commie friends who want to take out their own man. The weapon is supplied from their own support base. A Soviet sanctioned assassination. Pity the Soviet Union disintegrated some time ago.'

'You're correct. But there are still Russian arms lying around in the jungle and there *are* still commies waiting for the right time to take this small but vital nation for themselves. And there's nothing like subterfuge to cause infighting and to destabilise a political party. You also forgot to mention that the few bullets you're about to let fly at the general cannot come from a silenced weapon, because there are no silencers that can suppress the flash your gun will make and hide where we are. There's also the trade-off between the accuracy of your weapon and the ability to conceal its muzzle flash. People don't want you to miss, no matter how ridiculously cumbersome the weapon is. And lastly, silencers aren't readily available in the jungle. You got all that, Buddy?'

Fitzgerald sure knows his plays. 'Yeah, I got it. I could hit him with your pistol four times before he hits the ground from here.'

'I'm sure you could,' he says seriously. 'All right. Are you ready to make your mark in the history of this nation?'

'Well, when you put it like that…'

A casual grunt of laughter. 'There he goes. We're just waiting for him to have another cigar with some cognac by the window. Bastard probably has it with ice.'

'Sacrilegious,' I mutter, viewing the large target through the scope.

An assistant brings an ashtray to the table by the window. The general takes a seat with an aide. He is a wiry man that could be confused for having a cocaine addiction as he perspires profusely inside an air-conditioned room. There are a couple of other aides or advisors with them. The guy closest to the general has only a couple of patches on his shirt that aren't shaded by sweat. He is giddy and appears out of control.

'Do you see that man sitting beside the target?' Fitzgerald says.

'Yeah, I do. Guy must be tweaking beyond belief.'

'Funny that. He's actually a paid informant. He is shitting himself good and proper and will probably get a bullet as soon as the general goes down. I'm just waiting for a signal from him, then it's a green light. Got that, Buddy?'

'What's the signal?'

'He wipes his nose with his handkerchief.'

I almost forget Fitzgerald's last comment. I am focussing too much on the general and where my first shot will enter his body.

'You have to hit him centre mass. No headshots,' Fitzgerald commands. The comment averts my focus as I see Fitzgerald remove a camera with a high-powered lens from his satchel. 'Just in case they decide to try and cover up our work, these photos will go to the international press tomorrow.'

A real piece of work Fitzgerald is, just as much as his employers. I don't care to think about the political consequences of a scion for my country in a foreign nation. I've just got to do my job. Ethics and morals can be debated later. I train the rifle back on the general.

I adjust the scope enough for the aide to be in frame as well. Too close a zoom and I may have problems getting the second shot off and the kill confirmed.

Our mole is sweating even more now, because he must know what is coming next. He continues to talk to the general who is lighting another cigar, and being merry and animated about it. The butane lighter goes out, and so does the aide's handkerchief. It pats its owner's forehead and then wipes some sweat off the bridge of his nose. That's it. That's the signal.

I am in a state of grace. I consist of equal parts of calm and focus. Nothing has ever seemed as real as this moment does.

Fitzgerald starts, 'You have a green li—' he says and doesn't even get to finish before I pull the trigger.

The SVD 7.62 x 54 mm rimmed calibre bullet ejects with an almighty roar. Its trajectory is truer than any sniper shot I've taken in training. The muzzle flash is distinct in the night air, as if we set up 100 camera flashes and took a photo of the ordeal. Fitzgerald starts snapping the microsecond the bullet pierces the glass and cuts the general almost in two. I can hear the camera with the distinct sound of its shutter flicking repeatedly.

'Hit him ag—' he says, preempting the second bullet before the roar cuts him of again.

As the second round makes its way to its target, I see people in the room look in our direction. The second flash from the SVD removes all doubt of our whereabouts to our remaining audience. The bullet crashes through the glass almost exactly where the first did, so much so that the entry holes overlap. It pierces his head and the sheer size of the calibre of bullet rips through the general's face from his temple. Half his head explodes and shatters like a dropped watermelon. There is only the bottom layer of teeth left as viscera flies across the room in a splash of crimson. Some blood, bone, and brain even reach the glass vase on the table at the other end of the room.

I realise that I just broke orders with the headshot. 'Shit, I'm sorry,' I say.

I am greeted by severe snorting from Fitzgerald. My faux pas has him in hysterics. 'Don't worry, Buddy. I've got enough photos of him when he had a head and face.'

I contain a snigger…barely. At least he has a sense of humour. I immediately start cleaning the rifle.

'Hey, fuck that, Buddy,' Fitzgerald taunts. 'We've got to move. They'll be up here in no time, and we have to get out ASAP.'

I peer over the scope at the hotel room and can just make out the advisor, shaking uncontrollably as he traces stray hair from his comb-over back over his head. The other men in the room are yelling and pointing at our position. We may as well have set up a beacon.

'C'mon, Buddy,' Fitzgerald says, already at the access door.

I take the rifle and follow. We descend the stairs in leaps, taking as many steps as possible. It is a dangerous game to play as one bad step could lead to a sprained or broken ankle.

After we pass the twelfth floor, almost halfway down the building, the noise at the base of the stairwell reverberates harshly. There are armed troops at the bottom making their way up. Fitzgerald takes the lead by entering the tenth floor instead of facing an inevitable massacre.

We sprint through the corridor to the elevator.

'You've got to be kidding me. They'll have it covered,' I protest.

'We have no choice.'

The floor indictor displays a pixelated number eight. With the SVD, I jimmy open the door and prise it as far as I can.

'You're going to have to go first,' I say.

He takes his cue and jumps to the stationary cart, falling awkwardly from the distance and sprawling himself over the roof. I join him a second later, the fall paining my ankles, especially after the punishment on the stairs. The door closes behind us and we are in darkness. I open up the small hatch and see the car is empty. If it weren't, the people inside would have known we were above them.

'What now?' we both say.

'I guess we're going to have to ride it to the bottom floor and hope for the best. If they're smart, they'll have every exit covered, but maybe not in time. Someone will eventually check the shafts and we'll be sitting ducks. Ain't that right, Buddy?'

'Yeah,' I agree. 'Give me your gun. I know how to use it.'

Fitzgerald snorts and hands it over. I lay the Dragunov down, as we won't be requiring its services anymore. The elevator descends, and we count the floors. It heads straight for the lobby, making me want to yell in good spirits at our luck. I hear the door opening but can't make myself open the hatch to see who comes in. Once the door closes, I lift the lid slowly and see a portly man in a shirt and vest...an employee.

I signal to Fitzgerald to wait and as soon as he nods, I carefully open the hatch and swing into the cart. Before the employee can turn around, I have a gun to his temple and a forearm around his neck. Fitzgerald joins us after I press the emergency stop button with the barrel of the gun.

'Ask him to speak English,' I say.

'*¿Habla Inglés?*

'Yes,' he replies.

'Access card?'

He burrows into his jacket and removes a nondescript, thick white card. I grab it and swipe it on the panel. Fitzgerald takes over and hits B1 for the basement.

'What's on the basement floor?' I ask.

'Storage rooms…and the car park,' he says as the smell of urine wafts up to our nostrils.

'Do you have a car?'

He doesn't answer me but instead goes back into his jacket to remove a set of keys.

'You're going to show me where, then we're going to let you go. Understand?'

He nods in terror despite my assurances. If I were in his shoes, I'd feel the same way.

The elevator stops, and my experience in urban operations automates my actions. I point the gun at the door for anybody who may be waiting on the other side when it opens. I use our poor friend as a human shield. But when the door opens, we are greeted with silence and an empty floor with nothing but parked cars that are tightly and orderly arranged. I check the areas around the doorway but find nobody. No ambushes waiting for us to exit and no trained snipers by the exit ramp. We are clear, but that will all change very soon.

'Show me where your car is and fast. *Run!*'

We rush to the end of the floor where all of the staff vehicles are. He points to his beaten-up white Ford.

'I'll drive,' I offer.

'No. I'll be driving, Buddy.'

I hesitate, mentally confirm Fitzgerald is higher up the chain than me, and toss him the keys. I push the employee to the ground and dash for the passenger side.

He reverses fast and spins the car's front wheels before jamming the gear stick in first and taking off for the ramp. He snorts the whole way.

'Ha ha. We're almost home free!'

'Keep your eyes on the road. Don't look at me, Fitzgerald,' I warn.

'Relax, Buddy. That was one hell of a trip.'

'Like I said, we're not out of it yet.'

He thumps his foot on the accelerator to get us up the ramp. We turn the corner and can see our freedom until we spot a BT-60 armoured personnel carrier in front of us. The machine-gun turret points upwards aiming at the roof we once occupied. Instead of braking, Fitzgerald accelerates and does supremely well to avoid crashing into its side. He swerves right and clips the APC with the rear corner of the coupe.

More laughter. 'That was close, Buddy. Really fucking close,' he says. '*Wooooooooo.*'

At the next intersection armed police stand behind barriers with shotguns raised. Fitzgerald picks a gap between two police cars in the blockade and accelerates towards it. I fire a couple of rounds at the policeman standing in our way, and he rolls to one side to avoid being run over.

'We're almost there!' Fitzgerald screams before passing the line.

Suddenly there is a tearing thud and I cower from the sound. If it were aimed at me, there would be no need to hide as the pellets would tear through the weak steel the car is made of like a ball bearing thrown at a large piece of paper. Instinct, that's all it was.

But the shotgun blast didn't come from my side. The force of the blast and the range with which it was fired projects Fitzgerald onto my lap, almost in pieces. The driver's side door has a gaping hole in it.

The car begins to slow. Fitzgerald's right arm and leg seem to be attached to the rest of his body by string. They are limp, and thick blood and morsels of flesh are strewn around the car and on me. He is conscious, though, and my thoughts are not only that he is about to die, but that I need to take control of the car to get out of here or I will follow his likely fate.

I've got no time to think about Fitzgerald, so I let him flop over my seat as I straddle over his body to the driver's side. Another shotgun goes off behind us, and the shell hits the boot with enough force to jolt our car forward. The car stalls from our switch, and I rush to restart the motor, the key turning and stammering the engine to life. I stomp the accelerator and swerve left to avoid the corner of a building. The right front of the car connects ever so lightly, and I'm relieved it's still driveable. The moist air whips into the cabin around my calves and shocks Fitzgerald like a cool breeze stings a freshly made graze.

'Ssshhhiiitt!' Fitzgerald yells.

'You've got to calm down!' I scream back. 'Otherwise you'll go into shock.'

'I can't feel my legs, Buddy.'

'Well they are there, pal. I don't want you to worry about that right now. We can get you fixed up, but you need to concentrate. I need you to navigate our way out of here or we'll never make it out alive…Are you listening to me?'

Fitzgerald doesn't answer. He is too busy looking down at himself, checking to see what is and isn't a part of him anymore. I slap him hard across the face to get his attention.

'Listen to me. You need to help me drive this piece of shit to the rendezvous point. Do you understand?'

He nods.

'I'm going to help you up so you can see the road. It's going to hurt like hell, but I need you up to know where we are going. You've been briefed on the exit strategy…I can only fucking hope.'

He groans and cries out as I pull him up in one quick and intense movement. He doesn't say anything as we hurtle through the quiet streets at three in the morning. The police and army will be mobilising and gathering resources to hunt us down. We were lucky they were disorganised and had not prepared interceptors. But it distresses me how quickly they came after the assassination. Did they get a tip-off? I make a mental note to question my superiors—if I make it out alive.

I slap Fitzgerald again with the same heavy hand as before. He seems to want to go to sleep. The slap wakes him up.

'O-o-OK,' he stammers.

He scrutinises our surroundings with intent although struggling to breathe.

'I know where we are…we're not too far off. Turn right at the next light, Buddy. The pickup point is a junkyard near the fire station just outside the city limits.' He smiles. 'Perfect place to store a helicopter brought in under wraps on the back of a semi.'

'That's pretty ingenious,' I say to nobody.

He has enough spare energy to snort a little.

'Left here.'

Sirens blaze behind us. Shit! There's no way I can beat their cruisers for speed.

'Keep going. High speed, Buddy. It's at the end of this road. You can't miss the junkyard.'

I throw the car into the fourth and highest gear. Thank God for the ghostly presence on the streets. I need to swerve around only a couple of stationary vehicles at red lights. We motor by huge billboards filled with Spanish advertising of the trappings of a first-world life. Sugar-laden soft drinks and exorbitantly priced fashion, all localised with distinctly Latin models. I almost laugh. Commercialisation is able to touch even the most resistant of societies. This could be anywhere in the world if there were no slogans.

I finally see the piled-up cars and a very tall chain link fence with spirals of barbed wire coiled on top. I slow down, then make a sharp turn into the yard. Fitzgerald is spot-on. It is a makeshift fortress with the build-up of mechanical carcasses surrounding the perimeter. A truly excellent place to hide a chopper just outside the city.

To my disappointment, the once-far flashes of police lights are noticeably closing in. We will have to be quick or our chance of escaping will vanish. As we enter the property, two armed men are standing guard with assault rifles and torches, shining them in our faces and flapping their arms to show us where we need to go. They must have known of our impending arrival from the police scanner.

Fitzgerald slumps in his seat, quietly playing with his bloody torso with his good arm.

'We've got to hurry,' I say to him.

'I'm not going anywhere, Buddy.'

We both know he's not going to make it, and it hits me in a way I haven't felt in a long, long time. He doesn't deserve this. Sent out on something so dangerous without cutting his teeth on something he can handle.

I can't hide that I am affected by his courage.

'What do you want me to do?' I say. I don't even try to conceal my emotions by wiping my eyes.

'Block the entrance with this car and give me a rifle, Buddy,' he whispers. 'You better load it so I don't need to. They'll shoot down the chopper if I don't give them a distraction and something to aim at.'

Sniffing, I nod as I get out of the car.

'Give me your gun!' I scream at one of the attendants.

Back in the car, I can hear the whorl of the chopper's blades spinning into life.

I take the wheel and the car almost spins out of control as I position it to cover the entrance. Loading the M16 and making sure the safety is off, I place it in Fitzgerald's good hand.

'Be careful. It's loaded,' I sob.

'It would be wrong to be in this job and not take a life with me before I die, Buddy,' he snorts back. 'Here.'

He hands me his camera. The bulky thing is as heavy as the rifle even without the telescopic lens that I have no idea when he discarded. He has the nerve to hand over the one object that got us into trouble and him into a bloody mess. I can only treat it with contempt for what it has caused. Spots of tears drip onto the camera body as if it started to rain. But the night sky is starry, and the moon is as loud as it can be, screaming light across Fitzgerald's scared face.

I instantly blame the second shot and this fucking camera. The need to record evidence of the kill and the stupid need for a second bullet to be fired to make our mission more complicated than it already is.

'You better get out of here,' Fitzgerald says.

I back out of the car and begin sprinting to the chopper, hidden around the back behind a wall of cars.

'Buddy!' Fitzgerald shouts.

'W-w-what?'

'Can you adjust my aim?'

I barely make out his request over the whooping of the chopper and the screams of 'Hurry!' from the agents already packed into the Black Hawk. I might not make it if I go back. But I can't just leave him there.

I lean through the passenger side window and over the door Fitzgerald slumps against to adjust the rifle he's cradling. I carefully fine-tune his sights when I feel a bullet whiz by my ear and into Fitzgerald's stomach, centimetres from my head. He sighs heavily.

I look up and see a policeman and press Fitzgerald's index finger onto the trigger to fire off a couple of rounds. Both bullets pierce the cop's head, and his brain matter flushes out the back.

'Thank you,' Fitzgerald grins.

A gush of tears fall on his shoulder. His dazed presence rips my twisted morals into an unexplainable paradox. I don't want to leave him here, but joining him in death won't help the situation. Any healthy body that can escape should. That's basic training. My legs buckle a little before I am in full stride. The finish line is the precarious safety of the chopper.

I follow an agent who had been waiting in the distance to the chopper. Its rotors are at full spin and ready to take off. The blades whip loose debris and dust into a tornado of junk. I am surprised that it hasn't lifted heavier car parts as well. As soon as I get in I am berated by the pilot.

'What the fuck took you so long?' he shouts over the noise. 'You're jeopardising our escape.'

I stare death straight into his eyes, quietly threatening to knock him out of the seat he's buckled into. Grudgingly, he raises both hands up apologetically and motions me to strap in. Now is not the time to nit-pick. I faintly hear the clatter of an M16 going off in the distance followed by a few automatic bursts from an AK and then nothing as the chopper lifts and banks away from the action. I have just enough time to see soldiers and policemen traverse the car in which Fitzgerald's now deceased body lies and in unison snap their heads up towards the chopper with amazement. I don't have time to know if they are shooting at us as the pilot picks up speed and we fly away unhindered. The whole sequence is an inconsequential haze.

So many minute events led to this fuck-up. Couldn't we have just needed one bullet instead of two? That's what a fucking sniper rifle is for: one-round kills. The bullets make such a mess of human flesh and bone that it is enough to kill with only a partial hit. I am certain I fired so true that I cut the general in two with the first shot. There was no chance he would've survived. Or was it the pathetic exit strategy devised by our superiors? Or the willingness of Fitzgerald to take the wheel? I shouldn't have listened to him. I should've taken the driving duties and started the engine myself. He wouldn't have complained given the hurry we were in. I had advanced driving courses under my belt, but he insisted. Maybe he had those skills, too? Judging from his driving, maybe not.

I can't stop crying and make no attempts to conceal this to anyone else riding with me. I am well past the point to be saved. Fitzgerald didn't need to tell me that we were doing this country a disservice on a whim. I'm not going to need the compulsory blackout of media when I return to my private quarters at the barracks to know the camera footage I will hand over will make the front page of broadsheets around the world.

It's all too much. I can no longer be a pawn for a government wanting to control other nations, while at the same time professing to protect its own people's free will. My life has been wasted by helping my country achieve these ends. It has cost me more than enough pain. And it cost Fitzgerald his life.

Fitzgerald was just a lowly ranked intelligence officer. He never signed up for a mission like that. He was a glorified interpreter for fuck's sake! He was nothing like others I've served with. Operatives with hours and hours of trigger time and training for missions like this. No, he didn't deserve his end. He was expendable, just like me. The fix was in…we were never meant to come home alive.

I stare out into the night sky as the chopper flies away.

There's nothing left that I can do. I'm done. I'm out.

The first thing I'll do when I get back is quit. This was the last straw. I didn't need any extra motivation to begin with.

As my eyes dry, they begin to sting. I look down at what I'm holding. I still have the camera and the film inside they so desperately want.

I toss it out of the chopper. They'll need a submarine to get it.

CHAPTER TWO

I wake with a jerk from the shock of reliving the past. I must have been sleeping for around an hour in the car. I grab my phone out of my pocket and switch off the alarm that was one minute from going off.

It's a haunting past I will never be able to escape. But why do bad memories always surface before working?

I have to concentrate. My reputation is on the line, and without this I am nothing to my employers and to myself. Once I step out of this rental car, I cannot let any emotion affect me from doing my job. I am a professional, and this is what I *must* do.

The clock flashes 1900, and I give myself time to adjust my hair like a narcissistic prima donna. I know there is a higher justification. Yes, I am probably suffering from obsessive-compulsive disorder over something that could be considered trivial, but the extra attention helps settle nerves. It's all right, nobody will notice a minor imperfection, but I'm not moving from this vehicle until I am satisfied. The devil is *definitely* in the details, and it's not my job to fuck things up…my hair and appearance is just one of them.

I am satisfied three minutes later, or so I think. An inkling of frustration tugs at my sanity, making me slightly uncomfortable. This is going to be difficult. There are so many factors, so many things that could go wrong. I am about to walk into a well-lit public place and leave my image and my face for witnesses to see and cameras to record. The heavy rain tonight is just another variable that I can only sneer at as it pelts angry bullets over the city. But I knew this already when I painstakingly went through everything over and over again like I always do, and this is why I can take these jobs and be so successful. It's all about planning. I concentrate on my breathing, push away any negative thoughts, and annihilate them. I refuse to let the ever-reducing protests of a conscience get in my way.

I take my briefcase and umbrella and get out of the car. I parked on the second floor of a multi-story car park a short distance from my destination because I know this car park is far more accessible than anywhere else in the area. Also, the exit is located on this floor, which lends itself to a quick getaway, and that is just as crucial as its convenience.

My expensive wooden-soled leather shoes crunch the broken glass into finer shards as I make my way to the stairwell. The concrete walls are scrawled with gang tags, and half the ceiling lights have been smashed since I was here last week. These random acts of vandalism prove my theory that this city is in such disrepair that if it can't control the misdemeanours of misfit youths, how can it possibly control more heinous and organised crimes? Short answer is, and almost all of this city's populace will agree, that it can't.

At the bottom, I open my umbrella and step into the rain. Crossing the laneway, I enter the deserted courtyard. During normal hours, this area would be packed with lunching workers, but people have more important things to do on a miserable Sunday evening.

I'm glad I don't.

I stroll past the brass bust of a saint in the middle of the courtyard. His hands are forgivingly open as if receiving grace from God for miraculously curing the incurable. I wonder if he ever had the same doubts in his ability as I do now? Of course not; he had God on his side. Large droplets of rain hang impossibly from the tip of his nose, defying gravity by not falling to the ground to join all of the others as a puddle on the pavement.

I trudge through the rain to the dominantly lit building in the area. It acts as a beacon for me to enter. The large letters spelling 'Mercy Hospital' adorning the entrance are barely visible without sunlight. Instead, bright rows of fluorescent lights illuminate the floor-to-ceiling automatic doors directly below.

I've been through these doors many times, but never with the sense of purpose they give me now. Stepping through the threshold has a new feeling, washing away any thoughts of turning back and forgoing the intentions of fulfilling a job I've done on many occasions and spent hours planning. I am ready for whatever comes. The small gripes back at the car mean nothing at this moment. I project that I am a professional and that I am the best at what I do. This is the only motivation I can accept. It's the only stimulus I need.

I am familiar with the long lobby and the unmanned service desk halfway to the secure double doors at the end, next to a set of lifts. There are a few palm trees in pots scattered evenly along panelled walls with portraits of the building throughout its inception, construction, and renovation. I know this because I have looked at each at least five times in the last month as people flowed in and out during daylight hours.

Before heading for the lifts, I conceal my umbrella behind a pot. The blue chequered carpet will be saturated by the time I leave. At the lifts I wait patiently for the first available and take the time to look through the Perspex window of the secure doors, which beyond that is accessible only by security-cleared healthcare professionals. There's an attractive female doctor chatting to a male nurse, directing her conversation towards a metal clipboard, and pointing to its contents. The nurse nods in agreement with her verbal prognosis, is left with the clipboard, and takes off in a hurry. I wonder what could have been so important that he needed to leave so quickly.

The 'bing' of the elevator's doors giving way reminds me of the job ahead. The carriage is empty. That's a good start. I take a quick look back to see if there is anyone coming that may be sharing my ride and have the chance to bother me. All clear. I enter and poke the tenth floor call button with a gloved index finger and wait for the doors to close.

They start closing when the attractive doctor I had just observed swoops into the lift to my sombre surprise. Shit.

Admittedly, this situation was *completely* unavoidable. How could I have possibly averted this chance encounter? By pretending to hang around in an empty lobby? Security would've been called eventually, and I would've been stuck in an even more awkward conversation. No, this is completely unavoidable.

She enters smiling as if she is having a good shift, while I keep my poker face hoping for the best but at the same time, planning for the worst.

Maybe I should act like a foreigner or play a deaf mute? What a stupid idea considering I have my doctor's credentials hanging from my suit pocket.

'Hello. I don't believe we have ever met,' she says while pressing the panel for the fifth floor and craning over to read my identity card. She continues to squint to evidence this and find out my name by reading the miniscule print. I would have preferred anyone but this inquisitive doctor.

'It's Dr Kruger,' I say extending my hand.

'Dr Kruger,' she smiles back, reciprocating my handshake. 'I haven't seen you around this hospital, and I like to meet as many peers as possible. Are you new to Mercy?'

'I've been here before but never as a resident. I run a private practice specialising in cardiology and very rarely make clinical visits.' I nod, remaining curt but pleasant, hoping to end any more conversation.

She smiles back radiantly but a little put back by my attempt to cut her curiosity short. Any other time, I could have a pleasant conversation with such a beautiful girl, but this is neither the time nor place.

'Oh,' she waits, searching for another opener. The elevator seems to be as quick in its ascent as if I climbed the cable cords myself. 'Why did you specialise in cardiology?'

'No reason. I just sort of fell into it.'

I gaze longingly at the number five she pressed and rummage through my memory to discover that I know what happens on the fifth floor. I can't be too much of a prick. Just enough to be unassuming and unmemorable but considering that she will probably never meet another doctor she doesn't know on an extremely quiet Sunday night, that premise was thrown out the window to begin with. What would a normal male doctor do in this situation?

I read the tag attached to her coat: Jessica Ward. 'It isn't as exciting as medical research, Dr Ward. Level five…is where the cutting edge *real* medicine happens.'

She giggles with her ego inflating just a little, hinting to me I may have overcooked the compliment, although it is better to put the attention on her. 'Well, thank you. I would be lying if I said I wasn't excited about the breakthroughs going on. You should be hearing about it sometime soon. Keep your eye on the journals.'

The bell rings for her and the doors open, to my relief. There is no waiting room or corridors to speak of, but a heavy glass door, clouded with a frosted finish, and a key-card entry system for access.

The floor is especially secured for a reason. The hospital boasts a research laboratory of world-renowned doctors and scientists in conjunction with the state's top university, a short distance down the road, working on ground-breaking projects that my new, attractive acquaintance is involved with.

'Nice meeting you, Dr Kruger. I hope to see you soon.'

'Likewise.'

She pauses, her gaze at me is too long for my liking. Maybe she is surprised to see a doctor she doesn't know? Maybe she is attracted to me? Any reason is not a good one. Stupid me for continuing to look at her instead of averting my attention. To what? The elevator panel and buttons? My watch? Any heterosexual man would be taking every opportunity to soak her up for as long as possible, and this is my only recourse to play it safe and predictable. Asking her out would be too much in this situation, as well as throwing in some gay mannerisms to deflect any interest.

She is certainly beautiful, though. I can't help but notice her golden blond hair tied up as if odd strands are an unnecessary obstruction to show off the soft and delicate features of her face. Her perfect skin glistens with faint foundation and eye makeup, even under the harsh and inescapable lighting of a hospital. On initial impressions, though, it is her voice and the way that even after what may have been a stressful time commanding staff, she can sound relaxed in a conversation only minutes after. I can't remember what carefree feels like as the doors close on my short-lived reverie.

They shut my connection to another world like a slap in the face and I'm left to return to the task I set myself to do. No amount of female distraction will ultimately disturb my goal and my sole purpose here.

The lift now seems to be moving like a Ferrari as I arrive at the top floor. I take a deep breath to clear any thoughts and feelings, and I'm as calm as ever. Stepping out, I see the main reception desk attended by a night nurse who is bent over at a filing cabinet. I walk by the desk without saying a word and into the main hallway. There's no reason why I would want to disturb her any more than she would want to be disturbed.

The tenth floor is post-operation recovery. Patients are at their weakest and carefully monitored for signs of complications from serious surgeries and procedures. Why they must be on the top floor is something to ask the hospital administration. I would've thought if there were any risks, these patients would want to be closer to the surgery theatres. This and it would've made my unwanted dalliance with Dr Jessica Ward conveniently cut very short.

I make a right-hand turn and spot the room I need to enter. Seated are two steroid enhanced thugs, more suited to a bodybuilding contest than a hospital. Nevertheless, they signpost my destination. I approach them with confidence and an air of intellectual superiority.

'Good evening, gentlemen.'

'Who the *fuck* are yoo?' the bulkier Italian heavy asks.

'I am Dr Kruger, the cardiologist to see Mr Luigi Baresi.' I smile back, handing my credentials to him to inspect, provided he can read, of course.

'Never heard of yoo,' he barks. 'Where is the regular guy? Y'know, Dr Carter?'

'Dr Carter has taken a leave of absence for a couple of weeks. I believe he is beached on an island somewhere halfway around the world. He has informed me of Mr Baresi's condition, and I'm here to do a few checks on his post-surgical condition.'

'We haven't been told of yoo…Fuck off!'

'Louis. Calm down,' the other guard says. 'I'm going to check with the boss. Just wait here and keep an eye on him.'

'I don't trust him, Mike,' Louis says, staring me down with bulging eyes from a boulder-like head perched on top of a mountainous torso. He certainly is one big unit who would be hard to take down without a firearm.

'Then just *watch* him, idiot,' Mike vents.

The door is left ajar as I overhear Mike explain the shady circumstances of my appearance to Mr Baresi, but I know the right phone calls have been made and coming here hasn't been a waste of time. The conversation ends abruptly with Mike coming out, disappointed he didn't have the opportunity to, at the very least, tell me to go and fuck myself.

'We've been told to look through your briefcase…Mr Kruger,' he says sheepishly.

'Good,' grunts Louis, snatching the case from my hand. My patience begins to wear thin. 'Put yoo hands on the wall and spread yoo legs.'

'There's some very sensitive equipment in there,' I object, while Louis frisks me. 'Some of it is quite expensive…and I didn't attend eight years of medical school to be treated this way just to see a patient.'

'Tough shit, pal.'

Mike rummages roughly, removing a box of syringes, vials, and anything that could harm his boss. I am unimpressed. It is akin to taking a hammer from a carpenter. How am I supposed to work like this?

'I find it highly irregular to be requested to perform a checkup without the necessary equipment,' I protest.

'What's *irregular*, shithead, is the person you're checking up. Anything happens to him, and you…are…dead.'

Time to be smart about this. I take a nervous gulp, giving the impression that I've just shat my pants. 'OK. I'll do my best.'

He ushers me in. The ward is bare. No flowers from well-wishers are allowed, and his drip has been recently changed by the night nurse. Half of the bed's privacy curtain had been drawn to shield the patient from the exposed window, which has rain streaming down the thick glass. The TV, perched on a bracket from the ceiling, is muted and flicks colours onto the pristine white cotton blanket the patient is resting under.

The old man sitting up in bed is more alert than I thought he would be. Most surprising is the gun he is holding. The barrel is aimed at my centre mass, and I can tell from his eyes that he is very capable of pulling the trigger.

Mike stands in the doorway watching my every move.

'Hello, Mr Baresi. My name is Doctor Kruger.'

'Yes,' he croaks in a weak, but confident voice. No doubt he indulged in too many cigarettes over the years. 'I was told there was going to be a replacement for Dr Carter. But you must understand that I would be a fool to not take precautions these days.'

'Understandable.' For what happened to him, I would have come to expect no less. But does he really need to point a gun at the vetted doctor giving him a routine checkup?

I look over my shoulder to see Mike hanging by the door, wanting to inspect my every action.

'Privacy, Mike.'

'But sir—'

'Leave us. I have everything under control,' Mr Baresi says, waving a Smith & Wesson variation on the iconic Browning 1911 in the air.

Like an obedient lap dog, Mike leaves, shutting the door behind him.

'I just want to run a few tests,' I say. 'Blood pressure. Pulse. General health tests to see how your cardio system has stabilised since the operation.'

'That's fine, Doctor. But if anything is out of the ordinary with your procedures, I will put a bullet in your brain. I don't trust doctors, and I certainly don't trust you.'

His gun is pointed straight at my head as I dig through my briefcase. Out of the corner of my eye, I see him tire, barely able to keep his pistol steady. It's as if my arrival was all he could bear and it has exhausted him.

I remove my leather gloves. Whether or not he can see, I have flesh-coloured latex gloves underneath. I carefully pull out a mercury manometer and tear the Velcro fastened cuff apart.

'Sir, you're going to have to change hands holding the gun.'

He obliges slowly so I do not have to walk around the bed.

I pull the cuff up his withered and wrinkly arm, squeeze the rubber bulb repeatedly until the main artery is completely occluded, and take his measurement.

He strains slightly from the pressure on his arm and slowly lowers the firearm. This is the fleeting window of opportunity I have been waiting for.

I cock my left forearm and crash it into his chest. Mr Baresi lets out a large whimper of air with little noise. The shock of blunt violence forces him to recoil and lose his bearings—and control of his gun. I anticipate this and lunge across to save it from slipping off the side and clattering on the ground, an event almost guaranteeing to alert Mike and Louis outside. My fingertips scamper along the pistol's slide. I throw my right hand to grip the gun and in the process almost fall right over the bed. I pull myself back up and on sure footing, cock the hammer, and reverse the balance of power to my favour in under five seconds.

'You move, scream, or do anything stupid, and I pull the trigger,' I warn as calmly and quietly as possible. Even with a firearm, I don't want two additional guests to join us. 'Nod if you understand.'

His frail body takes a few wheezy breaths, but he complies with gentle nods. A few decades ago, he would've been able to handle a situation like this and put a person like me in my place. But he misjudged his abilities, putting his pride before reason. I want to gloat but have respectful restraint for the old man. How the mighty have fallen.

We stare at each other in silence for what seems an eon. A proud man almost always in control now in front of an unknown quantity, pointing his own gun back at him.

During our standoff I can only guess at what he might be thinking.

The notoriety of being a *Capofamiglia* must change a man's mindset as much as changing religion. He's been on the front page of the daily newspapers countless times with rumours of his underworld war with Vincenzo Varetti, a stoush that has claimed fifty or so lives and almost his after he was shot leaving his mansion for a quiet walk six weeks ago. Gunning for the head of a traditional Mafioso family or even a *Sotto Capo*, an underboss, is anathema in this criminal society. The rules are changing, though, and quickly enough to destroy the respect of a man with Baresi's importance. His son has already been kidnapped and is presumed dead, but without a body as evidence, nobody can say for sure. Every now and then, a random body is found washed up in the bay, strangled, or shot in a hotel room. The papers have a count for the calendar year for as long as I can remember on the second page below the index, and it's only a rough estimate as those figures are all confirmed deaths while the editorials plead for the public to be assured of their safety. But not even the great Luigi Baresi is safe. Nobody is safe. *Ever.*

He stares at me as if peering into the vacuum of my soul to try and find leverage or something, anything to turn the tables back in his favour. I don't attempt to harden my gaze back at him. He will find nothing there, but being the head of a major criminal organisation, he will surely try.

'If I yell, Mike and Big Louis will crash in with guns blazing. So why shouldn't I scream?' he says.

'For one, you do not know who I am and the reason why I am here. Perhaps I am here to warn you, and cannot do this through any legitimate channels. Secondly, I have faith in my abilities from just getting here that in the time it takes for those two dumb shits to react, you will be the recipient of two bullets in the chest and one in the head. And lastly, Mike and Big

Louis can only guess where I am in this room while I know that they can enter only through one door, and when they do, they will be shot. If only one dies, Mr Baresi, rest assured that the other will not get far if he runs. But you should think of yourself and the collateral damage done if you do not follow what I say. The second-best possible scenario for you is that your next bed will be made of polished steel a few floors down in the hospital morgue.'

'My bed is already made it seems.'

'That's confidential,' I say. 'But Mike and Big Louis's will be up to you.'

After letting his predicament sink in, Mr Baresi murmurs in Italian and quietly chastises himself.

'I should have listened instead of laughed at them,' he says, dismissively. 'I should have known that they were right and that I should have been more prepared.'

'Who are you talking about?'

'They warned me. They said they were sending the best. Some freak of nature. A grim reaper.'

'I do not know who you are talking about.'

'Yes, you do. You fail to see that I know. I know they sent the best...'

'Who told you this?'

Mr Baresi raises his trembling hands with effort at me. '*Vincenzo Varetti* sent you.'

'Pardon me?'

He hyperventilates, struggling to speak. 'You...were sent...by...*Varetti*...to finish...off a job...he couldn't...do...himself! They said they were going to send the best. The *very* best.'

'I don't know who *they* are, Mr Baresi.' There's no point in hiding from the truth. 'I don't talk to them. I don't meet them. I don't speak to them.'

'I know.'

The standoff continues. The silence between us is something I've never experienced before with anyone I'm so unacquainted with. Is he full of shit? Is this some clever trick to buy time and hatch an escape? Should I shake him down for his sources or will my intrigue waste enough time for Mike and Louis to barge in? If they do I will be in trouble.

'I don't suppose a bribe is out of the question? I'll give you double what they are paying.'

'No chance.'

He nods, defeated. I try to sympathise, but I can't. The dawning of his regret is lost on me because I struggle to pity him.

'May I…' he says, his chin quivering. 'May I ask you a favour?'

'You can ask, Mr Baresi.'

He straightens and sits up higher in his bed. I check his hands as they swim under the sheets, but he rests them empty and on top of the blanket. 'I cannot change what you will do to me, but you must spare Mike and Louis. They are just lackeys and do not deserve such a fate. Louis is my nephew, and a little stupid. He should not have his simple life rubbed out on my account.'

The gall of a man who still thinks he holds power. I *must* spare them? I've learnt to never give guarantees.

'If they don't attack me, I can fulfil your request.'

'All the killing…all the deaths,' he mutters. 'As you may know, my son has been kidnapped by Varetti.'

'I know.'

'I believe he is still alive.'

'How do you know?'

He ignores me, instead straying off on a tangent. 'Do you know why there is a war going on between the two biggest crime organisations in this city? The media has it all wrong…'

'Not that I care, but underworld wars usually have to do with competition in illegal commodities like drugs. With the amount of drugs you and Varetti import and sell, I can only believe the media and say someone is stepping on the other's toes.'

'Then *why…why* would we be fighting over it now of all times? We've coexisted for years running drugs. And people think it's such a bad thing, too. All we do is meet demand. *No.* It has to do with something much more.' He keeps shaking his head in disillusionment and shock. 'It has destroyed many lives. Many more lives than you can imagine…including my family.'

I want to tell him off. I want to ask him about the lives he destroyed by 'meeting the demand of his customers?' What about the people addicted to his drugs? What about the crimes, the burglaries, armed robberies, and even murders his customers had to commit to get the money to pay him for the low-grade shit he peddles? His hypocrisy is woeful.

He begins to sob, but frankly I don't care. The longer you are in the vices game, the higher the chances are that someone with a grievance will want your blood. And unfortunately for Mr Baresi, that someone hired me to see it through with professional accuracy. I wonder whether I should feel anything, but I don't. He, of all people, should've known what he was getting himself into. For someone who has controlled a gang of criminals responsible for some vicious acts, it takes some nerve to want to repent, and the truly pathetic ones repent when faced with extinction. I place the gun on a chair away from arm's length, reach into my briefcase, and pull out a solitary, right-handed leather glove, casually slipping it on.

'I just want my son to be safe,' he weeps. But I am not an angel. 'Can you do it? Will you save him?'

'I don't…do…independent contracts. It all goes through my agency.'

'Of course…of course,' he mutters. 'My *consigliere* is looking into it as we speak.'

He wears my patience thin and I scan the room. His two bodyguards, for want of a better word, confiscated the tools I was going to work with. In not wanting to alert them, the gun is less than useless, but it isn't hard to improvise.

'I don't think there is much left to discuss about your condition.' Time is ticking away and I cannot entertain the notion that he was warned of my arrival. It *has* to be bullshit. There is no way there could be a leak. I walk to the empty bed next to Mr Baresi and remove a pillow.

Fear begins to take hold of him. 'Somebody needs to stop these people,' Mr Baresi pleads. 'It's *not…about* the trade of *drugs*,' he desperately bawls, alerting me that he may be attracting Mike and Louis.

'Then *what?*' I say, advancing, bearing down on his already frail body, my fist coiled back and ready to spring forward with venom. 'Arms?'

Mr Baresi's eyes bulge. '*No…People.*'

I stop, temporarily halted by his profound reply. What could he possibly mean? What people could he be talking about? More games, they have to be!

I unleash my fist, connecting violently with the old man's jaw. The leather glove cushions some of the sound the bone-on-bone connection makes. The crack becomes more of a low-frequency thud. He is out cold. I use the pillow to smother his face. He cannot struggle, as his body is prohibited from replenishing his lungs with fresh oxygen. I kill him mercifully, more mercifully than what he did to some of his victims over the years. I feel no remorse, even for a man who pleaded for his life and am not surprised at his change of heart. This is a natural reaction for humans. First, the desperate calculations on how to get out of the situation, and then hopefully, finally, acceptance. As I check his pulse to confirm the kill, I am disappointed he couldn't accept his fate like some of the many he brought to an end by his hand. He lived by his sword, and has died by it as well.

But I shouldn't think about it now. I have a hospital to exit.

CHAPTER THREE

I prop Mr Baresi's body up on the bed and adjust the oxygen tubes to fit snugly on his upper lip. Picking up the gun, I release the hammer back to its less lethal position. Should I remove the bullets? But what if Mike or Louis checks? What about the safety? The now-dead old man was waving a gun around with the safety off…no wonder he was so careless.

I grab my briefcase, quickly adjust my suit and think about checking my hair before I leave. I need to play out my exit correctly. I have no room for error and will need a little luck. Three things can sink me: Mike or Louis noticing the click-like noises from the mechanically administered oxygen stopping, Mr Baresi's gun, and the potential swelling of his face. Any one may instigate further query and trouble.

I clench the pistol by the barrel instead of the grip, hoping this will give the impression I am either very naïve at holding weapons or have no intention of a confrontation, or hopefully both. I end up leaving the safety off and open the door. As I step out, I try to casually close it behind me, but Louis jams his hamburger fist in the gap, surprised that I'm holding Mr Baresi's gun.

'What the fuck?' Louis says, seizing my gun-holding shoulder as a defence mechanism.

'Mr Baresi is asleep at the moment. I thought it would be best you have the gun. I think it would be safer this way.'

Louis takes the gun and switches the safety off before ejecting the magazine to check the rounds.

'Stupid old man leaving the safety off,' Louis chokes. 'What a crazy bastard.'

'*Louis!*' Mike says. 'Show a little respect, you moron. Check Mr Baresi.'

Louis peeks into the ward to see how I left him: looking dead tired.

'Mr Baresi said he was drowsy and has taken a nap. My visit was too much excitement for one day. He said that he would be *very* angry if he were disturbed,' I warn.

'Did you give him anything?'

'He asked for some pain relief medication, which I administered. Its main effect is drowsiness, which is why he's asleep at the moment.'

'OK,' Louis grunts.

'Dr Carter will be back next week, so my work here is done.'

I smile politely and head to the elevator. That was tense, but I did the best job with the obstacles placed before me. Can't congratulate myself just yet. See the job through first. Do not let your guard down and don't do anything foolish. Always tell yourself this no matter how many times you have been successful. Just being alive at the moment is only the start.

The receptionist is still at her desk, reading a chart and taking notes and she doesn't look up to acknowledge me. Two minutes later I exit at the ground floor, pick up the soaking umbrella behind the pot plant, and walk out. No need to run and give security something to think about.

The rain has stopped. The lull of the night is mesmerising and for the first time, I can appreciate my surroundings without the hassle of always being attuned to my task. This is my favourite time of night. A moist air remains after a deluge with speckles of stars poking through the benign clouds in the sky. It soothes me and despite my actions, I am as emotional as a Buddhist in meditation.

I exit the car park the same way I came in, and just as calmly. No need to speed. No need to do anything stupid. I am not even disturbed with getting hit with every red light on the way out of the city. Two marked police cars, lights and sirens blaring, whistle through a set of lights in the opposite direction, probably on their way to Mercy Hospital. I pass the sign for the city driving up a hill. The black 'H' for Hillbay City has been scrawled over with a thick red 'K.' This is not far from the truth. Over the past few years, 'Killbay' has come closer to describing this city more than anything imaginable.

Hillbay was named because of its geographical features. Surrounding the city is a delicate mountain range that gradually evens out and leads to the bay. A capital city spews from the bay inland from the major industrial port that provided its greatest economic benefit during settlement. Even during this time, 'Killbay' was labelled because of the settlers who slaughtered the indigenous population. Now it's gang wars and random acts of violence that the city is unable to combat, let alone deter or control.

Five million people live from the ranges to the bay with a bustling city centre, a major port with industry, no beach, and growing areas of a ghetto-like existence. The people living in the two-mile-squared business district survive in high-rise apartments. The affluent shifted out long ago to 'The Hills,' living in luxurious manors and mansions away from the rest of the city. Apart from this rich community, there are a few suburban boroughs that buffer the rich from the poor and the central business district.

I drive through The Hills. Each mansion must be sitting on acre blocks or more. High brick fences and wrought iron gates conceal everything but a view of their roofs. In all my years living in Hillbay, I have never seen a 'For Sale' sign here. Houses aren't just acquired here. This is old money, and nobody can just buy one of these gargantuan estates without some vetting procedures beforehand.

I'm sure people drive through here to gawk and dream, but I am simply passing through. It's just another community on my way through to Pine Lake: a secluded lake and camping ground with a small forest that trails around some of the ranges and eventually makes its way to the bay. It's a busy camping spot in warmer weather but in these conditions, I expect it to be deserted.

Once parked, I get out and check for any people in the area that may take an interest in what I'm about to do next. It's all clear. I pop the boot and remove a small wicker basket and lighter fluid and head over to the brick bench where there is a hot plate. The leather gloves go into the basket along with the item of my evening's discontent, a wig of expensive human hair, to be incinerated. Finally I am able to run my hand over my buzzed hair and attend to a few itches the wig irritated whenever I cared to notice. The fluid is sprayed on the pile before a Zippo is used in the cloak of night to set the whole basket ablaze. The leather gloves take a while for the flames to catch, but they eventually succumb to the heat. As fantastically crafted as they were, the unique prints of the leather could easily connect me to the death of Baresi, just as if I hadn't worn gloves at all. The wig is always a precautionary measure and is the only thing that may divert the scent off me tonight.

There can be no evidence to link me to the crime. It feels a little fucking pointless now, as there are three people I'm now at the mercy of: an incredibly attractive, intelligent doctor who, as a matter of course, should have developed excellent powers of observation, and two thugs who may be able to give a description, but possibly won't out of humiliation that they were so close and let their boss's murderer get away. I shake my head in disbelief. So this leaves one person likely to be giving them an accurate description at this current moment. What a fuckup!

I get back into the rental and drive to the city to drop it off. I am still wearing the latex gloves I wore to the mark, but I always destroy these at home so I don't leave any prints behind or spend any more time wiping down things I don't have to.

The exit from a hit is *never* as nervous as coming back. If you're going to get caught at the location of the mark, you would already be dead or in custody. That's poor planning and even worse execution. No, the escape is never hard. Those who haven't prepared or are devoid of nerve will panic and shit themselves. They speed, do stupid things, and get caught. The ride back is the worst. It's when the mind plays games on itself. It's breaking through the invisible barrier of the city limits that trigger waves of paranoia. During my escape, the cops would be falling over themselves piecing together what happened. Roadblocks may be set, but unless I'm caught in the act, the police will not know who to arrest or apprehend.

By now, they would've had time to review the CCTV footage from the hospital and may even have an idea of my appearance. The general public will slowly be informed by radio and TV, and by tomorrow, the newspapers will be filled with the death of one of the most notorious crime figures in the history of the nation. Witness statements will be recorded and compositions will be drawn. How close they are to my appearance will depend on the gapingly large mistake of riding an elevator with that one viable witness. Is this the end of my career in this city? But what could I have done? Searched her out and killed her because she's a witness?

It's best not to think. I turn the radio on and flick to a station playing classical music for a distraction and to avoid any news bulletins that might interrupt commercial stations. I enter the outer suburbs, sticking to the main roads. I sit at a set of lights at a major intersection. In my rearview, a cop car motors casually behind me. Just fucking great! The intersection is quiet with only another car on the other side, waiting, like my neighbourly policeman and me. A car flashes past in front of us to catch the amber. The cop doesn't pursue. Why? It was clearly an infringement. He was speeding, it was easy to tell, but I sense the cop is more interested in me. Maybe he is lazy and doesn't want to interrupt the end of his lonely shift with paperwork by pursuing a law-breaker.

The light turns green and I accelerate with caution. What is he doing? He tailgates, maybe checking the number plate of the rental. I know what I have to do. It's time to take the necessary steps to protect myself. I reach under the seat and grab my Heckler and Koch USP with a homemade, disposable silencer and place it down the side of the driver's seat, easily within distance while still remaining hidden. The cop turns his lights on for me to pull over.

I've never killed a cop, well, at least not in my own country. I do not want to start now, but I may not have the choice. If it happens, it will only make matters worse and therefore make my night and the rest of my life impossible. Killing someone like Luigi Baresi is hard enough, but the truth is, society doesn't see men as equals. If I kill this cop, I offend society even more than if I just killed Baresi. This cop passed exams and tests and is honoured to be an instrument of this state and its people. He's out to do their bidding by keeping the streets safe. If I take him out, the police will stop at nothing to track down the person who killed one of their own. And the society I am reintegrating back into will be so jumpy, so on edge, I'll have to disappear. This is the problem I now must confront.

If he is the second person I have to kill tonight, so be it. It's either him or me. And I am sure it won't be me if it comes down to it.

I oblige his request by double-parking. He shouldn't have any issue with this, as there is not a spare curb to legally park for as far as I can see. I dangle my hands between my legs and over the seat and slip off the latex gloves I've worn for most of the night. I throw them as far under the seat as I can.

Eventually the solitary officer, a thickly built male who stretches his shirt by simply breathing, lumbers out of the squad car and approaches my driver's side window.

'Good evening, sir,' he says.

'Hello, Officer.'

'Licence, please.'

He brandishes a large Maglite and shines it into the cabin of the rental. I burrow into my suit jacket and retrieve my wallet. He inspects the picture, glances at me, rechecks it, and glances again. How many times do you need to check a photo against the person who's right in front of it? Is it instant memory loss? I can try and convince myself of these stupid observations, but this situation is only going south and I need to be ready for alternative arrangements. Maybe there will need to be two deaths tonight because there's no way I'm going to be apprehended. I have the upper hand. I have the drive, the initiative, the element of surprise, and most importantly the willingness to act first with lethal intent. I move my right hand over to beside the seat, casually gripping my pistol. 'Any reason why you'd be using a rental car, Mr Drummond?'

'It's a business write-off,' I say, cocking the hammer quietly.

'What line of work do you do?'

'Financial consulting.'

'Financial consulting…and you work on a Sunday night?'

His tone makes me want to take my chances right now. Do you know this could be the last thing you say? How will you be able to reach for your gun if I pull mine out and point it at you? Your hands are nowhere near your pistol.

'I have some pressing clients in The Hills.'

With my free hand, I dive back into the same pocket and extract a business card. He takes his time inspecting the card. The gold embossing and impressive simplistic layout may have done the trick.

'Got any investment tips?' he inquires, either half-heartedly for advice or to see if I'm a sham.

He won't be dying tonight. 'Of course. You can't go wrong with anything to do with sustainable energy. You know how politically correct this world is becoming. They're guaranteed excellent yields. How much are you considering investing?'

'About $20,000. Not much for you big players,' he says, more relaxed.

'Big players were all small players at one point. Why don't you take the card, do a little online research on the firm to see if we match your needs. If you want to know more, give me a call sometime and I'll be glad to set you up with one of my juniors for a great investment portfolio.'

'Think I might do that,' he smiles. 'You better be careful driving home…we've been told to pull over random cars this evening.'

'Oh. Why?'

'The crime boss Luigi Baresi has just died at Mercy's.'

Has just died? 'Oh, wow. What happened? The papers say that he was doing well after the operation.'

'I don't know. I read the same thing. To be honest, at the station he is a touchy subject. I mean, are we supposed to care about him if he's done terrible things to people? Is it right to let someone like him die? The circumstances around his death are very suspicious to me. The details are still sketchy about what happened. Maybe it was all of those surgeries; maybe it was something worse. They're still trying to determine the cause. All I know for now is that I have my orders, and my orders are to check randoms on my beat.' He leans over and I think he wants to check what's in my briefcase, sitting innocently on the passenger's seat, until he turns his head and looks down the side of the car into nothingness. He wants to tell me something in confidence. He bends over and whispers, 'You're a smart guy. If something didn't happen, why would they be asking me specifically do random checks? I mean c'mon. Don't you think these orders are fishy? Until *something* is confirmed, every cop's going to be thinking the worst. I'm on the lookout for anything, or anyone suspicious, that's it. I report to the sergeant if I think anything isn't right.'

'I wholeheartedly agree with you about everything. You, as a cop, have been asked to protect a man when usually you're protecting society from people like him. It's a moral conundrum that's hard to resolve. And your orders are certainly strange if he died of natural causes.'

He nods. 'Oh, well. Not much I can do about it now…but enough of my problems,' he says, handing me back my licence. 'Be careful on the roads home.'

'Will do, sir.'

Only until I can see the cop safely in his squad car through the rearview mirror do I replace the hammer of the pistol still in my hand. It wasn't me who was lucky, but him. I feel like I have to check my nerves. No, I'm not stressed at all, and I raise and level my free hand just to prove the episode didn't affect me. Not even close to a shudder, let alone a shake.

I wind the window up, drag the gloves back from under my seat with my foot and pull them back on, then give them a quick inspection for incidental tears. I restart the car and drive on while the cop car follows me for a block and makes a left heading towards the docks.

I drop the car off in front of the rental dealership and take the time to carefully wipe down the steering wheel for prints with a clean cloth from my briefcase. *No need to stress. Do your job like you've done plenty of times before.* I go over the same items again just to be sure and even wipe the backseat, boot, and the exterior door handles, just in case. If the cop decides to call the card I gave him, he will be put through to the real Mr Alvin Drummond, stockbroker. And even if Alvin is to be quizzed with tonight's events, with the current climate and need for clients, he'll do anything for extra brokerage fees. It's a pity he has no idea I stole his identity because I would expect a thanks for the referral. I break out a small DustBuster and carefully clean the floor to remove any soil I picked up from Pine Lake.

I unscrew the silencer and place it, the gun, and the used latex gloves into my briefcase. I take the time and check that everything has been accounted for. The rental car's keys are tucked into an envelope and dropped into a chute at the door of the dealership.

Before I go to bed tonight, I'll destroy all of my clothing along with the gloves.

Fog has smothered the city's skyline as I decide to walk casually to my apartment a couple of blocks away. I try and enjoy the empty city at a time when not many people are able to. After all, most will be getting up in about an hour for their nine-to-five desk jockey jobs. Normally, I'll be sleeping through until about midday and wait for contact from my handler, which is never by phone, to meet up in around a week's time.

Tonight's rest will be anything but normal. There's just too much on my mind.

It's the gaping holes I can't shake. Baresi's cryptic warning bugs me, but the ramblings of an old man begging for his life are not my primary concern. It's the woman. There's a good chance I'll be packing my bags and fleeing the city I grew up in and lived for most of my life.

Well, my perfect record had to end sometime.

CHAPTER FOUR

I've slept a total of eight hours in the last seven nights. Since getting home from the Baresi hit, the TV has not turned off. I haven't done myself any favours by periodically switching between all of the major channels for any developments since the aftermath and funeral of Mr Baresi. Since then, nothing. The news said he died from complications from surgery. What bullshit! There's no way the cops could come to that conclusion. They would have needed a blind man run the autopsy for any chance of such a finding. And just because the media has dismissed the death doesn't mean I'm in the clear at all.

If the police don't have any good intel, leaking such misinformation would help them out. They want to lull me into a false sense of security. I'll walk out of my building and get nabbed as soon as they spot me. If the corruption in the force is as bad as it is, there'll be an overlap and a joining of effort to hunt me down. Baresi's men will be sharing police resources to get their revenge.

I'm not the type of person who gets cabin fever, but this is testing my limits. There hasn't been a hint of a manhunt or a description or police composition of me anywhere for any unrelated or fictional crime. It just doesn't add up. I still have a large bag packed and waiting on the chance that I'll need to flee in a hurry. It's impossible, I know, but maybe the police have tracked me down to my apartment; maybe they're taunting me before storming in and cutting me down.

'Aargh.'

I'm too tired to think about it. Why am I still here? Why haven't I moved on yet?

I know exactly why. There are loose ends to tie up. As I sip on a flat white from my espresso machine, I see the telescope by the French window in the living room. It's a burning reminder why I haven't bolted from Hillbay. I've got to make contact with management. I've got to make contact with my handler.

I walk over to the telescope and am careful not to interfere with it in any way. Its current settings are important, and I crouch down and carefully readjust its focus to check it once more to confirm what I saw yesterday. I'm so tired I don't know what to think. Was it real?

The viewfinder is pointed straight at a lamppost a number of blocks away. One small shift and it will take me a while to retrain the telescope into this position again.

I look through it for the third time today, conscious that sleep deprivation may cause me to hallucinate. Yep, the masking tape is still there, with two rows neatly wrapped at around chest height. The sign is as obvious as the sun. He wants to meet, and it is safe to do so. Contact has been made and agreed upon for 1400 today, which is less than an hour from now, hence two circular rings and not one or three.

We have other codes and signposts for signals through the city, but this one is important. My handler doesn't know where I live and neither does the agency. But we prearranged *that* telephone pole for contact after any job. He knows I can view the pole from somewhere or that I walk by it on occasion; he just doesn't know where or when.

I have to expect the worst. And the worst is that it's over. What my handler will tell me is the agency's intel from within the police department is that they are looking for me. This will force me to take flight. He'll confirm the balance of payment for the job and not ask for anything else as no work is available or will be in the future. In other words, it is time to move on.

I look out of the window of my studio apartment, down at the white-collared workers below, scurrying about in their business suits to lunch appointments. In the week since Mr Baresi died, I'm half a million dollars richer. My largest single payment will probably be my last. But in truth I never did it solely for the money. I was gifted in a craft that is getting harder to be great at.

I followed the code to the letter and had the discipline and skills to succeed. I thought everything through, planned appropriately and adapted whenever and wherever it was called for. Certain times called for certain measures. Fluidity and measured responses to the curveballs are critical. Sometimes it's needed to even get to the mark. To be able to get behind that closed door requires abilities beyond standard military operations, but social skills not normally associated with an assassin. No two situations can be treated the same way. Sometimes it's best to be an extrovert to avoid suspicion, or as with Dr Kruger, somewhat fearful when pressed by a heavy. Sizing up obstacles and people is more important to avoid bloodbaths and witnesses. And, of course, sometimes these are unavoidable…my most recent encounter is a perfect example. It was just bad luck.

This impending doom won't leave me. My whole life had been set up for this line of work. Small decisions carefully lighted my career arc. How could I do anything else? This business reflected my life, and my life reflected my profession. From birth I was heading down this road. I was raised in a Catholic orphanage on the slum outskirts of this city. I was never told about what happened to my parents. To this day, I don't know if they are alive or dead. My education was poor, and I graduated from high school with little direction.

What was I going to do after graduating? What could I possibly have chosen as a career? I was too poor for further education and had no employment prospects during an economic downturn. I was broke with no guidance and hungry. I could've been Mike or Louis at one point. At least one of my classmates was groomed for a life of crime.

There was no other pathway guaranteeing a pay cheque and the chance to see the world for free. So I did what any desperado school-leaver would've done: I joined the armed forces. I was seventeen at the time of enlistment, and the discipline suited me. A strict Catholic education prepared me for it. It enabled me to excel at times when others cracked. I had no relatives who would've missed me if I took a bullet in some far-off shithole. I spent four years as an infantry grunt and a further six and a half in the Special Forces, picking up all sorts of weapons training. It was great.

We had to be proficient in everything, including firearms our country didn't buy or produce, and train for situations we could never conceive of being in.

Our unit was the most active in the army. We were dropped into some hairy situations by a military brass that didn't give a shit about our predicament. At the time, neither did we.

I loved it because I didn't have a care in the world. My fate would always be in my own hands, which is where I've always wanted it, and it travelled as fast as a runaway locomotive. So many times our platoon was dropped into hostile environments, and our training and survival instincts took over. We did black-op assassinations, kidnappings, rescues, convoy protection, border patrols, and everything in between in countries for economic interests, ideological interests, and sometimes, for no foreseeable interest at all. Most of the time, we didn't even know where we were going, and sometimes we used to wonder why the fuck they would bother sending us at all.

Even then it didn't matter. We were all lost souls, spectres of normal people with deficient emotions, with no real family and dispensable friends. We had death wishes and didn't care about the consequences. It was a crazy rush until it changed. It always changes. And it will soon change again…

Fur brushes against my naked calf and pulls me out of some fond and some frightful memories. It is my black-and-white cat, Buster, scenting himself on me arrogantly, simply because he can. I took him in from a deserted alleyway about three years ago when I began to resettle in Hillbay. He was just a stray kitten then—almost dead, he was that skinny. I bend down and knead his head. His soft, short fur and beauty belie his penchant for petulance and misbehaviour. He rocks onto his hind legs to greet my hand, purring gratifyingly at the attention he seeks. But I can't indulge his whims for long. I have to front up to my handler and finalise everything before I leave this city in a hurry.

From the signal left by him in the last week, I know the day of the week, time, and place we'll have our debrief. I'm sure he'll understand that it would be extremely unwise for me to operate in Hillbay or even this state anymore.

I grab a large winter coat and head for the door. Buster sighs in distress and I look at him for a moment before shutting it behind me. I leave the TV on because he likes to watch it sometimes.

It's going to be hard leaving everything behind. This is the first time I've felt this way even after I gave up on the military. Barracks can never truly feel like a home. They're just living quarters and even after ten years, I still considered them temporary.

Despite my actions being a small splash in the violent ocean of this city, I feel settled. Maybe the high crime rate relaxes me more that it would anyone else? Maybe it's because it took me such a long time to find a glimmer of happiness to revel in?

Take where I live. It took months to decide on the fourth-floor apartment I own in full. I thought of everything before buying. It was well positioned at the front of the building with a nice view of the city and a convenient and discrete external stairwell, for emergencies, that doubles as an escape route. The steel skeleton winds its way down to a quiet alleyway from the bathroom window. The building is in a great location as well— never too crowded for cars, but it also has enough foot traffic during peak times to be able to blend in if needed. Sure, I could have bought a larger apartment on a higher floor, but four levels up was enough. Four flights of stairs to descend if things ever got too much. That sort of reassurance is indispensable.

The profession takes a mastery of restraint and ego-checking. I was never seduced by temptation to fall into one of its many pitfalls, and there are more pitfalls for a hit man than with any other profession I can think of. The want or need to flaunt any financial success can be the end of an operative in this game. I own a car, a four-year-old Ford, but it sits in the basement car park and I never use it. I could now splurge on something luxurious and fast. The paradox of my work is not being able to enjoy the fruits of my labour. Not until retirement. Being paid in $250,000 chunks is a problem. People will ask how I managed to come across such a windfall if I were driving around in a Porsche. I would stand out in this neighbourhood with a sports car or luxury saloon. And standing out from the crowd is never a good idea. If I decide to retire, then I can find some way to funnel and excuse a sudden fortune. No, it's best not to consider an upgrade or move elsewhere, even if I can afford it. I'm close to my targets in the city, and the suburbs are mundane. It's doesn't take a genius to figure out that anything used for work needs to be disposable. There are no special guns, cars, or anything else for me to hold dear. If there was, I would be gone.

Dispensable tools are everything. I need to be able to walk away and not have an attachment to anything, including my apartment. I can be certain that if I were outlandish, I wouldn't have survived this long. It's a contradiction many people can't grapple with.

Before I know it, I've ambled a few blocks. The overcast day is whipping chills through the main streets as my neck and face begin to lose feeling. When I notice, I quicken my pace and head straight to the meeting point. It's a small bar on a lower ground floor of a large but aging commercial building. I enter the establishment, and the rundown décor seems to mirror the city and my mood for the past week. Seeing as it's still the early afternoon, there are only a handful of unemployed drinkers and a couple of suits having a few quiet beers on an extended lunch break. I order a J&B Scotch on the rocks and take a seat in a secluded booth, away from prying eyes and ears. But as I wait, I can't help but listen in on the conversation over at the bar.

'Urgh. I'm over it, Tommy. I've had enough of the politics. I'm sick of that fat *fuck* Jack Prendergast taking all of the credit for my initiatives at work. Fuck *him*.'

'We've been through this before. A million times over already. There's no point in whinging. There's nothing you can do about it. Nobody's hiring out there. You've got nowhere to go if you quit. And you know you're not going to be able to get the boss's cock out of his mouth. Jack's chin isn't red from his psoriasis, but from the constant whacking he's getting from Dean's balls. And there is not a goddamn thing you can do about it.'

'Bullshit! One day I'm gonna *kill* that mother*fucker!*' he shouts, not caring if anyone hears.

His colleague laughs. 'You're not going to do shit.'

He lowers his voice into a more serious, quiet, focused tone. 'That prick Prendergast has cost me at least a hundred grand in bonuses over the last three years. That's *my* money. *My* hard work…he doesn't deserve any of it. Well, we'll see who'll be laughing soon. Don't think for a second I haven't thought about it. Y'know, getting rid of the son of a bitch.'

'Oh. And how are you going to do that exactly?'

'I'm gonna go out a buy a gun and shoot that piece of shit when he's walking into his house.'

'You don't have the heart to do it…Don't be stupid. You're a pussy.'

'Fuck off. I'm hard. I'm smart. Random street crime happens all the time in this city. There's a fucking gangland war going on around us for fuck's sake. I can get away with it. You watch. I'll blow you away with the shit I can do…'

I have to chuckle. Well, there's always someone who might be willing to pay for my services if I get out of prison!

But seriously, going rogue is a fool's game. It's one thing to do something everyone else deems abhorrent; it's another finding the clients who want you to do it for them.

My handler, who I only know as Lloyd, enters with his unique limp and a leather-bound presentation folder that I expect to contain severance papers.

His limp is interesting and so was his story behind it. He told me once he had a decorated career in guerrilla psy-ops and took a stray bullet to the knee on an advisory mission. I don't know if I can believe him. In my days in the service, people always like to put a spin on how they were forced out. One great story after another. Arrogance will get the better of everyone eventually if not checked.

He orders a beer. Wish I could continue eavesdropping on the stone-cold killer at the bar. 'You're stupid to think you won't get found out. It'd be easier to just pay some bum off the street…'

'Jesus, Aaron. You look like shit,' Lloyd says with a smile that instantly pisses me off.

'Can you fucking blame me?'

'What? Did the money not come in yet? It should've been cleared to you by now. You know the drill. One week's grace and you get full payment. Do you need me to check with management?'

His concern over something I now consider trivial pisses me off even more. Is he playing some fucking sick game with me? Does he know my means-to-an-end is over? My livelihood? My career? My life?

'No. I got paid, that's not the problem. Something happened on the job.'

'Like what? You fucking nailed it! All our sources confirmed there were no eyes, or rather none that were forthcoming. Did you actually think Louis and Mike would make a statement that they were asleep on duty while their boss died? Did you *really* think that? C'mon! They'd be the laughing stock of Hillbay. They'd become celebrities for fuck's sake. Celebrities that were so shit at their job that they've probably set their organisation back a decade.'

'And there was nobody else?'

'Who could there have been?'

'You tell me.'

'Are you slipping, Aaron? Is paranoia striking you hard? Don't you think there would be a press release for the killer of the old man, even if that old man were one of the worst sons of bitches in the country? You know the police can't distinguish between a good and bad person and who they have to protect.'

'Of course I know that!'

'Then wouldn't you be on the news for the last seven days if there were a scrap of evidence to show for it?'

'That's what I expected.'

'So then?'

'Then what? Maybe they didn't want to release that information?'

'You *really* are losing it! That's not protocol and you know it. All they have is some grainy CCTV footage of a man walking in and out, which we both knew was going to be unavoidable. You are living up to your tag as "The Grim Reaper." As far as the police are concerned, they've closed the case because they have two witnesses that say nobody went in or out of his room that night. One went in to check on him and found him dead…that's it. The case is officially closed. Do you want the police report? No autopsy, nothing suspicious. A seventy-six-year-old man died from complications from surgery. He was lucky to survive the previous attempt on his life if you ask me.'

'And you're sure about this?'

'One hundred percent! They've got squat on you.'

I'm a little dizzy at the revelation. Seven nights of barely enough sleep all for naught. The best feeling in the world is relief, and it piles on me so quickly that I can't bear it. It takes all my effort not to crack a smile because I don't want Lloyd to know that I've been petrified for so long. But why didn't Dr Jessica Ward say anything? She has absolutely no reason to not give them a description, a name, and everything else. Was the police that shit at their job that they didn't even bother asking? There were no CCTV cameras around the elevators, but they should've done their best to question all of the staff that worked that night. Did my employers have something to do with it? Maybe I need to have this confirmed with people I know? It's possible that a turn of luck can happen, especially when you least expect it. God knows I experienced it in my army days. But I just can't let this go without being sure.

'Something else happened,' I said.

'Like what?'

'The mark knew I was coming.'

'Oh. How so?'

'He told me. It could've been a fluke or a wild guess but he was waiting for me. You need to seriously look at this. Whoever hired me shouldn't break their agreement and let important information slip. I should be furious about it.'

'I'll look into it,' Lloyd says, as seriously as I thought he was going to be when he walked in. He slides the folder towards me. 'But right now I have something more important for you.'

'Like what?'

'I have another job. And the client has *specifically* requested for the best. This is unprecedented. I asked the firm and this hasn't happened to anyone they have, or had, on their books…ever. I've seen the write-up and intel and you need some serious balls to want to take this on. If you think the last one was hazardous, wait until you read up on this. Extreme risk, but I think you'll like the payoff.'

'What are we looking at?'

'Two million,' he says coolly. 'Complications like this we don't offer to resolve even if we have someone who's suicidal. Finish up. Let's take a walk.'

I don't know whether I should be concerned, outright offended, or extremely lucky for another assignment. Even *I* know it's usual practice for a contractor to 'cool off' before another assignment. After that scare, perhaps I should be considering retirement anyway. I'm still a free man and can enjoy all of the liberties that come with it. I can get out with everything earned. I have investments and can use my funds wisely to leave and find some pissy job to whittle away the years. But why haven't I done this already? What keeps me in this dangerous profession that can only ever end in my ruin? I know the answer, but I'm too ashamed to even think it.

I slam down my scotch, and Lloyd impressively skols his beer like it was water. I turn to the corporate conspirators still at the bar. The 'killer' is sobbing into his beer while his friend stares into the distance and takes a swig of his drink, embarrassed to be sitting next to an emotional wreck.

This is the reason why it's never a good idea to go independent. There are too many unknowns. I knew a few people I served with who probably would have approached the sobbing man and eventually let on that his problems could disappear with their help. But there are too many things that could go wrong. Even though the man could well afford the hit, who's to say he would not break under the guilt of his enemy's demise? The threat of being convicted with conspiracy to kill is the only deterrent that can pacify that anguish. And if he breaks, whoever fulfilled his Machiavellian wishes wouldn't be coming out of prison, ever. Seeing his pathetic state before me, it is more reassuring when there are people who find the work and can assign it, and keep up the Chinese walls of anonymity on both sides. Aaron, despite Lloyd calling me that, is just a name I picked out. It is *not* my real name.

We leave the bar and head out onto the cold street. The city has died a little. Workers are back to their offices to finish off their day. It's frosty enough for steam to drift from the stormwater drains as we stroll towards nowhere in particular.

'So why is the bounty so much?'

Lloyd hesitates. 'This assignment is a little out of the ordinary.'

We pass a few pedestrians. It's one of the strangest things. Lloyd and I are having a conversation about killing someone and snippets of information don't mean anything. It all seems so innocent. But if these pedestrians were to stay within earshot longer, they may just be able to piece these bits together and discover what morally reprehensible work I do, except our combined tradecraft would never allow this to happen.

If I don't say yes, there are others willing to pick it up. Simple laws of economics assert that if there is a demand for a product or service, there should be someone keen enough to come along and supply it. Illicit drugs and organised murder follow the same laws as fuel for a car or toilet paper.

'*How* out of the ordinary is it?'

Lloyd clutches my arm uneasily and hastily ushers me into a random alleyway. We stop behind a large skip.

'It's not a run-of-the-mill assignment. We shouldn't even be offering this to you. This is a case for law enforcement, *not* an assassin. But seeing as they won't help, and you've got a death wish, I've been instructed to run it by you.'

'*OK*. But fuck. What's got you spooked?'

'It's a rescue operation…with a target thrown in for good measure. One mill for the rescue and another for the mark. Fifty thousand kitty for equipment and whatever you want. Those are the terms.'

'You have sufficient recon?'

'It's hot. And you'll have to see the brief for yourself. We were going to throw in a helper, but we know how much you like your privacy.'

'Correct. No partners.'

'Yeah, we know your stance on hired help. And the problem is you've got to move quickly. And when I say quickly, I mean *fucking* quick. Two weeks.'

'This *is* a suicide mission,' I mumble.

'You will want to commit suicide when you read the finer points. Like I said, this is highly irregular. We always give our people at least three months grace to back any heat off. But we've investigated this thoroughly, and you're in the clear. There's only the grainy video from the hospital, which they can't identify you from anyway. You're a fucking ghost. There are guys at the firm that want to meet you. Even the Chairman would gladly give you a blowjob.'

'I'm flattered.'

'Just let me know in a week,' Lloyd says and slaps the folder into my stomach. 'Me thinks you're crazy enough to say yes.'

As Lloyd hobbles away, I'm forced to yell over an incoming ambulance's siren, 'And what happens if I say no? Who's going to do it?'

'Nobody,' he yells back, then disappears around the corner.

CHAPTER FIVE

I guess I was wrong. Perhaps there are a very small amount of tasks that only one person has the balls and the ability to pull off. And it seems that in this case, I am that one person. This is the complete opposite of how I thought the debrief was going to turn out.

I look down at the folder. Holding one of these always fills me with trepidation and opportunity. The feeling I have now is something else, something completely different. It is sheer dread and morbid curiosity. What's in this folder that could spook Lloyd so much? No, don't open it, there's no point. I'm strangely excited and intimidated by its size and weight.

When I emerge from the alleyway, I quickly check to confirm Lloyd has disappeared and pull out my phone. Before I can consider anything, there's one guy I need to consult and confirm about the Baresi hit. To hell with being cautious. If Lloyd has said it's all right, then it must be.

I text his current number: 'Location?'

I begin to walk where I expect him to be minutes before getting a response: 'Usual place. Downtown.'

It's a bit of a hike to get there, but it'll be worth it if it means peace of mind. If there's anyone who's got the inside scoop on the dealings of the underworld, this is the guy. The only other way to confirm Lloyd's version of events is if I went to a police station and asked the captain myself. At least my man will have the inside track from the other side of the fence.

The underworld will not only know if the police are after me, but also if Baresi's organisation is too.

It takes around thirty minutes to trek through the city. I head straight for the derelict districts of the city's central business district. It's a hundred-metre block of a mixture of abandoned buildings with barely any windows and empty industrial properties filled with rubbish. The common theme is graffiti. Graffiti is everywhere—gang tags and people's lame attempt at being artistic. The police have surrendered the area to the homeless and drug afflicted alike. It is a sign of the times and the shift from being a manufacturing powerhouse to a finance and service-driven city. In order to make the transition, there had to be losers. Unskilled factory workers were out of a job. Those that didn't recognise the downturn and quickly retrained turned to other means of survival. They banded together and now prey on the weak who dare to tread on their turf. They mark their territory with a spray can and in some places, their urine.

As much as I am not fearful of some roughhousing, today is probably not the best time to be sucked into any form of violence. That would be impractical. I don't hurry to my destination, either. I don't think it would be a good idea for me to rush as it may be mistaken for fear. I set a casual, yet workman-like pace and am thankful it doesn't take me too long to arrive.

It's a redbrick, single-storey building where my contact calls work. He was once a player and got out clean, but he still keeps his head to the ground.

I step into the narrow doorway and can barely see the end of the corridor, as no lights are on. I hear a pair of expensive shoes making contact with the hardwood floorboards. 'Curious' George emerges from the shadows with a hand out to greet me.

The infamous 'Curious' George got his name from high school. He was a bright student who loved to tinker with electronics and craft his own recording devices to use on his classmates and blackmail them. One day when he was toying with some equipment, it shorted out and caused a fire destroying a hundred-year-old school building. From the most innocent of accidents, George's trajectory into crime was set.

He was quickly drafted into Varetti's syndicate and became a sensation. Feared by not just those he was told to keep an eye on but also those he worked with, he never did shake off his desire for extortion. It all came unstuck when lightning struck twice and he overloaded a circuit at one of Varetti's safe houses, destroying the premises and five million dollars worth of drugs and cash. He created an incendiary beacon that led the police straight to the apartment. It was too big an embarrassment even without the financial loss, and Varetti had no choice but to cast him out of the organisation.

'Good to see you again,' George says.

'Likewise.'

'Come, let's go to my office.'

I follow him even though I've been there many times before. I can just make out that the lights are on around the corner. I don't know why he has a completely dark corridor all of the time. I guess he wants nobody to know there is a nerd's bunker in the middle of a seemingly derelict building. At the end, the room opens up into a wall of monitors and high-tech gear I could only imagine the names for.

George is his own intelligence factory. 'Curious' is a double-edged moniker. He is renowned for his ability to hunt down information on people and particularly criminal gangs that not even the police can pick up. He also has an obsessive compulsion to record and document everything that might be useful later. A wall is lined up with arch-lever folders and scrapbooks, which is presumably a log of every conversation stored elsewhere. I would hate to think of how much electronic data he has amassed.

When he was tossed from Varetti's organisation, his parting gift was to impregnate a street boss's new wife and join Baresi. Vincenzo Varetti was so incensed he approved a hit ordered by his offended employee. George's scalp must have been worth it at the time because it almost started a war between the two families as devastating as the current one. But George was always one step ahead. Having the inside scoop on what they were planning meant they never were able to catch up to him. He left a calling card consisting of a courteous dump in a paper bag for his belated pursuers. He was extremely proud of that. Shitting was his masterpiece of taunts akin to the embarrassment of receiving an open-handed slap in public. He told me there was something about leaving something so disgusting that it eventually became demoralising.

In the end, they had no choice but to give up. By that time George was a hot-enough potato that Baresi didn't want the hassle but certainly didn't want to hand him over as demanded countless times. There are only so many bags of shit a man can receive before being humiliated into surrendering.

George turned to freelancing, which was disastrous for the private investigation industry as he quickly cornered the market. Ex-cops wanted him gone, too, but by that time, they knew he was untouchable.

'Can I offer you a coffee?'

'No, thanks. How's business been?'

'Pretty quiet. I've got some major insurance clients who pay the bills and then some, but never anything exciting. You know the drill. It's a boring game, but it pays well. How's print journalism been treating you?'

'Articles write themselves in this town.'

He and I both know the rules: assume everyone is above board and just take their money when they ask for something. Of course he knows I'm not a journalist, but he's also not stupid and won't bite the hand that feeds.

I met George through a shady sergeant in the service and when the question came of what I did for a living, the awkward pause was broken by the sergeant who claimed I was a reporter. It was the most useful introduction I ever had in Hillbay since returning. We bonded after I paid him five grand for my first-ever outsourced intelligence job. Even though I sparingly require his services because the agency has its own write-ups, he has always come through with the goods over the years. His impartiality towards organised crime has been refreshing, not to mention his strict adherence to confidentiality. To him, I could be a handler or a hit man.

'Is this a business visit, or just a courtesy call?'

'I was just in the neighbourhood and thought I'd drop by. I might have something for you very soon.'

'Good. I'm getting bored of looking at cheating housewives and people whose backs are out but can drive a golf ball over a fairway. It's not a challenge. I get restless easily these days. Jesus, give me something good.'

'It's that bad?'

'Not really, but when you had an action-packed life, settling down is always going to be hard. For some, *this* shit is actually exciting.'

'I know what you mean.'

'I'm sure you do.'

I rack my brains about how to broach the subject and get the information I want out of him. He'll be able to tell me if there has been even a whisper about Baresi's hit, but I don't want to draw any suspicion.

'Have you been reading the news?' I ask.

'What about?'

'They say the crime statistics are preparing to fall, because your old boss bought the farm.' I couldn't think of any other way to be as direct as possible.

'Some say he was killed,' George says.

'And what do *you* think?'

'Natural curiosity got the better of me, so I checked it out. He died from complications from surgery. All my sources tell me that. I don't know why people start these bullshit rumours. He was an old man, and he was lucky to survive that long.'

'I don't know. Maybe that's what they want everyone to think, that he was the victim of an elaborate scheme after surgery.'

'An elaborate scheme? Varetti must be one crazy bastard if he wanted to go after the old man again. How much does he want to kick the old dog? They kidnapped his son who "does no wrong" in his father's eyes. If they wanted him to suffer, they would have wanted to *keep* him alive and weak. If it was Varetti, it would have been complete overkill.'

'So you think the war is over?'

'As good as over. I don't know what they can possibly do to get back at Varetti. They've been smashed and will be small time from now on. There might be a few bodies turning up here and there. It's inevitable there will be some in-fighting with what's left of Baresi's organisation, but there won't be any more war. That is as good as done. Whoever takes control is only going to be hanging on while they slowly slip away. By all accounts it was the last straw.'

'Isn't that going to affect your business?'

'In the short term, yes. But there's always someone who'll fill the void. This is a big city, my friend, and I'm sure there's a gang out there who'll make a play for the big time soon enough. But only time will tell…Surely there's something else you want to talk about than a dying dynasty and my business's financial outlook for the next five years. What's in the folder?'

'A write-up for a story I'm doing.'

'Of course it is.' He grins.

I don't bother trying to convince him otherwise.

George was telling the truth; there's no reason why he wouldn't. The official line is that Luigi Baresi died from complications of surgery and I got off scot-free. The truth will never see the light of day and I am extraordinarily lucky. I shouldn't dwell on this anymore. Chalk it up as luck and know that it can go both ways.

We chat a little more about nothing much before I see myself out.

As soon as I step out onto the street I crouch over in relief. Nobody is gunning for me, and I have nothing to worry about…except for what's in this folder.

What could possibly be so important that my employers would want me to take a case on so badly? I hold the folder up and stare. Should I ever open this now that control over my destiny has shifted back to me? It can't hurt to just read the brief, can it? Even if I will say no? Why do I need to remind myself that I am in control? I have the final say, and I can refuse if I want, which looks most likely after that scare. But what about the payoff? This onetime grab will tip me over the edge. Maybe when it's over I can work with George and 'settle down' into some mundane surveillance? Or maybe I don't need to bother? Financial freedom will have its perks. But is the risk worth the reward? My threshold of what's risky is a little more than what Lloyd might believe, and the only way I'm going to know is if I take a peek. The only place I dare to do this is back at home, and it's probably best if I get back there fast.

CHAPTER SIX

On my way home, it seems fitting to cut through Freedom Park and save time. Freedom Park is a garden oasis slapped in the middle of a concrete jungle. In summer, it is packed with tourists and workers keen on vitamin D and a quick tan at lunch. Its paths trail around urban forests with dewy sports fields in the middle. The dense collection of trees is thick enough for beggars and the homeless to set up camp without attracting police attention. The trees also ward off some of the cold when it comes. Today, not many are brave enough to battle the chill.

I'm almost around one of the quieter trails when a man in his early twenties walks towards me, his hands in the front pockets of his hoodie. Judging by this expensive jacket and his arrogant swagger, it appears he obtained the clothes on his back through illegitimate means. His face is gaunt and blemished enough to show signs of meth abuse.

'Sir, do you have any spare change?' he mutters, his eyes wandering behind my shoulder.

'Sorry, I've got nothing in my wallet.'

He steps threateningly into my path. 'Care if I take a *look?*' he insists, pulling out a switchblade he had gripped in his jacket.

I am not impressed. This little punk thinks he can stand over me with only a switchblade? There's nothing I can give him except a couple of hundred bucks in my wallet and this folder, which he will have to kill for. And if he manages to do that, he can be certain that someone will be chasing him for it. He'd be alive for twenty-four hours, if he's lucky. My employers will take every measure possible to recover this folder. These files are more important than *my* life.

He startles when he realises I haven't reacted the way he wanted me to. He seems confused and a little doubtful, finding it difficult to process that there is someone that isn't scared of him.

I move a hand to my coat's front pocket and fist a few coins I know of have. He is mesmerised at my relaxed demeanour, maybe starting to realise I have had a lot worse pointed at me in the past.

Taking advantage, in one quick motion I remove my hand and flick the coins at his face.

This might be a life-or-death moment for him, but this is playing out in slow motion to me. I've created my distraction and it doesn't matter that I'm unarmed; I now have the upper hand.

I seize my chance and run straight for him, shouldering him like a charging bull. My inertia and the surprise of my attack knocks the switchblade from his hand and lifts his skinny body into the air. He lands on his rear, and the chain of his buttocks, torso, and head follow like a whip and I hear a small crack as his head connects with the pavement.

I retrieve his knife a few metres away and bear down on him. In seconds, I notice a few pedestrians who witnessed the incident from afar start to walk over and gather around us. And I didn't even drop the folder.

'I should kill you,' I whisper loud enough for him to hear.

'*Stab* that piece of shit!' a passerby says.

'Yeah. Teach that prick a lesson,' another adds.

The crowd builds and yells for me to do something in retaliation. But the attention is unwanted. If I wanted him to die, I would have killed him already. His throat would've been duly slitted by his own knife, and I would be fleeing from the scene.

The miscreant opens his eyes groggily. He stays still, fearful of the crowd and my wrath. He squeaks a few terse sounds as the gathering builds and the noise increases, but I remain quiet and motionless. At least twenty people mill around now.

I look up at an approaching uniformed cop. I pocket the switchblade, turn and move through the crowd, slipping past them gratefully inconspicuous to the officer.

'All right, all right,' the cop yells to the gathering as I make my exit from the scene.

I jog around the path and as soon as I'm out of direct sight, I bolt to the nearest road. The cop will, of course, be questioning who was responsible for upending the punk, and eventually an eyewitness would have pointed to me. Police attention is the last thing I need, ever. Perhaps I made the mistake of not giving the kid some money, but maybe he was going to try and rob me in broad daylight anyway? Either way, I feel confident I dealt with it satisfactorily despite wanting to teach him a lesson in respect.

My paradoxical situation proves itself again. Egos need to be constantly in check. There's no point in bar fights over girls or honing superior fighting skills on wannabe alpha males. It won't impress anyone except people who could recognise and report me to the police. Within the madness and illegality of what I do, I am sure and secure within myself to truly let little things slide. I have to. The handful of friends I see on an irregular basis are blind to my profession, but know of my background. It is difficult to lead a lonely existence, and I'm sure other people in this field have the same issues and some may have failed at this disciplinary necessity.

I finally reach my apartment still smarting from today's events. I take the elevator, and before I reach my door at the end of the corridor, the door of 4C opens right on cue.

'Oh, hello, Patrick,' the haggard voice of Mrs Rutherford, my intrusive neighbour, chimes. I have to be alert juggling another alias.

'Hello, Mrs Rutherford.'

'What a coincidence bumping into you at this time.'

I doubt this is the case. There have been too many coincidences since she moved in next door. If she wasn't eighty-something, I would be more concerned.

'Oh. Why is that?'

'Well, Patrick, I was wondering if you could assist moving a couch of mine outside. My daughter's boyfriend is picking it up in around ten minutes. Only if you are not troubled. It seems you've had a hard day already.' She points to a tiny drop of blood on my cream-coloured shirt.

'Oh that. Well…y'know, Mrs Rutherford, it's just another one of my bloody noses on the way home today.'

'You really should see a doctor. It's not normal to bleed so regularly!'

'I will make an appointment first thing tomorrow.'

'Would you like me to remind you?'

'That won't be necessary, ma'am.'

'I hope not. You should take greater care of yourself. You only live once and even then, you never know what might happen. People need to take care of themselves and others. The youth today don't care about things like that. I saw on the TV people doing crazy, crazy things to each other. Like killing others for their money just so they can buy drugs. Killing to buy drugs. What has this world come to?'

'You're definitely right about that, Mrs Rutherford.'

'Of course I'm right, Patrick. Now, quickly put away that case and give me a hand. But only if you're not too busy.'

She adds it as if it is an afterthought. But what can I do? I am at the mercy of an old lady, who has nobody in her life. Sadly, she is ignorant to the fact that her daughter is one of those 'crazy people' on drugs. I've noticed the telltale signs of a wired perception and sores on her face, which certainly is not acne, as she wanders through the building to her mother's at all hours to borrow money.

Mrs Rutherford does have her uses, though. Even though I have consistently suggested that she buy herself a lapdog or cat, she refuses. 'I don't need to be hurt again at this age,' she says. Instead, she will happily take care of Buster for me and spoil him rotten, making it harder for him to accept my meagre offerings when he returns. She acts like it is a burden, but I know she would keep him if I ever have to give him up.

I open my door and drop the folder and my coat on the couch, disturbing Buster as he snoozes in a ball in front of the TV. He flinches and meows, irritated, so I pat him until he gently purrs.

I head back out to help Mrs Rutherford, and she shows me the dated two-seater she wants moved. I tilt the couch onto its side and start pushing it to the front door.

'Now, could you please lift it, Patrick? I would hate for the arm to get dirty!'

The *real* test of discipline I face on a regular basis is to not show anger towards her. I peer down the length of the couch. It has to be at least twenty years old and she is concerned that an arm will get dirty?

'Sure, Mrs Rutherford.'

I strain as I heave this piece of junk, plodding it along one lunge at a time until I get to the elevator. While I'm here I may as well ask her if she is free for the improbable chance that I will actually agree to whatever is simmering in that leather folder.

'Say, Mrs Rutherford. You wouldn't be able to look after Buster for a week sometime soon would you?'

'Another business trip?'

'Perhaps so. I don't know if I will be asked to go yet, so it might not be required.'

'I would love to, Patrick, but I will be going away tomorrow for a couple of weeks.'

Shit. Well, no big deal. It's unlikely I will need to use her services anyway. If not, I will have to chance it with him, or give him up to Lloyd to palm over to her if I don't make it back. So much for quid pro quo. Looking after Buster isn't even a chore for her.

I manage to stuff the couch into the elevator and on the ground floor continue to struggle with its cumbersome form.

'You can just leave it by the door,' she says. I do as she commands and begin to head back to my apartment. 'Are you not going to wait with me?'

'I'm sorry, Mrs Rutherford, I really have to get going. I have a scheduled teleconference I am five minutes late for.'

'Oh…well, good luck to you, son.'

She doesn't even say thanks, and I don't really care. 'How is your daughter going to take this away?'

'Her new boyfriend, Daz, is bringing a trailer.'

'*Daz?*'

'Yes, but I call him Darren. Daz is so primitive.'

'And where will you be sitting tonight to watch TV?'

'They said they'll only need it for a while. I guess I'll use my dinner chairs.'

She looks down at the floor sad and ashamed, revealing to me that she knows what type of person her daughter is…the type of person she is so against and despises. I feel a tinge of sympathy as her small pension supports three people and she is truly lonely. I wish I could help her, but there is nothing I can do. I make my way back.

Picking up the folder carefully to not disturb Buster, I head straight for the study, close every curtain in the room, and switch on the small laptop sitting on the desk. Out of concerns for security, this computer has never been connected to the Internet, and all forms of wireless communication were removed by a tech expert shortly after its purchase. I finally open the leather folder to find a clear sleeve containing an envelope with random photos, diagrams, information, and a USB flash drive.

After removing the password protection on the drive, I am hit with the classified intel reports to accompany the photos and diagrams. I sift through them all. A sense of panic similar to that experienced over the last seven days grips my stomach.

There are architectural plans of a massive estate in The Hills. The second to last photo in the dossier is of Valentino Baresi, and the last is of one Doctor Charles Ward…

After taking an hour to digest everything, I pace around the apartment to cool off. Could this be? Could Baresi truly have known about his own hit? And why the *fuck* would someone want the same person who killed him to find and save his son, the heir to a crumbling family dynasty? Lloyd was right. This *is* suicide! Perhaps I should've let the old man say his piece? No, I had a job to do, and I completed it the way I always do, with murderous efficiency.

My mind boggles when I read the recon reports: there is a small unit of private security contractors all armed with automatic submachine guns. Numbers range from ten to fifteen people at any one time. But what could they possibly need to protect? I have a look at the satellite images. There's one mansion and a second building towards the back of the property on a massive 4,000-square-metre block of land. There are a couple of vague photos of a small and usually manned watchtower in the other back corner, obscured by tall vegetation encircling the rear of the property. The watchtower immediately poses a problem, as elevated positions are terrible unless they can be neutralised quickly.

I examine the read-only, detailed reports on the computer, trying to memorise every detail. There have been no sightings of Valentino, but all intelligence suggests that he is being held in the two-story rear building, judging from the regular patrols and general concentrated areas of action. There has never been any sighting of any armed personnel entering the mansion, so it may be off limits to them. They are observed coming in and out of that rear building. What could possibly be in there? For that question, there is no answer or even speculation. And what if Valentino is not there? What if he is not even alive? Should I just concentrate on Charles Ward and not bother with him?

Doctor Charles Ward's bio lists him as a distinguished research doctor. He lost his wife and unborn child to a terrorist attack while both were serving as medics and specialist surgeons in insurgent wars a decade and a half ago. Soon after, he received a general discharge, which surprisingly is classified. *That* doesn't make sense at all. He, like me, moved back to Hillbay shortly afterwards and did double duty as a brilliant surgeon while making career in-roads into medical research, before dropping surgery and becoming a consultant to a number of drug companies, including the largest producers of antipsychotics and benzodiazepines. He clocks in an average working week of seventy hours and is often spotted at the war memorial in Freedom Park.

This guy is a superhero of medicine. Just like that, he can snap his fingers and change career paths. He must be as brilliant as his resume. But beyond the absurdity of his life choices is the question of why anybody like him would be caught up housing scum like Valentino, *if* he indeed has him. And why in hell would he have armed guards practically living on his estate? It simply can't be a diversionary tactic. The expense would be astronomical, and the payoff wouldn't be worth it. There must be something in that building worth protecting more than Valentino. He reminds me of another crazy old man, Luigi Baresi…

Panic suddenly attacks my frontal lobe, pressuring the tops of my eyeballs into pain.

'Holy shit!' Was this what Baresi was trying to warn me about? Could a distinguished doctor go out of his way to hold people in a building on his own property? He cannot be that stupid. Why would he want to hold a smoking gun?

I think this through. *If* they still have Valentino, why would they specifically hold him there? Why?…Well, why not? What's the best way to hide something? Hide it in plain sight. Charles has control over all of his subjects on private property in a place that nobody would expect to look, so nobody will ever find. This is twisted and all too much…

After two hours of reading and rereading everything, I'm done. I take a hammer to the flash drive and make sure the memory chips are isolated until the pieces are minuscule. I collect the remains and scoop them into a small resealable storage bag, which I put in my coat for gradual disposal next time I leave the apartment.

I decide to work out a little while the evening news plays in the background. It's imperative I keep up a basic level of fitness between assignments. Due to the unpredictable nature of my work, every edge I can find must be trained to a competent level. Strength, endurance, combat with and without weapons, and general marksmanship with weapons from handguns to sniper rifles all need to be constantly exercised. Training is never for fashion but for function. The only discipline I skip is explosives, as I've never been called to level a building. I bench press a solid 100 kilograms for reps when news headlines flash in front of me on the TV. The female anchor resumes from a commercial break.

'In medical news, a father and daughter team from Hillbay has devised a treatment that permanently eliminates aggression in individuals. This scientific breakthrough has been hailed as a cure towards psychotic behaviour in hardened criminals with abnormal aggressive tendencies and other antisocial behaviour. Doctors Charles and Jessica Ward made the discovery by identifying a chemical agent that inhibits the specific grouping of neurons in the brain controlling aggression. They both recently received the nation's highest accolade for medicine, the Sullivan Award, which will be presented by the mayor of Hillbay at a dinner held next week for the family.'

So this is what Jessica was telling me about. The vision flashes to a makeshift press conference. I recognise Jessica easily from the hospital elevator. Her smile at the masses of popping flash bulbs demonstrates an underlying, humble confidence I rarely see. This is deceiving when I think back to our chance meeting. Why didn't she come forward and tell the police about me that night? Worst still is now I've been offered to kill her father.

I was told at the very start by the agency that I will not be able to operate above the law. I revisit this warning and reiterate that turns of fortune and lucky escapes cannot replace this fact with complacency. I can't bribe my way out of my crimes even if the agency has far-reaching tentacles deep in the law enforcement community. They have their own firewalls to maintain. Just so the paper trail can *never* lead to them, there is no contact between them and their agents except through handlers. They are even more protective of themselves than the secrecy of the people on their books, if indeed there are books at all. The truth is, just like with freelancing, we are on our own.

A fine example is the rumour still swirling about the Bennett killings a few years ago. The *Hillbay Times*, as poorly believed as a tabloid rag can be, reported a killer on the run contacting them through letters to explain why he killed Ricardo Bennett and his three daughters. Rival papers called it a hoax and a prank. Then all of a sudden the letters stopped.

Even though I can't speak for my employers and any other contractors they have, because I have never met or known of anyone else, I find it very difficult to not come to the conclusion it was one of ours. It was an insurance hit, made out to be a robbery, and the hired help couldn't find the emotional solace to deal with killing for someone else's greed. Mrs Bennett was conveniently on holiday while the massacre occurred and collected not only everything in and including a mansion in The Hills, but also a large payout from a secret life insurance policy he took out after they were married. She, of course, had no idea about it and amassed a nice fortune for herself, only a fraction of which she could've accumulated on her stripper salary had she continued to work. I am adamant the agency quickly put an end to one of their own. An allegorical tale if ever there was one!

I finish my workout a little earlier than I should because of the distraction. Something doesn't add up. I tried to dismiss Baresi's warning as a trick when he wanted to involve me in his war with Varetti with his cryptic hints. Although his conspiracy theory is insane, it has planted a seed in a chaotic disturbance I now have to resolve. His wish came true. Lloyd's advice on the mission is playing on my mind as well. I've had difficult missions before, but he has never tried to dole out any suggestions before.

The objectives are clear: find and evacuate Valentino Baresi...and optionally, void Charles Ward. I rewind the live TV to the news and their press conference. Charles Ward and Vincenzo Varetti teaming up. This is ridiculous! Sure, there's the benefit of holding Valentino over his father to gain insurmountable leverage in their stoush, but why in the hell would Dr

Ward, of all people, offer to house him? Wouldn't it be wiser if he let Varetti do the dirty work?

I pause on a close-up of Charles. His clean-cut image, freshly shaven face, dyed dark, slicked-back hair doesn't give one sniff of deviousness. Why would a person like him be mixed up in an underworld war? Surely he would have the intelligence not to risk being anywhere near Valentino, even if he holds a grudge against Baresi. It simply does not add up.

Charles's smile beams straight down the barrel of the camera. I stare and don't notice the folder sliding off my knees and onto the ground. The noise startles me into focus and I pick up the pages. From an unchecked pocket, an envelope falls. I pick it up and pry it open. In it is an invite for a Dr Spentz to the congratulatory dinner and the official ceremony for Drs Charles and Jessica Ward to receive the Sullivan Award. It's the only reconnaissance leg-up I have for this assignment. But it may be invaluable for intel.

I frame-skip the TV to the close up of Jessica. Is it possible for her to be mixed up in this? My morals should find it difficult to be able to accept a job where I would make a person of such high social standing an orphan. And what if she didn't tell the police on purpose out of pity for me? Is killing her father the right reward for her kindness?

I find myself knowing the answers to these questions: I leave the moral judgements up to others. Nobody would put such a high price on his head if they weren't sure and their reasoning didn't have merit. And if I do find they have Valentino, Charles's guilt is as good as proven.

I recline on the couch and stare at the ceiling to stop the room gently rotating from the news. Setting aside the facts, the burning question still remains: do I take this on? I look around, stare through the window out into the city, over to the TV at the frozen picture of Jessica, and then at the folder. In the silence I know the temptation is too great.

My decision has been made. I'm going to take this on. A scare is good enough to put me back on track to pulling off the improbable. This will set me up for life. The money is right, so damn the consequences.

Buster announces himself as he walks in front of me. He knows it's time to be fed but instead jumps onto the TV stand and is fixated on Jessica Ward's image before meowing.

'OK,' I surrender, and change the channel over to the Cartoon Network. He tracks the characters as if they were mice and takes a swipe at the TV. I get up to fix his dinner.

CHAPTER SEVEN

I am suspicious this could well be a trap.

I go over the objectives and the details, and brainstorm over and over again. I try to think of anything that could work out better than the previous best plan to improve my chances of success so many times it consumes my waking hours, and some of my sleeping ones as well.

I keep thinking about it as I sit in a café waiting for Lloyd. The filtered coffee is weak so it's my third cup. The venue is not too busy, and there are a good couple of booths between me and any other customer. Lloyd goes out of his way to be around fifteen minutes late to every meeting just to be sure there are no surprises when he meets with his contractors. He's almost as paranoid as I am.

I zone out, and think about nothing while looking at the cars driving by on the highway out of Hillbay, escaping the tumult of the city.

If I manage to get out of this alive, will this be the last way I think like this? Surely I've had enough excitement for one lifetime. Get out on top with my body and brain intact and I'll have succeeded where many have failed and fallen. That is the simple standard of success in this business: survival and freedom.

I know I am shouldering a lot of risk. This *has* to be the last. This is the furthest I can stick my neck out without losing my head. Just by taking on such an assignment shows that I am becoming complacent and sooner or later that will come back to bite. And when it does, it is never good. I've risked enough in my life to know when to call it quits. And that time is right after this last payday.

'Have you been waiting long?' Lloyd beams, snapping me out of my trance.

'You know just how long I've been waiting…I thought that was your fat, limping walk I could hear. You should wear rubber-soled shoes next time you enter an establishment with hardwood floors. Noisy shoes and an inconsistent stride make you easier to remember.'

'I don't need you to tell me how to dress,' he snaps back. He slides into the booth and helps himself to the coffee jug I have sitting on my table and pours himself a coffee with the extra cup I ordered for him. 'Have you eaten? Because I'm starving.'

He waves down a waiter and orders a steak with eggs and fries.

'I thought you were trying to lose weight?'

'I gave up a while back. Besides, how much running can I do with this knee? All I *can* do is use the rowing machine at home, and even that's difficult.' I don't reply because I don't care. 'Your list is ready. I haven't had any difficulties obtaining what you wanted. But I am a little concerned about your need to use a riot shotgun. Do you really think you can neutralise *all* of the guards with rubber and pepper bullets?'

'Like you said, this is a suicide mission. I have no idea how he is being held. Maybe I need a key or a code to open his cell. So the shotgun might come in handy.'

Lloyd nods and shrugs. 'Everything is prepared. It's all in the cab behind this café. I assume you have a contingency plan in case anything goes wrong?'

'You know what to do. You know the usual grace period is a week, so if I'm not back by then, well, you've got all of the things you need.'

'You've had the same envelope sitting in my safe for years now. You haven't made any new updates to your life that might need to be addressed?'

'No.'

We sit in silence while he eats his lunch. A grim mood sweeps over me. I face annihilation. This *is* crazy. I would have never taken such risks when I started. I've had a solid week to think things through, and I knew once I absorbed the information, once I read through everything, I would say yes no matter what was in that folder. It's an addiction I need to shake. My obsession eggs me on even if I have second thoughts. It isn't the fear of dying that scares me. That was crushed out of me in the service years ago.

I think through all of the intel again. Skilled guards patrolling with automatic firearms and a bloody watchtower to contend with. How can the neighbours not question it? I guess the rich can afford to spend as much on security as they want to afford.

And that's the other thing I find extraordinary: the unimaginable wealth of the Wards. They must be from old money to have such an estate. And that's just the start. Charles is able to dedicate a whole building to his research out of normal working hours *and* to house and maintain a twenty-four-hour roster of guards. That takes financial might and it irks me. He must be dedicating a large portion of his wealth to his goal, whatever that is, or Varetti is fronting the money and if that is the case, why? Why finance such a large operation?

I doubt Varetti would risk that much. If he is providing assistance, it would be supplying muscle out on the street and not at the estate. If it was the other way around, my job would be a hell of a lot easier with untrained and unskilled street thugs. But these guys aren't. Then there is also the medical support staff Charles Ward would need.

Lloyd scoops some of the runny egg yolk with his last piece of fresh bread and scoffs it into his chubby mouth. He wipes some yellow slime off his chin with a napkin and dumps it onto the empty plate. He looks up when he finishes and smirks.

'You *are* one crazy bastard,' he muffles, mouth half-full.

'Maybe.'

'But my gut feeling tells me you can pull this off. No rhyme or reason. You want my advice? I'll tell you even though you're not going to listen. Don't worry about the kill. Leave it the fuck alone. A guy with that much security who believes people are after him will try and protect himself to no end. Only a fool would go for the kill.'

'Thanks, I guess.' I gaze out the window dismissively. 'Just to let you know, Lloyd, I will probably be retiring after this. I think I've ridden my luck enough times. It's bound to run out soon enough. It is probably time I called it a day, don't you think?'

He freezes momentarily from the news. 'Yeah, sure. Of course. You've pulled enough scores to retire graciously. Better to get out on top than dead, right?'

'That's right. Maybe there's something more for me out there.'

'Sure. I've always pictured you in politics. Maybe you can run for president, or prime minister?'

Jesus, Lloyd can be a dickhead sometimes. 'Yeah…something like that.' I knew he wouldn't take it well. He'll lose his handler's commissions. 'I better head off. I've got plans for dinner.'

'Yeah. You better go. The cabbie is a surly prick.' We share an uncomfortable quiet. I thought he'd be used to it by now. 'You know, you've been the best contractor we've come across…I'm still amazed by some of your work. Hell, in some ways, you remind me of me…I guess what I'm trying to say is I want to give you one chance to discuss arrangements if you don't make it back. Is there anything you want to be put down on your lot?'

He refers to my gravestone, provided my body is found and able to be identified. 'Yeah, I do…A friend of felines and not much else.'

Lloyd shoots back a quizzical expression, while I get up and leave. I find the taxi, still idling, just as Lloyd says with the driver reading a newspaper. He doesn't notice me coming until I tap the window and say, 'I'm your fare. Can you pop the boot for a second?'

I hear a small click as the boot lid rises a little and holds. I open it and find three brand new cases lying flat on the floor. I don't open them but am satisfied everything will be there and close the boot. I slide into the backseat of the car.

'Where to?'

'Freedom Park.'

'Are you sure?'

'Yep. Just near the war memorial.'

It doesn't take too long to arrive, and I'm pleased I don't need to entertain the cabbie with small talk. I hop out and don't pay him because Lloyd already has. He pops the boot again and I grab the cases. I notice the largest case is particularly heavy as I begin to haul them back to my apartment.

By the time I reach my front door my shoulders ache. I should've told the cabbie to drop me closer. No, that's just being lazy. Evading the chance of jeopardising my assignment is always the highest of priorities. Everyone is suspect, including an innocent taxi driver. I lay the briefcases carefully on the couch, not because they contain fragile explosives but to not wake up Buster from his slumber on the seat nearby. I inspect the largest case, mulling over it with inquisitive respect despite knowing what's inside. I flick through the combination, landing on 6-0-6, then hearing the light snapping of the locking mechanism. I pull the tabs and the case's latch pops open with an unmistakable sound.

Inside is the unmatched image of a Franchi Sporting Purpose Automatic Shotgun or its common street name: SPAS 12. The folded stock cradling the barrel and the four unique holes bored into the stock make the firearm appear distinctive and futuristic. It's an imposing sight and intimidating enough to still be used in movies as a combat shotgun to be feared. It *is* to be feared in close quarters when it's set to its self-loading, semiautomatic mode, which fires twelve-gauge shells with each pull of the trigger until all seven rounds, as well as one in the chamber, have hit someone or something with devastating force. Lloyd must have pulled a few strings to obtain it, because it is illegal to be in possession of such a machine of destruction in this country.

As powerful as its potential is, I am not overawed by this piece of equipment like a gun-nut. Although it would fetch a mint if I were to sell it, it will be stripped and disposed of in an orderly manner if I get out of the compound unscathed. It is, like everything in these cases, a tool for a job. That's all they are. Specific tools for a specific purpose. I open the other two cases: the unregistered Glock 22C with two magazines loaded with .40 S&W pistol cartridges, gas mask, grappling hook, smoke grenades, night camouflage clothing, and enough distinctly coloured and various shotgun ammo of rubber and tear gas shells to bring down a large crowd.

I tie knots in the rope to make it easier to climb. I check all of the ammunition and inspect, clean, and lubricate every mechanical part of each weapon before storing them in the closet and pathetically laying a few bags over the cases. I shower and wet shave with a double-edged razor before dressing in a tuxedo, meticulously applying a completely different wig to the one worn by Dr Kruger, and head out quietly through the fire escape after feeding Buster.

I hail a cab without difficulty. The traffic falls in line with my mood. There's little resistance as the cab vacillates through traffic to its destination; like the centring of my thoughts, both are fixed and at ease. I am calm but sharp, as if I could hear a pin fall and be quick enough to see it hit the floor.

I tip the cabbie a block away and stroll to the town hall. Even from a distance, I see limousines pulling to the curb and photographers standing outside to take pictures of guests for the social pages. I give them a miss and slip through.

Once up the steps, I get looked over by a model: a tall brunette in a black dress who checks my invite off a list on her clipboard.

'Thank you, Dr Spentz,' she says warmly. 'Here is your nametag.'

I smile at her as she tries to put the nametag on my jacket. Funny, I didn't see her do this for any of the guests before me. As she flounders, I grab the tag off her and pin it on.

'It's OK. I've got it.'

She keeps up her look and I notice she is feeling awkward, so I plainly nod and proceed to the reception area. I've never set foot inside this building before and baulk at the opulence and sheer excessiveness of the room and the service. A daunting crystal chandelier dominates the foyer like an omnipotent overseer of its patrons. People are celebrating with Verve Clicquot and intricate canapés served by pretty waiters, males and female, who seem on the whole inexperienced and hired for their beauty instead of their skill.

I take an offered glass of champagne and scan the crowd in the hope of not being surprised by any sudden encounters, although there is little chance of that. I recognise nobody. It would, however, be a complete disaster if I encounter Jessica Ward *and* she recognises me.

Guests huddle in small familiar workgroups, which suits me fine as I roam through the crowd to the far wall, purposely removing myself from any introductions or discussions.

I consume my champagne very slowly, almost a quarter of a sip at a time while appearing to gulp mouthfuls. This is pretty boring stuff but I better not leave. The reason I'm here is for intelligence and even the smallest titbit could be helpful.

Finally, the Wards enter the room to strong applause. I try to observe Charles, but my attention strays to Jessica who is dressed in a dazzling one-shoulder crimson chiffon dress with matching pumps. I don't think any heterosexual male or lesbian woman within view would be looking elsewhere. After wasting vital moments just to take this sight in, I stare intently at Charles, but his expression is bland. If only it were as easy as wearing a sign confessing his guilt. Nothing is forthcoming and he is remarkably stoic. He doesn't even let himself smile at his own awards dinner. Meanwhile Jessica is the complete opposite. She beams excitedly and waves to friends and colleagues who are cheering. Father and daughter couldn't act any more differently.

'What do you think of this?' a man beside me asks.

I don't pay much attention until I realise he directed his question at me. 'It's quite an achievement.'

'I'll say. More like a miracle if you ask me.'

The disgruntled sarcasm of his tone bates me. 'What do you mean by that?' I say, taking it hook, line, and sinker.

'What I mean is that for anyone else working on a substance like Aggredisol, it would have taken decades to create. This is a bolt out of the blue. Think about it, a chemical, permanent solution to some of society's greatest problems, almost stopping short of barbaric mental conditioning. It is insane to consider. They got this drug up and running in such a short time it's almost impossible…and I should know…I'm in this field. Miracle cure? More like Freeman's lobotomies.'

This guy must be jealous, but he does make an interesting point if true. The drug surely must work. It would've needed to pass the scrutiny of clinical trials to be approved. It's inconceivable to think any problems wouldn't have been detected during this stage.

Camera flashes illuminate the guests of honour while they are greeted by the mayor and his silicon-enhanced wife. Both couples walk through the audience to the end of the foyer where an attendant opens a set of double doors to reveal a large dining hall. There's an elevated stage with seating for eight, akin to a bridal party's wedding table. Everybody follows the guests of honour and are directed to their tables by courteous ushers.

I'm glad to find the table I'm assigned is to the side of the main stage. It's tucked away in a dark corner and affords decent cover and a great view of my target. I sit with nine other doctors, all of whom don't know each other apart from a husband and wife team, who chat among themselves while entrées are served.

I become increasingly attentive to the Wards because I am completely at odds with their behaviour. Charles slouches most of the time with folded arms and hands closed. He doodles on a notepad with long arcs out of boredom from the speeches the mayor and other dignitaries for the Sullivan Award give. After the main course, he tries to look around in the audience, but I'm doubtful he can see anything beyond the stage as it is well lit and the rest of the room is in comparable darkness. It appears he'd rather be in his lab. He's restless, as if he needs to get back to work straight away on whatever medical breakthrough he has planned next.

Jessica, though, is eager to receive her accolade. She sits up and leans on the table with her feet under the chair legs gently bouncing in excited anticipation. She is all smiles and converses vigorously with the mayor's wife while being captivated by the speeches made about this fascinating product.

My mind races at the prospect of sorting these signals. Is it possible Jessica knows nothing about her father's underworld meddling? Is she being kept in the dark, or wilfully ignorant? The biggest problem I have with all of this, which I keep revisiting, is why all the interest with such a criminally connected hostage in Valentino? How much is there to gain to involve yourself in an underworld war? His relationship to Varetti must be so important that he is willing to risk a leak of the association to the media and ruin his reputation, life, and legacy.

I peer up at the balcony and notice a number of male faces overseeing the whole procession. He arranged his own security team to keep a watchful eye over all his guests. Now that I'm aware, the number of security personnel on the floor is excessive for such an event. Lloyd was right! This bastard is paranoid enough to carry a squad with him wherever he goes. There is no latitude to snipe his head off from a distance and take only half of the reward.

A sensation flutters throughout my body at this logic that the spoon I hold flickers and almost falls out of my grip from realising the magnitude of such an adversary. Charles is an enemy I could easily lose my life to. He is incredibly smart and will be a capable foe. I carefully lay the semimelted ice cream back onto the dish and sigh. The sigh quickly forms a smile when I picture Charles Ward as a cunning villain. I may have met my match.

My natural curiosity also gets the better of me. I need to know what is in that second building. Even if Valentino is there or not—or dead—there is something there that Charles is going to great lengths to protect. If he is willing to risk his livelihood with what he is hiding, there must be something of importance to him and Varetti.

Nobody on the table notices the clang my spoon makes with the fine china bowl. They are all obliviously occupied with small talk. I retract and head for the bathroom before Charles gives his speech, which I don't want to miss.

I try my best to freshen up by splashing water on my face. The nametag is a little crooked, so I remove it completely. I'm sure other guests have, and I can always put it back on if requested by security. They aren't slouches either, constantly alert and patrolling in regular patterns and intervals. No guests other than myself would be any wiser to their calibre from the freshly licensed, inexperienced guards usually hired for a token presence.

As soon as I am halfway down the narrow corridor to the reception area, I am confronted by Jessica Ward passing me to go to the ladies bathroom.

Holy shit, not again!

For a split second, I have no recourse and am frozen, like a deer in headlights, not knowing what to do next. Should I walk back to the men's room or pass her with blind ignorance? Will only a different wig pass me off as someone else if I continue forward? Both will make me out to be a fool, but it's only with the latter that I will know if I got away with it. Either way, I'm pretty much fucked.

I am just able to hide my surprise with an awkward gaze that only prompts her to become inquisitive.

'Oh,' she says, 'We've met before, haven't we?'

I cough, only to give me more time to prepare myself. It's a confirmatory question and not a wholly rhetorical one. This gives me an angle. 'Sorry…' I say, in a complete departure from my regular voice, adding a twang of sophistication while lowering it half an octave. 'But you've mistaken me for somebody else.'

I stick to my script and pass her without giving it a second thought. Out of the corner of my eye I see her shrug and throw my correction away as if being wrong didn't bother her. Using a different wig tonight is my saving grace. I don't dare look back, but I feel her gaze linger on me before I turn from the corridor and out of her sight.

But I stop. I stop because I find even spending the total of less than two minutes with her on two fleeting occasions has made me attracted to her personality. What's not to like about a confident woman? Both times it's her that instigated harmless banter. Shy people won't do this to a stranger unless they are asking for directions. She can also be gracious when she is mistaken, and this is even rarer in a self-fulfilling world.

I shouldn't do it, simply because it is unprofessional. And secondly, I have more respect for women.

Against my better judgement, I turn back around the corner and take a mischievous peek at Jessica walking to the bathroom.

The only examinable flesh I have the pleasure to dwell on are her lower legs because they aren't covered by her expensive dress. The lines of her calves are fantastically shaped in heels. The muscle definition is subtle, yet captivating and certainly impressive. It is easy to tell that she takes the time to conform to a rigorous fitness regime. In a different world I could fantasise about fostering a relationship with her. It's moments like this that cause me to pity my career path because of the sacrifices I have to make. It is simply impossible to be in a relationship in this line of work.

I mope back to my table where Charles has already started giving his speech. I can mourn over my life choices some other time.

It is much clearer to me now. The security guards surreptitiously gather around the stage, no doubt to protect the principal. There's no way a sniper's bullet will be able to take him down. He's too covered. Likewise with Luigi Baresi, Charles is taking the necessary precautions. I don't believe he knows what is coming to him. If he did there would've been thorough checks on everyone who walked into the building tonight. It seems the extra protection is more routine than mistrust. Lloyd was right; going for the hit will be problematic. But how does a man like Charles explain these measures to his daughter? What would she think of all the heavies in her family home?

Charles goes to great lengths to detail his work, using mostly professional jargon that flies over everyone's head except his immediate peers. I am disheartened by it all, mainly because he doesn't reveal any insight into himself except a neurotic flair to justify his team of hired guns.

Meanwhile, Jessica sneaks back on stage. She has great timing because five minutes later, she is accepting the award from the mayor. There are more flashes from the press docked just in front of the stage. But I've had enough for one night and decide to leave before anything else happens. Tomorrow night, I will make my move.

CHAPTER EIGHT

I've mentally prepared myself in the same manner I always do. I am lost in focus, waiting for the time to hit eleven before I embark. I used to have adrenaline pumping through my veins at moments like this, but by now, through routine and repetition, the edge has worn off and has been replaced by a dull, workman-like clarity of what is expected and how it is going to be achieved. I prepped my kit bag last night as soon as I came home after the awards dinner. I could imagine nothing worse than to hurry through something so important.

I have a deadline of course, but common sense tells me breaching the property the night after the dinner would be easier than on the night. I have a psychological theory why.

Charles feels secure on his property, and judging from his trained guards, he would be naturally vulnerable whenever he travels. Of course, when he does leave his property, his men will be on the lookout for anything suspicious and will naturally be on edge. The night after, though, they will be resting easy knowing that Charles is safely contained within his compound. This, to me, is why tonight is the better option. And if I'm going for both objectives, I need to accomplish them on the same night. If I rescued Valentino last night, the chance of coming close to Charles would be next to nothing. And I definitely could not have skipped the dinner to save Valentino and wait around for Charles to show up. A simple missed phone call to check in would have scared off my mark. I have to claim his scalp and the only way to do this is to do them both within the same hour.

My plan sounds ludicrous: get Valentino out, kill Charles, and escape. All of the variables—the guards, the state of the targets, and even the location of the estate—make it a crapshoot with that many armed men. Back in the forces, this would be a cakewalk with even a small squad of trained soldiers. But I do not have the luxury of helping hands and extra trigger fingers. I can only rely on the few surprises I can spring and hope they will be enough.

I know I shouldn't but I visualise the financial freedom I will have if I am successful. I swear I will never look back and endanger my life again. The dream of retiring to a peaceful existence has taken hold and is now closer to grasp. Two years ago, I would have dismissed the idea without a second thought. But I feel I have made an impact in my life or at least certainly in this vocation. It's time to move on.

For my next incarnation I want to live in solitude. I think about moving away from Hillbay for long stretches at a time to a small, seaside town where I will not be bothered, and cannot be found or questioned. My longing to leave the city has been reinforced over the last few months. Big city living is not all that it has cracked up to be. The punk trying to mug me in Freedom Park is a shining example of that. It makes sense to me now: as the population swells so does the potential for crime. Maybe people lose their identity among the swarm and lash out because they feel unimportant. Why? Who knows? Nobody is forgiving these days, and people are mostly self-absorbed with little respect for others. It's quite strange I feel this way, seeing as I thrive from these 'problems'…

Everything is set as I leave enough dry food out to last Buster a week. He is asleep on the couch and it's probably best I don't wake him. But I can't resist. I gently stroke his head and he opens his eyes gingerly and closes them again. He fidgets until he flops onto one side and stretches out. Even though he's awake, he doesn't make a sound as I unlock the front door and leave.

I sigh momentarily because of that petulant ball of fur. I just don't have the capacity to despise animals, even the frustrating ones, as much as I can despise people. Buster's reasoning is his own, and it would be my fault by not conditioning him properly if he wrongs me. But humans, they have the capacity to be responsible for their actions and to reflect on them and recognise the error of their ways. Buster doesn't have that luxury, so I can't blame him.

On second thought, I should have told Lloyd to ask Mrs Rutherford to take care of Buster if I don't make it back, and I should have set aside enough money for her to take care of him and see him out. She wouldn't say no, not that she would use most of the money I'd give her on Buster anyway. Once her daughter got so much of a whiff of her windfall, it would evaporate just as quickly as it fell into Mrs Rutherford's lap.

Lloyd will have a hissy fit if I don't make it back and Buster is left under his care. The little guy will piss all over his new owner's furniture before he has his first meal. Unfortunately I found out the hard way about Buster's great need to demonstrate his territoriality. It's only proper that Lloyd doesn't receive the advantage of any prior warning.

I lug the heavy bag to my rental car a block away. The car I hired yesterday before meeting Lloyd is thankfully untouched. I wasn't happy leaving it here, but the clean, bare interior and a car alarm would've put a dampener on any thief's intentions. It's also the most basic, common, and cheapest of hatchbacks to rent. I doubt I'll be required to tear up the streets in a quick getaway tonight.

The drive is quiet, and I feel confident after a late revision to my plan. It's a change not even Lloyd would be able to anticipate. Operational methods are best kept confidential. It is always better for handlers like Lloyd to be left in the dark. If my suspicions are correct and there is a leak somewhere, if it involves the agency, changing plans and leading Lloyd astray will not be a wasted pastime. Lloyd might have a rough idea of what I intend to do, but his forecast won't be exact because he wasn't my only supplier. Misdirection can always play a role no matter whom it involves. In this instance, Lloyd will know exactly where I will be striking, but for the when and the how, he can only guess. And just because he is my handler doesn't automatically make us best friends.

The words Luigi Baresi spoke before he met his end are more worrisome than anything he could have ordered or otherwise done to me while he was alive. Until this gets resolved, nobody will be granted a pass from my suspicions. I know this doesn't help my situation either. Such doubts should not be hanging over me before any mission, let alone one as difficult as this. This is a cluster-fuck of the highest order, with the worst timing imaginable.

Nevertheless, I'll stick to my game plan. I park one street behind the Wards' estate. I trespass through the property backing it, marking a path with small bursts of a spray can to create a subtle trail for Valentino if he needs to leave without me.

There are no typical wooden fences separating properties, but there are three-metre-high solid walls to protect privacy.

I sneak to the adjoining wall and settle myself for a moment. I have plenty of time and take a moment to gather my thoughts. For the inexperienced, the calm before the storm is the time to fret. It's the nerve-racking moments right before action and imminent violence. The tipping point at which there is no going back.

For me, I'm just getting my breath back.

I lay the kit bag down. As I open it, the two ten-pound satchel charges I picked up today from Curious George reveal themselves as if a dirty pleasure smiles at me. Two separate remotes, set at different frequencies, are taped to each charge. They are not just an aid to more effectively extract Valentino; they are also my insurance policies. Lloyd's jibe that 'this is a job for law enforcement' made me realise that this *is* the time to get the law involved. How can Charles adequately explain that he is keeping a man against his will if the police come knocking? The explosions are there to make enough noise for at least a few neighbours to call it in and hopefully have the police respond in kind. It is time to have the authorities on my side for once.

I place an explosive on the wall closest to me. I quickly dash along the wall out of sight of the unmanned lookout tower with the other charge. I couldn't see any CCTV cameras craning from the tower, but I suspect there must be a number of them around the property relaying a feed to a central security unit. Otherwise it would need to be manned. I fix the second charge on the other corner and sprint back to my initial position.

While catching my breath, I holster my Glock into a duty belt, then grab the SPAS 12, smoke grenades, and gas mask and head to the large oak tree on the backing property, taking cover behind it. The thick trunk of the tree will protect me from flying debris. It's now 0030 and a better time, if any, to start. The explosions won't be large enough to bring down the whole wall, but they will make sizeable holes that a human can hobble through.

I grab both remotes and crouch for the coming detonation. I arm the triggers, exhale, and detonate the charges simultaneously. There is a quarter-second delay before a wave of noise rips through the quiet night. I let the dust settle for a brief moment before I emerge, shotgun in hand, and run to the fence. Faint yelling can be heard from deep within the property.

At the wall, I notice security has not scrambled yet. If I were in command, I would do the same thing. I need to go to them and not the other way around. If they are smart and not just slow, they know this, but if I don't push on, at some point they will have to send somebody over to investigate why two separate holes have been blasted through their back wall.

I step over the crumbled section of the wall closest to me, crossing the imaginary threshold, committed to not turning back until my job is complete or I am dead. As planned, this particular blast was blocked from sight by the rear building with only a dissipating cloud of dust merging with the faint fog to give any indication the wall has been breached. I scope both sides of the lane between the wall and the building with my sidearm raised, cocked, and with the safety off.

I shoulder the SPAS in preparation for an onslaught. I make my way to the corner of the building while crouched to reduce my hit size and be ready for a number of guards. Louder shouting comes from around the corner, but they are still some distance away. I'm yet to reach the corner when a guard runs just in front of me and stops to peer down the small alleyway. His silenced MP5 points safely to the ground as our eyes meet. My SPAS, however, is not. His eyes open to an impossible degree as I pull the trigger, unloading a shell into his chest. The impact lifts him off the ground. As he flies through the air, I wonder how long it will take him to realise he survived being shot only a couple of metres away with a shotgun made to split him in two. The discharged baton round will break his skin but not tear through his internal organs the way a buckshot round would.

I can make out commands from afar and as I pop my head out from cover to check their position. A few compressed bursts of an MP5 erupt; one round hits the corner of the building in front of me and a horizontal geyser of dust sprays out from the brickwork.

I take cover and watch the rear corner for guards sneaking around the other side. I have to keep moving or be a sitting duck. Sheer numbers will suffocate me. I reach for a couple of smoke grenades from my duty belt, pull the rings, and blindly toss them in the direction of the now quiet guards. I don't risk losing my head by finding out exactly where they are, as the grenades have a decent spread. I wait for the 'pop' of its discharging gas before grabbing another and tossing it down the alley over to the other rear corner of the building to protect my six.

I duck my head out again and see the smoke covering a vast area of the yard. There is no noise apart from the hiss of the canisters. I load the SPAS with three rounds of pepper spray and fire them into the haze. I overhear a guard incorrectly scream, 'It's all right. It's only *smoke!*'

I slide the gas mask over my face, take one final deep breath, and take my chances against a reckless order to fire blindly through the haze. If that order is given, it will take a miracle to survive.

But they're unprepared. I'm halfway to the entrance of the building when I hear a couple of guards spluttering and crying out. I have no time to smart over the pepper spray rounds. I hope more than anything that I have not been seen. The confusion of my whereabouts is an advantage I need to regain after revealing myself by shooting that guard.

The large double doors are luckily unlocked. Just as I assumed, the inside is reminiscent of a prison. There is a large hallway barred and gated with the unmistakable uniformity of doors on either side facing each other at regular intervals. I am buoyed at the prospect of finding Valentino; however, there is the obstacle of getting through the prison-style gates and into the rooms.

I load up the SPAS with baton shells and stride menacingly into the small office just before the gate. I fire at a prepared guard too slow to pull the trigger. His body vaults through the room like a catapulted dummy. A young orderly crouches under the operating desk, gripping a pistol in such a tentative manner I have to believe this is the first time he has ever held a gun. I remove my gas mask and sneer at him.

'Where is Valentino Baresi?' I demand. He shakes his head. 'You'll be in *more* trouble if you don't tell me than if you do.'

'C-c-cell four.'

A stroke of luck! He is here and alive. 'Lose the weapon, slowly, and open the cell or you're dead.'

Placing the pistol on the ground, he gathers himself and pulls a lever from the control panel he was hiding under. There is a pneumatic hiss, and I see in the corridor a cell door open.

'Thanks,' I say before striking him at the base of the neck with the butt of my firearm. He moans before collapsing to the floor.

I hurry until an antiseptic smell hits me. This is not merely a prison, but has the sterilised aroma of a hospital.

As I approach the door, the powerful and repugnant acrid stench of a raw sewerage plant greets me. I suddenly doubt if Valentino will be able to walk out of here.

His cell is poorly lit with only a flickering fluorescent light illuminating his gloomy predicament. I am witness to a depravity of the human condition. This isn't a prison cell hospital ward but a torturer's holding room.

Valentino is propped up in a corner wearing a dirty hospital gown with his arms folded and head down. He doesn't even realise I have entered the room. Faeces have been strewn all over the white-walled cell. Urine stains the floor as well as fresh pools of blood. But the most horrendous sight is not the state of the room, but the rotted corpse hanging in the opposite corner. I am transfixed on the figure. Is it a male or female? It's genitals and head have been removed, and where its head was cut, the skin on its neck is blackened at the edges and turns purple a few centimetres from where it was severed. Below this, the person's colour is a shade of decayed green around their centre mass. The corpse must have been there for a while, as chunks of skin and flesh have been taken from its sides and both pectorals or breasts, whichever they were, leaving a gangrenous border. All except one limb has been torn off; however, there are no bones or any traces of the removed appendages in the cell. The remaining limb, the victim's right arm, has flesh removed to the bone around the bicep and wrist and only has a thumb in place. The skin has rotted as well.

Jesus Christ! I look at Valentino for a moment and vomit. He probably cannibalised some of the human in front of us hanging by wire from the top of its spinal column. Who could make somebody willing enough to do such a thing? In all my times in combat, I have seen some disgusting sights on the battlefield, particularly in third world countries where lives mean little. But the vile nature of this cell in a 'supposed' civilised society has shocked me beyond what I thought could be achieved as the depth of human treatment. Someone was responsible for this, and I certainly think their wickedness must know no bounds. Charles *must* be behind all this. For that, he deserves to die. Such a bastard instantly earned what is coming to him.

But first, I have this sorry soul to extract to safety.

'Valentino Baresi!'

The pittance of a human I see before me is void of any response and emotion. I grab a fistful of his hair and yank it back to see if he's conscious. A pale and pasty face with gaunt cheeks, some boils and cuts, and glassy eyes stare vacantly into God knows where.

I don't have time for this. How long will it take for the guards to realise that I'm in here and shoot us both? Shit! My fears have come true and I have to try everything and anything and quickly. I slap him hard once across the face, but a tiny response doesn't satisfy me. It's time for drastic measures. I dig into a lower pocket of my cargo pants to pull out a rectangular case. In it is a small prefilled syringe of norepinephrine and methamphetamine. I pull up a dirty sleeve and inject the mixture into a clearly visible vein on the inside of his elbow. I pull him up and shake him by his shoulders, hoping the drugs will speed through his system that little bit faster. The effects are almost instantaneous.

'Valentino! We've got to get out, Valentino!' I scream.

'What?' he mumbles. At least he can acknowledge me.

'I'm here to get you out of here.'

He starts tweaking to life with a surge of instant chemical energy coursing through his bloodstream. He quickly becomes aware of his situation. He inhales a tornado of relief. 'Thank God,' he sighs, struggling to put together words. 'I thought I was going to die here!'

'You will soon if we don't get a move on,' I say, hurrying to the door and scanning for guards.

I run back up to the entrance. The smoke and gas has begun to clear outside. We don't have much time, and getting out will be tough, seeing as there is no other exit. The rear door I thought could be an escape is bolted shut and looks as heavy as a vault door. It is not an option. I eject the remaining three cartridges and load three smoke shells followed by more baton rounds.

'Put this on,' I tell Valentino, throwing him a gas mask. 'There's a hole in the wall behind this building you need to run through. I've marked a path with reflective spray paint on the property behind that you'll need to follow in order to get to the main road. You need to climb a couple of fences to get out, and don't worry about being seen by the neighbours. Just sprint through and don't look. They should already be frightened by the noise and have probably called the police. This is a key to a rental car on the street about fifty metres down from the backing property. You can't miss it because it's by far the cheapest car in this suburb. It's a silver hatch. Can you do that?'

He nods.

'Tell me you understand?'

'I understand,' he affirms.

I fire the three smoke cartridges in the vicinity of the position the guards took earlier, hoping they haven't made any progress. I hear some shouting.

'On my mark,' I yell.

I peer out and almost get my head taken off with a range of blind fire zinging past me.

'Now!' I scream, turning the corner and firing wildly into the artificial fog to cover Valentino's escape. I hope the ferocious power of the shotgun will create enough noise to force the enemy to take cover.

I can faintly hear Valentino sprint behind me over the noise of the shotgun. Seeing the horrific way he was treated only steels my determination and offsets the glaring warning Lloyd gave me to not bother with the kill.

How can I possibly turn a blind eye now? I had a basic plan and was fortunate with Valentino. Luckily, he is alive and didn't need to be carried out. If I'm going all the way, I have a small force to negotiate before trying to take Charles Ward out.

But as soon as I turn to see Valentino run through the gap in the wall and to freedom, I instantly regret not following him. A million-dollar pay cheque is running from me and I may not be able to enjoy it. As much as I want to right a wrong and fight for something I believe in, I cannot let it conceal the hard realities of how to achieve this aim. I'm fresh out of ideas on how to proceed.

In truth, the mark has kept me up at night. Not because of the qualms I may have in killing a doctor or the witch hunt that will follow after the world finds out, but the pious sense that my pride thinks I can succeed when I knew it was high risk before and next to impossible now.

I realise I must let go of the idea of perfection like a prized trophy dangling tantalisingly over a net and just beyond my reach. My personal salvation and retreat from this lifestyle is intertwined with this job. The rewards are as equally substantial as the immense risk. And now, running out of ammo for this weapon and not following Valentino out of here just closed the lid on my own escape.

I fire the last shell. My smoke screen is clearing and I am out of options and don't have enough ammo. There is no point in being anywhere near this building: Valentino has been extracted.

Surely, it is now a fruitless endeavour wanting to pursue Charles. He has probably been warned and fled to safety. There is no point. It is too late. I have to leave fast or die here.

I wait for the slightest break in gunfire.

I decide to backtrack and follow Valentino if I still can. As I approach the end of the building, a guard almost collides into me. Innately, I swat him with the butt of the SPAS. The impact connects with his jaw and grinds it sideways before snapping back like a pulled elastic band. He collapses to the ground in a heap. I peer around the corner to see armed guards positioning themselves for an ambush. There's no way I can beat a hail of bullets to get past them and through the wall.

I have no choice but to retreat back to the building.

For the first time in my life, the fight-or-flight adrenaline is nowhere to be found. I gasp, stuck feeling that I will be summarily executed or subjected to a treatment on par with Valentino's…or maybe worse. I pull my Glock and, for a second, consider turning it on myself to prevent any worse fate that may befall me if caught alive. But I am a soldier and a professional.

I will be dying tonight or worse, this is the only truth. It's not death that people fear, but knowing that death is imminent. A tiny moment of panic reveals to me that there is something human in me after all. I brush these thoughts aside. I've been in this game long enough to know better. Go down fighting and never give up. It's time to face whatever is coming, and in the most tactically beneficial way possible.

The corridor to the cells is a good way of funnelling guards to be picked off one by one, but I don't have enough ammo to walk out alive. Hiding is my next option, but it's impossible in this building. There is a secured door leading to stairs that is too complicated to open. I have no idea from all the buttons and levers at the operating desk, and the door is too heavy to smash open.

I decide to go to cell four, and I have no idea why except to buy time. The irrepressible stench has already burned its familiarity into my head as I almost seize at the thought of reacquainting myself with such hellish surroundings. My pulse elevates like it should and I feel trapped. The dread of being suddenly executed pulls at me again and I cannot force myself into the cell. It's the only cell available, but I cannot enter because my sense of smell prohibits me. I realise it is fear.

Instead, I can't help but look through a small observation slot into the next cell, just to gauge the room. *What the fuck is going on in there?* I am shocked to see what is before me. My mind swirls trying to take hold of a reality it can anchor to.

Foreign footsteps are heard at the entrance, but I don't care. I cannot even turn my head, run for cover or brace for death. *This is a fucking abomination!* My Catholic upbringing would not be able to justify the thing in front of me, except that it is the work of an evil beyond my understanding.

I make out a naked and sickly man, in such tormenting pain a quick end would be his first wish if he could think at all. His skin is diseased and parasitic and droops with so many sores, boils, and lacerations that I cannot see a single patch of skin that isn't affected. He moves about the room in such a deranged manner that I want him to stop because he is harming himself with his excitement. Skin flicks away like droplets of water flying off a wet dog shaking itself dry. Blood and melted skin spray around the cell, and I am amazed he is *still* alive after all of this. He is excited to see me stare at him and rushes to me. His bloody face crashes against the viewing glass. He smashes his nose against it and as he pulls away, his nose detaches and sticks to the glass, not even budging from gravity acting on it. It hangs there momentarily and as he shuffles away, it slowly slides down and out of sight.

Is he a sick joke? A ploy? An experiment of warfare chemicals or a clinical trial gone disastrously wrong? *How can someone do this?* There are so many fantastic ideas to try and explain but none can begin to rationalise it.

As I try in vain to comprehend, a stinging sensation hijacks my train of thought. They fucking shot me in the leg. I was supposed to come out firing. I barely notice with peripheral vision a wall of guards clamoured together with their weapons pointing at me. I collapse awkwardly as I realise I am not bleeding from a bullet wound but stunned from a tranquiliser. The dart tore through my thigh as I roll on the ground and yank it out. I leave my dropped weapons out of reach and am too weak to retrieve them.

'Stand clear,' someone shouts.

My guns are kicked away from me. I can't move, unable to even struggle as I pass out from shock. The last thing I hear is a guard say, 'Subject neutralised.'

CHAPTER NINE

I wake to a numbing punch to the side of my face. Even after this I am still groggy, so an even harder slap gushes across my other cheek.

'This is for Johnny, motherfucker!'

'Enough,' a voice orders.

The taste of blood fills my mouth. I swallow it along with a dislodged tooth as my eyes strain to open. My body screams in pain, but I have no energy to even whimper. Trickles of blood seep from my nose, dripping onto the mat under the chair, and I suspect my nose is broken, or at least my sinus cavity has ruptured.

When my senses come to, I run through a mental checklist learned from my military days. My hands are bound behind my back and I feel around them to gather they are bound by zip ties, but my feet and head have full mobility. I don't try and struggle because there's no point and apart from my nose and general muscle strains and joint aches, I am fit. I am assured that they want me alive for something because if not, I would never have woken up.

Gaining my bearings is a slow process after my initial checklist. What was the last thing I remember? A monster in a room? The smell of piss, shit, and rotting flesh. The basement and holding cells of the building on Charles Ward's property.

I can tell that I am not in the basement anymore. The overpowering stench is gone.

Instead, I am in a small room with a marble floor and not much else. There is a curtained window, a large Baroque painting with Catholic undertones, various liquids, tools, and a telephone sitting on a table. Two men are in the room with me. Both are dressed in tactical night gear, the same my foes were wearing last night, or this morning, or even a few days ago. I have no idea.

One, a supervisor, stands a fair distance behind with his arms crossed while my attacker grabs a jug of solution that he pours over me. I can taste vinegar.

I scream in agony as my skin burns.

He pauses and then pours again.

I scream and tremble involuntarily the second time. I can't think of anything to replace the unwanted focus on the pain.

'All right,' the supervisor yells. 'He's awake.'

The door knocks.

'Let me fuck him up a little mo', boss.'

'Not now. You'll have plenty of time soon.'

He opens the door and talks to a man I can't recognise. The conversation continues long enough for me to see the mystery man flash brilliant gold cufflinks while motioning with his hands in the doorway. Is it Charles? His shirt is so white that just his cuffs illuminate the room.

He leaves and the door is shut. 'All right. Clean him but keep him bound. After that's done, call me.'

I'm left in the room with this thug who is disappointed from his orders as he grabs a bottle of Betadine and a box of wipes to make me look respectable. The stinging of the Betadine is a cakewalk compared to the vinegar solution.

'After your lil' meetin', pal, I'm gonna fuck you up. Yo'll end up being fed to the dogs, faggot.'

I don't speak a word. Maybe I can't. Part of me is still shocked and the other part is confused. I could try to put in a decent fight now even though my hands are bound and perhaps even gain freedom from his pathetic threats and my current incarceration. But too many questions need to be answered. There is also the unknown waiting for me past the door. I have no idea whether there is nobody beyond the door or ten guards waiting to gun me down. I also owe it to myself to find out what's going on even if I am going to die from it. If I see an opportunity, I will take it.

He almost finishes applying textbook, army-trained first aid when he mutters, 'Fuck it,' and delivers a vicious uppercut to my stomach.

I wince in pain as the air is smashed out of me.

'Oh, yeah,' he says.

He backs off and as I try to get my breath back, he front kicks me in the sternum. I hiss out any air I have left, and yelp a tiny bit, almost passing out. Both sides of my chest are in pain, and breathing is laborious, a good sign a couple of ribs are at least bruised, if not broken.

'Ha ha! Eat that shit!'

I moan as he walks to the table and picks up the phone. 'He's ready.'

A minute later two more guards enter and help me to my feet. My attacker picks up a silenced MP5 and holds it continuously at my centre mass, never relaxing his aim. My feet drag as I am carried down the hallway by two men holding me by my armpits, and it surprises me no blood spills onto the floor. My sweat does, though. The guards' shoes squeak but my prevailing thoughts are towards my thigh and the burning feeling from the tranquiliser dart I took in the basement. Can I move my legs? Could I walk out of here if I were able to? I try to put pressure on my shot left leg. Sharp pain emanates from the wound through my nervous system, but it is only muscular pain and not from a broken bone or torn muscle. There is hope.

We enter another room and I recognise the figure standing relaxed, hands clasped behind his back: Charles Ward. His apathetic gaze conveys no emotion. I am roughly propped onto a chair as pain flushes through my body in all directions. I'm afraid that if I pass out like I want to, I will be punished into waking up.

'Thank you,' Charles motions to the guards. 'I'll call for you soon. Until then, you can leave us.'

The guards hesitate a moment, then oblige.

Charles paces a few steps while they leave. He, too, seems uncertain, as if trying to figure out how to open his dialogue with me. He shows no nerves despite what I've agreed to do to him. And he is right there! I am *so* close to finishing off this job and getting out of this mess, forever. All I need to do is kill the crazy man standing in front of me and escape.

But my life is at his mercy, and I could be dead within the hour. Right now, any other life will do. The finish line is right in front of me, and it hurts more to know that than the physical pain I am currently enduring. If only I were healthy, even with my hands bound, I could be quick enough to kill him before he can let out even a yelp. I can only brood about how much I want him dead.

'It's been a while since I've been speechless…but you have me stumped for what to say.' He smiles. 'I guess you want to know what it was you saw down in the holding cells?'

'You're insane.'

He laughs. 'I'm afraid if people were to compare you and me, your record for destruction and murder would far outweigh mine.'

'Everybody I've killed deserved it,' I lie.

'Oh, I didn't realise you were a judge as well as a contract killer.'

'You know what I mean.'

'Not really. You think what we do isn't comparable?'

'You sick fuck. You want to compare yourself to me? I'm not mutilating or *experimenting* on people. Do you honestly think you can get away with this?'

'Oh, my! A man with ideals! You need to get one thing straight: I already *am* getting away with it…and I have you to thank.' He grins.

'What the *fuck* are you talking about?'

'Haven't you ever wondered how you received your hospital credentials, Dr Kruger?'

If I weren't sitting down, I would have been floored. How could this be? How the fuck can he know? There must be a rat, this is certain. But who? Finding this person is now the second-most important thing to me. There is one thing I want more: to kill the prick standing in front of me. *Nobody* should know the link between me and my work. C'mon, think! Who could it possibly be? Who are my suspects? Lloyd? Would he jeopardise a fat commission and certain death? All contractors are assured of meticulous levels of security. Is it someone Lloyd reports to? The agency is tighter than a drum. Counter-surveillance? Curious George? Maybe Charles Ward's personal platoon? Possibly. The corrupt police? Highly doubtful. I try to stare the information out of Charles's smiling eyes, but I can't even buy a clue.

'Still thinking are we?' he says with a smirk.

'*Fuck* you. You're not going to get away with this. One of your hacks will give you up to the cops, or the government, and they will shut you down and dispose of you.'

He bursts into laughter. His genuine chuckles resonate with sarcasm.

'They'll do nothing of the sort.'

He resumes pacing. 'I assume you have a grasp of basic history as I tell you this, because you seem an intelligent person on the whole. But perhaps a little too ambitious for your own good.

'After the Second World War, when Nazi Germany and Imperial Japan were defeated, do you know what happened to their high-ranking physicians when their bureaucracy crashed around them? Contrary to popular belief, most weren't taken to firing squads despite the best efforts of purveyors of justice like the Nazi-hunters. No, they were given a simple ultimatum: work for the winners or face prosecution. Of course, *some* were sacrificed in kangaroo courts, others were "magically" acquitted, and the most important ones, those that did the most ground-breaking work, were never found. It isn't hard to understand that most agreed to be utilised to the utmost of their expertise. They worked for the noble pursuit of science, regardless of their employer, and for them, only the leadership changed. These scientists were able to find the physical and psychological limits of human beings when given the opportunity and the circumstances to do so. They continued with their important research well after reparations were paid. They were dedicated to their work, to strive for a better understanding, and the victors knew this and let them continue. Nobody, bar the un-opportunistic Soviet Union, cared about persecution because, let's be realistic, war progresses technology like no other political climate. Four decades of progress from the Cold War is irrevocable evidence of that.'

'What does this have to do with you? You're not a refugee from the Soviet Union.'

'Does that really matter? Have you seen my achievements? Do you know of my record of excellence? You saw the recognition I received last night at the award ceremony.'

'If you knew I was there, why did you not think I would kill you then?'

'Hmm. There was a little luck involved I must admit. But we ruled it out because there would have been so many witnesses, and we assumed you value your pathetic life and wanted to keep its sad existence intact. We even scoured the building and put our own cameras in, just in case.' He lingers on his planning and technical brilliance. 'We did our homework and psychological profiling just as much as you did. You were cooked from the start.'

Son of a bitch! Further evidence to concrete my theories of betrayal. 'So why haven't you killed me yet?'

'Ah. Straight to the point! Now we're getting to the interesting part. And just for that I'm going to be blunt. I'm sure you're familiar with this country, what it stands for, and why its culture and prosperous society is at war with entities bent on the destruction and abolition of our way of life—'

'Do you want to get more intense with your hyperboles?'

With that insult, Charles's mood immediately sours. His face turns red with rage. '*Listen,*' he explodes. 'My daughter and I have more than made a little sacrifice to this world. She lost a mother to an attack, vaporised in an instant from military-grade plastic explosives given to her killers by a regime that hides from open warfare because they know they will be crushed. Instead, they decide to attack civilian targets, innocent targets, people who may not have even supported the war against them.' He clears his throat to compose himself. 'You see, we're both in this war together, using the talent we possess to help in the seemingly impossible task to rid this world of those who try to rid us.'

'Bullshit! I was coerced into my wars. That's what being in the military is all about. I didn't have a choice.'

'Just because you didn't care, doesn't mean that you aren't able to make up your mind to participate?'

I am silent because I know it is true. I didn't say no to my army service because it didn't matter where I was going and what I was asked to do. Even the socially crippled lifestyle I live today is more normal than my time in the military. But killing in a 'peaceful' society instead of a battlefield is unacceptable because I don't have a rank and am not given a mandate by a government to do it. But I have the joy of choice now, and I'm not constantly fed the line that I'm invincible or some super-soldier to tip the balance between rational thought and reckless aggression. Instead, I have what is at best a lame sense of autonomy. I do the bidding for less crooked but still incredibly sinful clients. But at least it is better than what I witnessed in those cells of his.

'And kidnapping people, leaving them to be cannibals, and burning the skin off unsuspecting citizens you do not hate will stop a war that is unstoppable?'

He smiles with approval. 'Finally! Finally we're getting somewhere. Unheard of? Absolutely not! Back in World War II, there was a Japanese secret medical unit known as Unit 731. They led the world in the research of biological warfare. All kinds of medical experimentations occurred that would have been frowned upon during peacetime. POWs had limbs severed and reattached to the opposite side. All known plagues were tested, including anthrax, mind you, not to mention testing archaic and primitive notions like that animal blood could be substituted for human blood or seawater could be a substitute for saline. And what do you think happened to that data? Do you think it was destroyed? Of course not. At least our friend, Boris in cell five, has the benefit of anaesthetics along with the careful extraction of any self-detrimental parts of the brain, such as pity and fear. It was such a shame you had to disturb him when the structural integrity of his skin was not stable. It will certainly slow down our observations. He is a great example of—'

A strong knock on the door interrupts his train of thought. Charles shows genuine surprise at the disruption.

'*Don't* say a word,' he warns.

He walks over and opens the door. Another hidden conversation with a person I cannot identify. It goes on for about two minutes with Charles nodding, seemingly subservient to the man he is engaged with. Maybe there's another factor, another person involved in all of this.

'There's a friend I want you to meet,' Charles says, after closing the door. 'He'll be ready soon.'

'I can't wait.'

'You should be *grateful!*' he barks, in a fit of anger. 'I can just as easily sedate you and turn you into the same hideous man as Boris. Or alternatively, turn you into his food.'

'But you haven't. So there's obviously something you need to tell me before you kill me. Because I'm about to die from all of your bullshit.'

Charles lunges and slaps a hand on my throat. 'I will kill you if you don't treat your situation and your *life* a little more seriously.'

I am saved by another knock on the door.

He takes a while to adjust himself and too long to salvage composure. It's as if he is ashamed of his outburst and lack of restraint. He fine-tunes his tie to its previously perfect state, blissfully oblivious to his moment of madness. He mutters to himself quietly, until the door knocks a second time to snap him into action.

He smiles menacingly.

'Are you ready to meet a good friend?' I say nothing. 'I'll assume that's a yes.'

He reveals the man standing on the opposite side of the door and shakes his hand. It doesn't surprise me to learn his identity. He couldn't have been more contrasting to Dr Ward, not only in appearance but also public standing.

'Good evening.'

The grin is unbearable. The sinking feeling wipes the colour from me quicker than I can realise. I stare at his impeccably white shirt and shiny gold cufflinks.

The epiphany of destruction of this city's underworld and my significant contribution to it sinks my stomach until my vision blurs and I almost black out. I don't though, and it takes the best part of a minute to regain myself and identify the newly most feared man in Hillbay, and possibly the country.

Vincenzo Varetti keeps his pleasant smile as he bends forward like a curious professor inspecting a wild, but tamed beast. He has aged well for his sixty-something years, despite choosing not to dye his silvering hair.

I've been played. It's that simple. Someone I know has sold me out and given me up to do Varetti and Charles's bidding. And my paymasters are here to rub it in. They're going to patronise me, and I can only sit here and take it.

'I don't know where to start with the praise I have for you,' Varetti says in English completely removed of any ancestral accent. 'But the main thing I would like to point out is that you, and only you, were able to remove my greatest rival to this city's unaccounted for wealth. Words can't express the joy I felt...well, *we* felt about the whole event, especially after we tried for so long to get to him. The only thing we were able to do was to inflict a tiny dent by kidnapping his stupid son and getting lucky with a wounding potshot. I'll never forget the morning I reached for the paper with the giant headlines of Luigi's demise taking top billing on the broadsheet. I still smile just thinking about it. You have no idea how your actions will triple my wealth, and how pleased we are for the demand people have to brighten up their lives with our products. The demand for ice is going through the roof, which is great for me because it involves heavy production compared to cocaine and heroin. And now, any start-up organisation will need to consider the muscle and reach I have and what will happen if they dare try and compete. And my good friend here is more than happy to supply me with the compounds I need.'

It all fits into place. 'In exchange for test subjects?'

'We all have backs to scratch. Most of these lowlifes are tweakers anyway. No-hope bums. Probably diseased, addicted, and don't have a hope of surviving the winter let alone the rest of their lives. How do you think Freedom Park has been "depopulated" of its bums so quickly? Dr Ward is achieving greater things with these people's lives through his research than they would have ever done on their own. In a way, we reduce crime and increase the quality of the lives of the people in Hillbay.'

'The crime you help to increase with the shit you push.'

Varetti opens his hands with cool resentment. 'Is it my fault people turn to drugs because they lack the life they want? Most people want fame and fortune and all of the trappings that come with it. But these accolades come at a price. For every millionaire, there are a million poor. For every famous actor there has to be a people to adore him. When they find out they can't get their slice of the pie, they become depressed, disillusioned with why they wanted it in the first place. They're mindless, impressionable people. Eventually they discover it's better to be high than deal with the reality of their failed ambitions.

'If you ask me, it's the media's fault. Television and the Internet have destroyed more lives than drugs ever will. False idols and false dreams dumb children through self-generating hype. Now there's the Internet to trap even more people into a sad grab for glory. Mass entertainment is the worst thing that could've happened to humans and their aspirations.

Professional sports is not far behind. All I do is make their transition to a *pragmatic* life more pleasurable.'

'Fine, whatever. So what the *fuck* do you want with me?'

They look at each other. 'We're offering you to decide your fate,' Charles says. 'And I'll be quite disappointed if you make the wrong choice.'

'Do you think we abducted that brat, Valentino, just to piss off Luigi?' Varetti insists. 'He served a couple of purposes. The ultimate one was to provoke Mr Baresi into a war he could never win. The other was to find the cream of the crop in the "subcontracting" market. And nobody has stood out with as much professionalism as you have.'

His words turn my stomach. Varetti didn't need to say any more. They have been following my career for some time.

'The Aquinas hit last year was the best work I've ever seen,' he continues. 'Making it look like suicide. That was *outrageous*. Everybody believed it. The police. The papers. I'd believe it myself if I didn't know the truth.'

Fuck! They know everything! Who do I know that could be in contact with him? It has to be George! He just jumped to the top of my list. He certainly has a history of betrayal. There cannot be anyone else. I thought I kept him at arm's length? I thought he wouldn't be able to track me? But he is the best at what he does, just like me…and he could've tapped me if he wanted to. I failed and deserve this punishment, but George, that fucking sell-out. I hope the money was worth it!

'I know we can't sway you with the idea that there are people here that work for the same agency you do,' Charles states. 'We know you've never come into contact with any of them. But what this should tell you is these people have been convinced enough to join us. I don't want to go into particulars, but this is important to the government. Your government. Our government. Of course, they like to keep their distance from our operation, so I've had to factor in security as part of the budget. And you would be a welcome addition to the stable. No more contracts. No more hassles. And once my research is completed, there is a lump sum payment for you that you could not dream up.'

'But why? What are you trying to achieve? Isn't Aggredisol finished? Aren't you done?' I ask.

Charles scrunches up his face as if I needed to question him. 'I thought you would've had a better idea. There are two agents I had hoped to design from the basic compound of the drug we know as Aggredisol. In its present and successful delivery system of a serum, we effectively poison the amygdalas of the limbic system, which has the same effect as surgical removal or precision lesions. The two amygdalas are not only responsible for aggression, but also sexual behaviour, so in effect, we have a neat population control built into the compound as well.

'Certain government agencies want a temporary airborne agent for obvious reasons, but this has been harder to devise when Aggredisol has such permanent effects. Nevertheless, with astounding progress, we are in the final stages of completing this work. For this nation's interests, this will be a far greater achievement than Aggredisol itself. They will be able to take any strategic asset they want and not leave a trace of any adverse effects to contravene the Geneva Conventions. It is the perfect weapon. Diplomatically, it will have no equal either. How can there be international uproar when there is no trace left behind? Devising an agent effective enough to administer was problematic, and our initial prototypes caused extreme and acute dermatological trauma that was irreversible. Boris had such an adverse reaction. We have some final testing to do, but I am confident that once it is successful, Aggredisol will pale in comparison to this achievement. The second agent, and what my true aim is, will be even greater…

'You may not realise what a fantastic microcosm of the global population Hillbay is. It is a peculiar city. Although not the largest city in the country, it has one thing that it is renowned for: it has one of the most diverse populations of any city in the world. And because of this incredibly varied gene pool, any genetic trait related to race can be studied easily…provided the subjects are willing enough to participate.'

'And you get Varetti to supply you with people.'

'Yes. Without their differing genes, it's hard to figure out and test what we need to.'

'A certain permanent strain of Aggredisol?'

'*Now* you're thinking. I was a little sceptical when we decided to release the formula for clinical use, but we are at the precipice of perfecting the product for its original intended use. Do you want to guess what our primary goal is?'

'You want to make it race specific.'

His dyed eyebrows arch with excitement at my deductions. 'Exactly! Of course compounds are incredibly finicky to match to specific race heritages. Gene drift, interracial coupling, and a delivery system that can saturate the population all need to be worked through, which will take more time. The temporary, unspecific strain is ready to begin trials across Hillbay, unbeknown to everyone except us and the government. It's quite clear that you were up against a force with considerable backing by *very* important people that will stop at nothing to achieve its aims.'

'And what's your plan?'

'Isn't it obvious? To be able to turn a whole race, any race of choice, defenceless wherever and whenever I choose. It is an internal security defence against religious radicalism that's impossible to escape. It's my contribution to freedom. Freedom to enjoy our civil liberties without being attacked by people who don't enjoy our way of life. Freedom to exact revenge on those who seek to destroy us. And most importantly, freedom to manipulate this world in such a way that will ensure our survival. This country will be free from any person, organisation, or whole nation that attempts to subvert our way of life.

'Even before the beginning of monotheistic worship, civilisations were struggling against foreign aggressors. Imagine if there were a way we could end wars, temporarily or even permanently, with strains of Aggredisol. Picture a silent crop duster dispenses a fine, harmless mist in the middle of the night over an entire village while known terrorists sleep, and by morning, they are harmless against the servicemen who arrive, disarm, and neutralise the threat and achieve all objectives without a single casualty. This might appear fantastic to you, but this will be a reality in the not-too-distant future. Some of your fallen comrades would not have needed to sacrifice their lives.'

'What you really mean is that you'd render a nation harmless and pillage it for all it's worth? And you want to self-administer a strain against our current enemies and control the country's population ratio by race at the same time.'

'I prefer my euphemism, thanks. You know, I was actually approached and initially financed to concentrate my scientific endeavours to help military departments *increase* aggression in its troops. But why bother creating a super-soldier when you can simply disable the enemy without them even knowing? Why create better fighters when you can wipe out the need to fight at all?'

'Because it would be used by a bigot like you for personal and political gain, and it allows you to hold people hostage to your whims.'

'But I could make this world a more peaceful place! *You* would be out of a job. Imagine if we *all* took the most potent of strains of Aggredisol? A permanent physiological solution that would align our behaviours with what is expected in a civilised society? It would eliminate any notion for conflict. No fighting. No violence. No anger? Perfectly harmonious humans in every way.'

'It's not natural.'

'*Define* natural. And while you're at it, define normal. There's no such thing. Communities on such a magnanimous scale have put an end to what sociologists can research and declare as "normal." I'm not normal. *You*, my sociopathic friend, *definitely* aren't normal. Which is why I can use you and make it worth your while. You would be a calculated risk, I must say, but I'm sure you'll find and know that this future in warfare is inescapable and, in the end, right. I'm bent on changing the world for the better.'

'That is such a lie. You never intend to administer it to yourself. You are only out for revenge.'

'Don't be so negative. I'll only be skewing the world's landscape into a more favourable position for the people who, above everyone else, advanced this world for the greater good to only see others exploit it. If it weren't for our European ancestors, life would've been much different. And I'm not about to let my country and society be victims of such atrocities merely because we have more liberties—the liberties people abuse in order to undermine and attack them.

'Multiculturalism has failed us. It has failed because people have been encouraged to *not* assimilate to our way of life. People who refuse to respect our rule of law and who do not care about our culture. How many do you see migrate *from* a secular democratic nation to a fundamental one? *None*! Because we know that our system of tolerance allows us to pursue what we desire. When people come to subvert that, then they must be stopped, and I prefer a nuclear bomb to a knife.' Charles shows his annoyance and anger with spittle pooling in the corners of his mouth. 'If you think for a second that this world is heading on a correct course in the state in which it currently lies, you are more ignorant than I could have imagined. And it all has to do with population drift. The reason to wage wars has come full circle. For centuries we have fought for religious beliefs. The only respite was in the twentieth century when political ideology became a focal point. Soon after, the "clashing of civilisations" renewed, just with different technologies at hand and now with much more at stake. It's not only between Christianity and Islam, but also between some predominant schisms within them. Serbia and Croatia, Iran and Iraq ring a bell? I'm not prepared to lose my rights and my life because we allow people to congregate for religious reasons. If they want to live under other repressive laws, fine. But like socialism set out to do, some fanatical elements won't stop until the world submits to their way of life. My research, our brilliance in medical advancements, will show who is superior in this world. We're going to reduce them to subhumans because without anger, they can only feel resentment, and when they come to realise their plight, they will only turn away from their beliefs.'

'This is ridiculous. You couldn't possibly be so accurate as to be able to cover a whole specific race of people? What about interracial breeding?'

Charles shakes his head dismissively. I realise I'm dealing with a lunatic not fit for an asylum.

'What people don't understand is that genetics carry our heritage, just as much as they carry our future. I'm not talking about just our parents; I'm talking about generation after generation. Our DNA has our history for longer than we can measure. With a blood sample, I can trace every known race that has entered your direct line of descendants. I *can* tell you if you have any of five traces of African, or twenty kinds of Asian, twenty-four types of Indian, or if you're almost a pure Aryan specimen…although that's impossible from just looking at you. We can go around in circles debating, but my time is precious…so I'm going to be as direct as I can. You can either be privy to it, or become a victim.'

'And if I refuse?'

'I have yet to decide your fate. But you can be assured that soon Hillbay will be my sample population in an experiment on one particular ethnicity which I've yet to decide. It will be good to test my delivery method and observe the viral qualities my germs can express. Of course, there will be some fun involved in all of this. A campaign of specific terror and intimidation is needed to properly establish the success of my findings. Who knows, you may even enjoy yourself and get paid handsomely for it.

'Right now, we have planned to begin testing our temporary generic strain and have test subjects already in mind. This certain fringe organisation will receive the shock of their lives when we trial our militarised Aggredisol in the next couple of weeks. A gas will be pumped into their clubhouse, and even though they will be heavily armed, my men will walk in there without guns and create a storm of violence and rid this city of one of the most heinous gangs while they can only act as punching bags.

'I wish I could give you time to think about this, but I'm afraid I cannot let you dwell on your decision. If you cannot be swayed when you are bound and with the fear of being executed within ten minutes, then no amount of time will help you change your mind. So, what will it be?'

What is my answer? See the beginning of the end or just my end? Charles is right about one thing. If I cannot say yes to him now with my life in his hands, there will be no other time when I would agree. The end of war and conflict? That's the utopian dream people have wished for since the beginning of time. How many people have suffered because of war? Millions? Billions? And one insane doctor who suffered claims to have the solution. What would life be like in a perfect world? Everything I did in the army and what I do now would cease to be relevant. It's true, I wouldn't be needed, and that's a good thing. But why is it that I want to say no, even if I will most certainly meet my death soon after?

Because I simply wouldn't be me.

Killing, approved by the government or not, has been my adult life. Conflict has shaped me to be the person I am. Conflict has shaped Charles to excel beyond what he could have only dreamed to achieve. Conflict will never stop. It's how we deal with it that will change if he gets his way. And he is blinded by his own vengeance, justifying it under the guise of helping the world. What would he be if he didn't experience the pain of grief? Happier obviously, but wiser?

I think of Fitzgerald. He wouldn't have needed to have died. If we had Aggredisol, we could've walked in there with gas masks and put a bullet into General Lopez's head and had time for tea before walking out. And I, I would not have been stricken with guilt for all these years.

But I needed that burden. As much as it still pains me, I learnt from it and grew to be a better person. Without that mission, I would've been still in the military and not dishonourably discharged. I would have made major by now or even a young colonel. Since then I've hated the military with a passion and my feelings haven't changed. The same brass that fucked us over will now use Charles to their own ends to exploit any situation possible except they'll do a lot less sacrificing. I know all too well that they don't intend to help the world but just themselves, just as the political parties that play musical chairs with the country's power.

There's no way I can be a part of that. Shame on me if I am fooled twice. I would rather die.

Charles waits, tapping his feet.

'Go fuck yourself.'

He twists his face into creased frustration with an aura of fury and contempt because I could not be convinced. '*You* are a fool. *Guards!*'

As the door opens, Varetti draws a Beretta Model 75 in self defence so quickly that I admire his guile. The weapon is unmistakable. A 4.2-inch barrel that extends past its frame and leads to the unique, sharp-edged sight.

'Proud of your heritage?' I joke, nodding at his Italian-made firearm.

'Very,' he replies as I am dragged away.

CHAPTER TEN

I am still alive…barely.

I can't remember what happened as soon as I was dragged away except that I was powerless to stop force being applied to the back of my head. Or was it my neck?

Urgh! I am groggy, but I need to stay alert and fight. I swing a fist and catch nothing but air.

I check my vitals. The first thing I realise is that I am completely naked. Taking my time, I inspect and test the flexibility of all my joints. Nothing is sprained, although there's bruising in many places, my ribs are tender, and breathing is difficult. Every muscle aches from fatigue and I am systemically exhausted. My skin is unbearably sensitive to touch. There are no new lacerations or contusions I can see or feel. But how could I feel this way from only being knocked out and dragged into a cell?

This doesn't make sense. Was it Charles? Did he do something? Was I placed under anaesthetic? Shit! Charles could've done anything he wanted to me. I don't even know what day it is or if it's morning or night. I could go insane imagining what Charles could have done to me without my knowledge.

A strong odour of antiseptic wafts in the air and is pungent enough to make me vomit in the corner. It is all bile and reminds me that the last time I ate was before leaving my apartment however many days ago.

There are no windows except a small slit in the door leading to a hallway. I don't need to guess where I am. It's the same building that once housed Valentino, maybe even the same cell. The heating is uncomfortably high.

There's no point in thinking about an escape. No Boy Scout tricks can get me out of here. There's nothing left to do but wait, naked, for someone to tell me what is next. I am left to a madman to decide my fate.

I can't think like that. I've got to put away the defeatist attitude and preserve what little energy I have left. I try and sleep in the opposite corner from the warming vomit, and underneath the small, vandal-proof surveillance camera that hugs a corner of the room between the walls and ceiling.

I begin to doze, almost falling asleep when the door opens and guards enter, armed with batons. This is by-the-book and planned. I have enough sense to figure that out.

It is the easiest and one of the most effective forms of torture possible: sleep deprivation. Why bother with physical punishment when mental torture is more effective? It also doesn't leave scars…well…sightly ones at least. I recognise the last guard that entered was the maniac who took great satisfaction in inflicting pain on me earlier.

'I've come fo' a lil' meet and greet,' he says, stamping on my ribs. I wheeze heavily, short of breath and defenceless enough to not be able to curl up and brace for impact. My ribs are on fire, adding to the previous agony this man inflicted.

'For fuck's sake, Harry. You know our orders.'

Harry doesn't react to the command and continues to stare with pent fury. The contemptible way his hulking body blocks my view of other visitors is testament to how much he wants to kill me, or at least try.

I don't know how I've wronged him. Did one of my rubber bullets cause a fatality?

Eventually the command sinks in and he storms out.

An orderly replaces him in the cell and gets to work cleaning up my vomit quickly. He mops with a solution high in bleach, which is a bad idea. If the ventilation remains poor, he will have to make a return visit. Another leaves some bread and water on a tray near the door.

'In his state, he's not going to hurt anyone,' the supervisor chuckles as he stands over me. 'Now listen here, my friend. Harry wants to kick the shit out of you because your little rescue effort rendered his good friend a paraplegic. Normally, I'd let him have you…but seeing as you are a guest of Dr Ward's, I have to let it slide. It's a shame really, as we always like to even our scores.'

What are the chances of that happening? A million to one? My last thought before passing out was there was no way any of the ammunition I fired could have damaged a spinal cord enough to render someone a paraplegic.

At least two days pass since I first woke in this cell, and that is just my best estimate. The clock is ticking and I have no idea how much time is left before Lloyd assumes I'm dead. It's a situation to avoid at all costs. My possessions, my life, will be forfeited if enough time passes. My apartment, Buster, healthy bank and stock accounts will all go. I've wasted too much of my life to give up. I've taken this assignment to get out, not hit the reset button. I have to move soon and try my luck.

The orderlies drop off food at irregular intervals, always with three armed men, and I'm not stupid enough to try and breaking out at these times. The menu varies, but one constant remains: apart from some stale bread at times, the rest are army rations.

After a feeding, the door opens in what seems an hour's time. I don't even bother to turn my head. Must be just the same group of guards to pick up the food tray.

'It's time to finish what I started!' the familiar voice booms.

Harry stands alone at the doorway, baton in one hand and the tray in the other. He closes the door behind him and drops the tray. Joy springs from his eyes and he flicks his wrist, extending the baton to a punishing length.

'It's time for a workout, yo' bastard.'

He advances. My instincts insist I ball myself from the sharp blows that are coming. He begins to wail into my sides, and the pain is more harrowing than I realise. The constant whips from the baton's movement cutting the air is as haunting as the sharp, slapping blunt trauma I experience on my ribs and back. The pain quickly changes from my ribs to my hands as I cover my tender sides because I know if they receive a well-placed blow, then they will go from bruised to broken. A small stream of blood oozes onto the floor.

'How does it feel?' he says.

I bite my arm from the pain and whimper. My teeth pierce my flesh as I draw more blood. After a few hits, he takes a break and circles. I get the sense that he is surprised at my ability to bottle the anguish. I peer through my bracing arms at Harry inspecting the large scars on by back from years past and similar cruelty.

'You sick fuck,' he observes with utter disgust.

I seize my chance by grabbing his foot. Summoning all of my energy, I yank it out from under him. His body follows as his torso, then his head, make a muffled thud as he hits the ground.

Harry's upending leaves him stunned, and I take the opportunity to grab his baton and clip him in the temple. I don't care whether the force does enough to keep him alive, although I want to finish him off. A little blood splats from his face.

There is not enough time to strip him for his clothes. I've got to get out of here! The clock is ticking. A countdown begins in my head as the CCTV camera in this cell would have captured everything. I rush to the door and look out the window for any fodder for my getaway. No doubt guards, armed with more than batons, will be on their way. The door opens and I check either side of the hallway. There's nobody there, so I close Harry in for a good night's sleep.

'Hey,' an orderly snaps on cue as soon as I shut the door.

He emerges from another cell, but as soon as he realises I am not a guard, he becomes frightened by my presence. So he should. He drops the mop he was holding as I run at him before turning and sprinting the other way towards the exit. The gate to the hallway is unlocked but two guards are manning the control desk.

They are surprised to see me sprint at them as one hits the switch to shut the gate. I can't let that happen. My legs haven't work this hard in years, pumping like pistons so I can clear the gate just in time to deliver a downward blow to the face of one of the guards and an upward slap to the other. Both reel from the pain of the baton and turn limp upon impact. The console flashes red, indicating a security breach. I don't need a second warning to tell me I need to get out.

As I reach the exit, I am relieved to know it's nighttime. I have no time to rest as the sounds of trampling boots on grass wake me to a higher urgency. I am in the same situation as when I helped Valentino escape. And like Valentino, there is the need to run a gambit full of chance to survive. I sprint around the corner as they open fire and I manage to make it behind the building. The part of the backing wall previously blown away by my satchel charges has already been bricked up but not yet painted. How could they have done this so quickly? Have I been stuck here for longer than I thought? The sight of the repaired wall is disheartening. I notice this before realising a searing sensation in my thigh and blood streaming from it. I look around to find nobody. I must've been hit running. There's no time to analyse the wound. I can still use the leg to hobble on, so the damage mustn't be too debilitating. A quick look down and I am lucky my femur isn't shattered.

The wall is dauntingly high in my condition. But I have no time to recoup and reassess. I have to clear this or may as well prepare for a last stand, which will be pathetic and short lived. I jump only to have a couple of fingernails hyperextend and snap off as I claw unsuccessfully at the wall on the descent and collapse in a bog of pain. I gather myself quickly, running on adrenaline and the will to survive. Footsteps become louder. They must be near. With their firearms, it will be easy for them to finish me off from such a short distance, or to make me suffer. My heart races with unbounded excitement. Although my leg has been shot, my need for flight trumps the pain that would affect me otherwise.

I leap high for my life. My hands slap on the ledge. I have a firm grip. I chin myself up and throw my elbows over the wall for a better hold. Orders scream to the side of me but I don't dare check. I am able to lift my right leg over and while grabbing the left to drop over onto the other side, I hear the faint duffs of silenced weapons as they fire and clip my calf. I roll mercifully over the wall and fall in a heap. I have to check my leg. My foot is still there but what is this? The gunshot wound to the calf hasn't drawn blood. Did they miss? Was it a ricochet from the wall? Did I simply tear a muscle? There is already localised swelling where I thought I'd been hit, along with pain and a severe graze on my thigh. I still need to get up and run.

I have to keep moving!

I struggle off the ground and limp as fast as possible, not knowing if they would shoot me in the back or not. I can't turn to find out either. My life is sparingly in the balance and at the whim of a private army and whether they would bother sending a shooter onto the wall to finish me. The pain in my left leg sears with numbness while I scramble through the adjacent property. Still naked, I can do nothing for the blood trickling steadily down my leg, no doubt leaving a nice trail for my attackers.

Thank God it is still dark. Provided I can make it onto the street, the cover of night will allow me to figure something out. I miraculously manage to make it to the corner of a small shed.

They must have backed down, but it makes no sense why they would be bound to just their property. I have no time to ponder it. Worse still, I am beginning to become lightheaded from subsiding adrenaline and blood loss.

I stagger over some fences, onto the main road, begging for a stranger, or anybody for that matter, to walk by to mug. I can only manage to hobble through the streets as the deep blue shades of the early morning begin to arrive from the east. I should apply first aid to my leg, but I have no time and there's nothing I can use as a bandage, except my dirty hand. A black SUV approaches with no headlights on. Without knowing if they have already spotted me, I throw myself painfully through a neighbouring hedge. The van's slow pace is unmistakeable. It is a patrol searching for me. I can only deduce that a project of this magnitude is more than capable of tying up its loose ends. Valentino must surely be on their list as well.

My thigh looks as if a knife had slashed its way across it. A 9mm bullet must have entered from the side and ripped through flesh on its way out the front of my leg, leaving a mangled tear. It isn't too bad. Oh, who am I kidding? It's horrible. I can still walk, but it is impossible without a limp. It will need medical attention, and soon. A good bandaging, a lot of disinfectant, and a few prayers.

I wander aimlessly just trying to get out of the area unnoticed and to find a soft target. It's hard in my state. I shiver as the cold morning starts to bite. Every so often a car drives by and I scurry into a bush to hide. It well may be daylight before I can find an unsuspecting victim and that will only be trouble. It is a race against time and the rising sun. More daylight, more chance to be spotted.

My prospects diminish as time goes by. My fears come true as the sun begins to make its appearance even if it's veiled by clouds. Shit. I'm desperate, cold, bleeding, injured, exhausted, and just like this assignment, fresh out of luck. I thought I would go down in a violent blaze or from of an unaccounted-for fatal bullet to the head, not comically without dignity, naked, and in The Hills.

But what's this up ahead? A figure is running towards me. A stray soldier hunting me down? It can't be. They're going too fast and they don't seem to be holding anything like a weapon.

I hobble behind a large tree on the nature strip.

It's a male jogger, a little taller than me, striding down the footpath. He's wearing headphones. Without his sense of hearing, I may be able to surprise him if I don't meet him head on. Only problem is if I mistime my assault, I will not be able to chase him down with this leg. I have a chance, and a small one at that. I should feel bad and dishonoured to have to mug an unsuspecting victim of his clothes, but if I don't, either the cold, the loss of blood, or the police will put an end to my misery, and all of those options are equally worse.

I set myself behind the tree. If he suddenly crosses the street, I will have no hope. I have to use the one thing he doesn't have to guide me. I have to rely on the plodding of his runners striking the pavement to let me know where he is. I take a mighty sigh and as soon as I see his leading foot a metre-and-a-half in front of me, I lunge with an almighty rush and knock him off balance with a ferocious shoulder barge. The force is heavy enough for him to career hard into the opposing fence. He slumps to the ground and doesn't realise I'm on top of him until it's too late. I land a punch on his chin, and what little defensive reaction he had ends with his body becoming limp.

I quickly disrobe the man, removing his sweaty T-shirt and shorts as well as his runners, leaving him in socks, underwear, and with his mp3 player. 'Sorry, Buddy,' I say, even though I know he can't hear me. It pains me putting on his shorts and wet T-shirt. They will do little to help battle the chilly air and the onset of pneumonia, but I have no choice. Why couldn't he have worn a thick jumper and tracksuit pants? I take the time to drag him into the open front yard of a house and into their bushes even though my leg protests with pain. There's no point in mugging a guy and trying to get away if someone is going to call the police as soon as they see his body on the footpath. In that case, it may as well be me instead.

I scamper through the neighbourhood and out of The Hills. I head to the city but I won't make it far unless I get a lift. I am at least twenty kilometres out. I should attend to this wound as well if I can.

I find a public park and hide among some trees. I roll up the black shorts and find my blood still flowing but now at a slower pace. Lucky my unsuspecting saviour was wearing a dark green T-shirt. I tear its sleeves off and tie a tight and painful bandage around my leg with one and clean up the bloody leg from the wound to my ankle with the other. I pull down my shorts to conceal my hasty and dismal attempt at first aid.

With daylight well and truly here, I have to find shelter. But where? I know nobody in the area who can take me in, and I can't risk breaking into a home for the day to have a nap and borrow their antibacterial medicine or alcohol for my leg. I can't call Lloyd, and I'd rather die than call George. The hospital is not an option because they will call the police, or the police will call them. I have no choice. I have to make it home, and I need to steal a car.

I look around and find a suitable car. It's old and in a poor enough condition to have a shot at stealing. It's a ruddy two-door hatch, with its original beige paint ruined by years in the sun. Without any tools, the task would be impossible. Thankfully, I have one in the car's antenna, which was formerly a wire coat hanger. I snap it off and bend it into a 'U' shape and slide it down the crack between the side windscreen and door. I jiggle it while scanning the area for anyone who might catch me until, after a few minutes, it hooks on to the latch. I tug the wire upwards, and the door's old plastic knob slides up simultaneously. I'm in, but the hardest part is yet to come. At least I'm out of the street and the cold. The ignition's pin tumbler lock isn't the hardest, but with just a coat hanger, I need to be fortunate if I'm going to get it started. I fast become frustrated with the time I'm losing. And because I'm leaning from the passenger side so no motorists can see me easily, any pedestrian walking down the same footpath can spot me in a second.

I feel liberated when my makeshift key turns and the starting motor whirrs like an emphysema cough. The engine turns laboriously and eventually catches and splutters into life. I carefully climb into the driver's seat and take off at a slow pace, but only because it's the only speed this car can travel. I am a sitting duck if a patrol or the police found me in this slow-moving metal coffin. If I wasn't shot, then I could've legged it home. But instead, I'm in this rust bucket. It could be worse though; I could be dead.

I drive the speed limit and am not stopped on the way to the city and to the sanctuary of my apartment.

I end up dumping the car in the alley beside my building and will have to move it somewhere else at a later time. I stagger up the fire escape to my bathroom window, unlock the combination lock attached to the frame, throw open the window, and fall into the bathtub.

With my energy expenditure deep in the red, I almost pass out for a reprieve when my survival instincts kick in again and I groan getting out of the tub. I close and lock the window, open the medicine cabinet, douse stinging antiseptic fluid and apply a proper bandage to my thigh. The sleeves that acted as bandages are dry to my touch with caked blood, dirt, and sweat. The burgundy stains on my skin are a welcome sign that only arteries and capillaries have been damaged and with a little rest, they will heal in due course.

It slips my mind to check, but as I enter the living room, I'm greeted with the surprise that all of my possessions are still there and Lloyd has not enacted our MIA clause. I grab a glass of water and notice the litter tray overflowing with semiburied pellets of cat faeces and saturated with clumped urine. It is a sure indication that I had been held prisoner for more time than I guessed.

The TV confirms six days have passed since leaving the apartment and just one before Lloyd assumes I'm dead. Walking to the bed, a weird stench captivates my curiosity. As I pull the doona back, I find Buster lying in a ball. He howls at my indiscretion.

I flop onto the bed.

'You little bastard…' I say, as I realise Buster urinated on the pillow my face is resting on. I don't even have the energy to turn the wet stain over.

CHAPTER ELEVEN

I've propped myself on a park bench, and I stupidly prod my tender leg with the unrealistic expectation that if I massage the area, the damaged nerves and flesh will magically repair themselves. I have grown accustomed to compensating for the injury and have managed in the week that passed to remarkably improve its condition. I took it upon myself to consume large quantities of red meat, and despite the constipation, I've recuperated faster from all the protein. The skin has at least covered over, leading me to believe that the injury is far less debilitating than expected, though the general area is still extremely sensitive.

I've been waiting for an hour for Lloyd's arrival and may need to vacate the bench. I've begun to gloss over the *Hillbay Times* for a fourth time now. Disappointingly, nothing was reported on my breakout last week, although there was a letter to the editor deploring senseless criminal acts. The author happened to have mentioned a case in The Hills where a jogger had been king hit and stripped for fun.

An hour. A fucking hour that fat piece of shit has had me waiting. I nearly die and he has the balls to leave me waiting. As rage boils, I question how I will react when I do see him. It almost certainly won't be cordial.

In the time I've been attending to my wounds, I've had the chance to think about Charles's proposal and the reasons why I reneged. When did I turn into a person with such upstanding morals? I am a gun-for-hire and had the opportunity to capitalise greatly by performing duties with far less risk. Why make an enemy when I could have shut up and taken the money?

I question it, but deep down I know the truth. All my life I have shouldered professional responsibility for my actions and decisions. Every one of them has sat with me whether I liked being responsible or not. I can't agree with Charles that taking away someone's personal autonomy is just, even if it would prevent a catastrophe.

I've seen the effects of what today's conventional weapons can do to human flesh on the battlefield, and can admit to contributing my fair share. But thinking back to any of my handiwork, no instance was so obscene compared to what I witnessed. I was clinical, and the product of my training. When I killed, it was done methodically and quickly. There's no moral reasoning behind it. I've never lingered on killing or dwelled on it for fun; it was my job to be as effective and efficient as possible. The quicker the kill, the quicker the exit. I simply eliminated the obstacle to achieve the objective. It didn't matter if that obstacle was an armed solider, a brick wall, or an unopened gate. Neutralise it and keep going until the job is done and I am safe…

I should go for a walk. I've been sitting here for far too long. I get up and wander over to a junior football game. I watch the game as these young teenagers show great skill. The intensity lifts from a few errant and malicious tackles from both teams. Parents change their chants of support into cries of protest to the referee to intervene and control the game.

'Sometimes it's best if you stay put according to plan,' Lloyd says, suddenly appearing alongside me.

'Sometimes it's best to know when staying put will get you killed,' I reply, shooting him a callous glare before returning my attention to the game.

'It's OK if on occasion things don't go your way. You'll still be rewarded for what you've done.'

That patronising, fat shit. I explode. 'I was *compromised*. They saw me coming, and they were prepared. I was a caged animal out there and lucky to get out alive.'

'And how do you know that?'

'The mark told me, that's how.'

Lloyd quietens from the news as the noise of the game reaches a tipping point, with shouting and shoving both on and off the pitch.

'Have you thought that you should follow the standard procedures you signed up for when you began working for us? Have you thought about following the code that you are *expressly forbidden* to use *any* outside assistance, be that supplies, intelligence, or actions for an assignment instead of blowing up walls with third-party explosives?'

Son of a bitch! So he has information sources that are close, very close, to know about my little surprise and damage to the estate's perimeter. That smug fuck! How else was I going to get him out of there? By fucking helicopter?

I have to hand it to Lloyd. They've probably got a file on Curious George back at the agency. And yes, I knew full well it was against their directives, but I had no choice. There's a leak, and I can't trust anyone. But now I know who it is and will be fixing it very soon. Even so, this dickhead is testing my patience.

'You know the drill, then,' he declares, pissed off. 'From now on you're inactive…pending an investigation. I'll be contacting my superiors to look into this immediately.'

Lloyd pulls out his phone and starts to text. He is on edge and is startled when a fight breaks out on the pitch between two players. Parents begin to scuffle on the sidelines. I act with similar immaturity and passion.

'And how do I know it wasn't you?' I say, turning and lunging at his throat. I squeeze the flabby sides of his neck as a warning about what I *can* accomplish if I want to. He flails a little and bends over backwards from my grip, the only thing in the way from an embarrassing plummet to the wet and muddy ground.

'Because,' he croaks, 'my handler would never allow it.'

'And who is *your* handler?'

'The Chairman.'

I freeze with confusion. The Chairman? He's more of a shadow and legend than anything else. They say he can influence any and every seat of power in the country and most of the world. My grip on Lloyd's throat softens involuntarily, as if I have already made up my mind that Lloyd cannot possibly have leaked me to Dr Ward and Varetti. He surely wouldn't dare cross a person and an organisation that could see him in pain and suffering for a very long time. This, more or less, confirms it. Curious George, once a personal friend, has to be the rat, and for that, he will suffer. Lloyd will suffer too, but only his pride and only momentarily. He falls to the ground with a thud.

I help him up and play it cool. I look around to see if anyone is watching. Nobody noticed our little fracas because all eyes are watching the large brawl in the middle of the pitch. Overprotective and unashamedly aggressive parents are trading blows on the sidelines.

'You know this'll reflect on me just as much as it will on you, you fucking idiot!' Lloyd yells, competing with the shouting in the distance. 'You don't think I'll be getting any heat from the agency for this? Activating a contract without checking to see if it is operationally safe to do so is a punishable offence. *I* have to rate and approve, not just you.' His words are full of spite no doubt fuelled by the embarrassing fall.

'Well, somebody didn't do their homework.'

'No, shit! Or perhaps you had a tail on one of your *trusty* surveillance trips? Who the fuck knows how you may have been compromised? That's what I'm here for…to find the leak and plug it. But if it's external and on you, then you're on your own.'

I know I've been careful, that's the problem. When it comes to my job, complacency will get me killed. But Lloyd's assertions help sprout the smallest amount of doubt. What if they had a counter-surveillance team I missed? Realising the formidability of my opposition, in hindsight, I greatly underestimated them, the connections they would have and who they could lean on for intel. And that is wholly my fault. I was lucky to flee with my life…

We walk away from the game, now abandoned by the referee, and take a winding footpath around the busy park.

'Do you have any idea about how connected this guy is? With organised crime? With the *government*?' I ask.

'You knew before you took this contract that you'd be dealing with something extraordinary. And no, I have no idea. But I can say that if you didn't succeed, then it's pretty fucking deep.'

I don't let on about the experiments, the state Valentino was in when I found him, or what should be done because I am defensive and hurt, nor can anything good come from telling him about it besides recommending a tactical airstrike on the estate. Nothing else will do.

'I'm sorry about your situation, I truly am. But we need to move on and rectify your predicament. Let's get one thing clear here,' Lloyd says, stopping our journey to nowhere. 'You do *nothing* until I get back, you understand? I can only imagine you must be deeply critical of our organisation, or maybe even yourself. But the self-pity ends now. And more importantly, your desire for *revenge* ends now as well. I know this may ruin a perfect record, but I need your assurance that you won't do anything stupid. *No* fishing for your own information. *No* trying to make up the contract and finish the job. That's how this agency operates, and if you jeopardise any of their operational procedures, you won't be having me to contend with. The agency's reputation rests upon these ideals and methods and will not risk its reputation by one of its contractors having another crack at his target. Are you listening to me?…*Hey!*'

He grabs my arm.

'OK,' I say, trying to calm myself.

'I know you're disciplined, and you must feel crushed that any target, let alone your last, gets away. But you can't help that now. I don't need to discuss with you the policies that are in place in these instances. Obviously others may be selected for the contract and may receive the request to terminate, but you are *out!* No ifs or buts. I thought I'd never say this, but you are. Stay put and lay low. Because there are probably going to be bullets flying over this, and I'd hate for you to stand up and get hit. As for your employment, seeing as you may have been compromised, there is always the chance you'll be discontinued.'

With those stern warnings, Lloyd doesn't even give me the courtesy of a good-bye before he shuffles off. I continue through the park to the bench where I started. Over at the football pitch everyone has left, and there are patches of blood staining the well-groomed grass.

As Lloyd vanishes through bushes, I'm left to stir his remarks and instructions.

It's early evening, and all I can think about is getting a drink. With the spray I just received from Lloyd, my already-frayed willpower has no chance to protest.

In my precarious state, I know I shouldn't do this. What happened to me? I used to have enormous discipline in the army. When the boys at the barracks were out chasing tail and writing off their R & R, I was reading books and hitting the gym at two in the morning. But that was when I had belief in what I was doing and a job with purpose. Now, I have none of those things. I know I won't stop at just one drink. I am reckless, and I don't care. Everybody has their breaking point, and I just passed mine.

It doesn't help that I am spoilt for choice. Like any major tourist attraction, there are plenty of bars and pubs around Freedom Park. The temptation is overwhelming. At the edge of the park, I see a quaint bar opening for the night as a bartender adjusts an A-frame spruiking its specials. I enter and the bliss of a pianist playing some smooth American jazz is music to my ears. It beckons me to drink scotch at a consistently fast pace and twist my recollection of recent events.

'Bastard,' I mutter under my breath, finally coming to grips with the severity of Lloyd's instructions. I don't care for my unblemished record at the agency. Who would care about nonsense like that? It's not as if my record would amount to anything but a legend when I'm gone. And being a legend in this industry is scant conciliation when the people who will respect me are the miniscule few that deal in its macabre corridors. In the military, I would be an officer of distinction. But this is not the military, and so it's just another footnote that will never be read.

I am livid about Lloyd, George, and this whole fiasco. This is my life's work ruined. After all the sacrifices and the incredible amount of risk I absorbed, the dressing down from Lloyd as the mouthpiece for the agency is a slap in the face after all the hard years of work. I'm never going to recover my reputation. My private sector career is now just as finished as my public one.

But you are out!

These words of rejection and disappointment resonate with me. Fuck them. Lloyd and his handlers. Failure was almost assured because of the welcome party that greeted me. His words haunt me to my bones, and the more I consider the effect they will have on my life, the more it numbs me.

But I wanted out, didn't I? Shouldn't I be happy? I can get out, buy a cabin, and fish for the rest of my life. That was the plan, wasn't it? That's what I wanted to do?

I know I have a problem. An irreconcilable conflict with myself. I want out, but on my terms. I want to exact revenge on George and prove to the agency that I was double-crossed. I want to fix the wrongs that were done to me, the best way I know how…by eliminating them with extreme prejudice.

I refuse to leave this way, marginalised by a third party. It was an outside force that shouldn't have interfered with my work. Without the heads up, I would've gotten away or even killed Charles Ward. I can still do it. All I need is one more chance.

But what about Lloyd and the agency? One more breach can't hurt, can it? It's not like I'm divulging their existence and unravelling their business. And after what I've done for them, they wouldn't dare chase me down. I pulled off jobs for their financial gain others can only dream of. I did things for them that went above and beyond what is required. Lloyd's right about one thing: I should be on the top of their roster. I'm their best employee. They owe me this freedom. They owe me the right to make amends and right my wrongs. And if they question my actions? Well, I'm doing them the job they'd have to pay someone else for.

In the end, it's a win-win situation. I'll be saving face *and* my reputation with the organisation responsible for my livelihood, and I'm saving them the trouble of investigating. How can *that* be so bad? And if the chance presents itself to knock off Charles, I'll take that too.

I want to catch George in the act. I want to see him *um* and *ah* at my accusations before I pull the trigger. But I need a plan.

Before I know it, I shuffle off to the bathroom and throw up from a nonexistent tolerance to alcohol. On the way out, my vomit coarsens my throat. But it doesn't matter. My head is clear. I have direction with what I need to do. But just to be safe, I'll sleep on it.

I stay for one more drink, and excuse myself and exit after leaving a more-than-generous tip to make up for the inconvenience of cleaning up my contribution to their bathroom.

By the time I leave, I judge it is around midnight. I don't want to call it a night just yet but head towards home anyway, hoping there will be something that will tickle my fancy.

It so happens that I accidently miss a turnoff and end up in the seedier part of the city. Sure there are reputable nightclubs in the area, but there are enough strip clubs and the occasional brothel thrown in for good measure. It must be a good arrangement for all businesses involved. Gangs of young men go out having every intention to get lucky at a nightclub. If they're drunk enough and strike out, they'll give in to lust and go to a strip club and eventually all the way to a brothel, leaving in the morning a few hundred dollars poorer.

Right now, I'm too hammered to bother paying the overpriced entry to a nightclub, and even more for their drinks, so I skip a step.

I consider my options and count five gentlemen's clubs within a hundred metres of each other with all six major banks stationing their ATMs within sight of all of them. I have no preference for the club I should patron. Economics would dictate that they should be similar in most respects: overpriced and teasingly underwhelming.

This is probably not a good idea.

'Fuck it.'

I stagger past the first club, aptly named The Spread with its sleazy entrance enveloped by two huge female legs and a poster of a girl looking more like a man in drag. Only two doors down is the club I settle for. I have no reason to be picky because I have never set foot in any of them.

There is no queue. That could either be a good or a bad thing.

'Just one?' the heavyset guard asks.

'Yep.'

'Have a good time,' he says, unhinging the velvet rope.

I pay the trashy girl at the front desk twenty dollars to enter and almost stumble on my way up to the main floor. A bright stage with a massive red curtain behind it is the centrepiece of the room. I scan the area as if I am still working. I spot five guards evenly placed in the room. The venue isn't as full as it should be on a Thursday night. There are a few semicomatose men in lounge chairs sitting by the empty stage. On two of the smaller stages, really just tables with poles in the middle, two girls are sashaying monotonously to inappropriately unsexy music. Tough night to be a stripper, I guess.

After grabbing a drink, I begin to get a feel for the place. A sensation begins to crawl down my neck when it finally clicks that this club is owned by someone I'm familiar with. All of the security team, except for one, look related. They have a style all themselves, and not in a good way.

'How's your night been?' a perky voice queries. The girl is directly behind me, so I have to turn to face at her.

'Pretty rough so far,' I say truthfully.

'Aww. It doesn't mean you can't make the best of a bad situation. I'm sure I can cheer you up—'

'How much?' I blurt, cutting to the chase, but as hammered as I am, I really don't care.

'Thirty for a song or fifty for three.'

'What will a hundred get me?'

'A good time,' she purrs.

'All right.'

She takes me by the hand and leads me to a glass enclosure with couches neatly arranged inside. She sits me down and slowly teases me by taking off the few layers of clothing she has on.

'Not much of a talker, are you?' she grins.

'What should I be saying?'

She flashes a smile and replies, 'I don't know.'

She then proceeds to grind on my crotch. It doesn't help that I have an erection and that her grinding begins to feel uncomfortable because of the way my hard-on shifts around under jeans and underwear. I adjust myself quickly when she gets off briefly so we can continue.

As she places her hands on my shoulders and presses herself high, brushing her body against me, I catch a glimpse of a figure going behind the bar in the distance. She floats back down and breathes heavily into my ear, which unhappily jolts the wrong neurons. I quickly recognise the figure, and the buzz I'm enjoying dissipates quickly.

I place my hand on the small of her back, and she lets out a whimper of protest.

'Hey! No touching,' she complains.

'Listen to me carefully. I want you to turn around and tell me who the man is behind the bar.'

I can feel her deflate at the thought that I don't find her as attractive as she believes and she isn't worth the $100. Or maybe that the person sitting under her with an erection is a cop, or worse? She moves slowly away with an obvious look of fear. She turns and sits back down on my lap, pretending to play with herself.

She leans back and whispers, 'That's Val. He's the owner.'

'How often does he come in?'

'Every now and then. Three times a week maybe? He stopped coming a while ago, but now he's been coming in fairly regularly. He told everybody that he went on holidays after his father died.'

'And what do you think?'

'Ah, um…I don't know if I believe it.' She pauses. 'Are you a cop?'

'Of course not,' I reply reassuringly. 'Would a cop want to be caught drunk in a Baresi strip club getting a dance from a beauty such as yourself?'

The sleazy line worked and the tension eases. She continues her seductive dance. 'He just comes in to score some coke and deals to his friends, regulars, and some of the girls.'

'What's through that door just beyond the stage?'

'That's the staging area for the girls, and further down the hall is the manager's office where Val goes…Good luck getting through if you want to talk to him.'

'Relax,' I say. 'I'm an old friend of his…in a good way.'

I don't lose sight of Valentino as she slinks around in front of me. His conversation with a security guard becomes more animated as he takes money from the till and throws a rubber band around the wad.

'Everything's been real hectic around here since he came back,' she says. 'They've got a few more security guards around the place. It's like he's scared of someone. Maybe the cops, but he usually has people that he pays off, you know, to get protection from them. I've seen him have meetings with cops here at the start of some nights. But I don't know. He's more careful about things now.'

He makes a move out of the bar and I stand up and quickly dig into my wallet for another fifty. She says nothing as I hand it to her.

She smiles dourly, not knowing whether to believe that I am not a cop or someone worse. I make no attempt to explain as I leave the room while she puts her clothes back on.

Val heads through the mysterious door with its *Staff Only* sign, and I follow him. A guard is backed into the nearest corner, doing his job and observing everyone. When I mosey over there to get a better view of the silicon-enhanced beauty on the main stage, he doesn't look too concerned. This changes when I flash through the door and walk down the hallway.

There are girls applying makeup and adjusting their clothing who aren't too surprised to see me until I am chased. I sprint towards Val, who is at the end of the corridor. I am not even three metres away when he faces me and I come to a sudden halt in front of his aimed, compact H&K USP, safety off and hammer cocked, not more than one metre from my face.

There is a brief pause as our eyes meet. The guard behind me grabs both my arms, but he needn't have. Even if Valentino is drugged up to his eyeballs like it appears he is now, one simple squeeze of the trigger and it would all be over.

But he doesn't do it, and his memory works in my favour. He smiles and lowers his firearm.

'Well, I'll be damned! Could it be? I can't believe it's you!'

I flash an acknowledgment his way as he scrunches his face into a ball of wrinkles and begins to shed tears.

'I can't believe it's you,' he mumbles.

'Boss?' the guard says, completely perplexed.

'Fuck off!' he barks, and waves him off with his gun.

'I thought we should talk,' I say.

'Yeah…sure. Come into my office.' He fumbles trying to locate his keys with coke-fuelled confusion.

Inside his office is a jewellery box full to the brim of powder on his desk. If this is his personal supply, then I have low expectations for how much he is selling.

'Want a line?' he asks as he falters to sit down on his massive executive chair.

'No thanks.'

'Oh, yeah, sure. I guess a guy like you isn't interested in stuff like this. You know, to keep your wits about you.'

'Something like that.'

'Sure. Look, hey, I can't thank you enough…for getting me out of there.' He chokes up and begins to sob openly. Sobs quickly turn to tears as the haze of cocaine lifts and Val perhaps realises the tragedy that has befallen not just him, but his family's empire. He shakes his anguish away by racking up a line of coke and snorting it with confidence. He takes a few minutes to let it kick in before gracing me with a wry smile.

'I've got something planned. Something big. I want you to come and give me a hand with some of my heavy hitters.' He pauses to concentrate on chopping another line on his desk. 'We may not be able to get the old man, but we can certainly get him where it hurts. Funny to think of it like this, but I'm going to do to him what he was planning to do to my dear old pop.' His eyes glass over with sadness, but the emotion quickly evaporates. He stoops down to emphasise his point, 'I'm going to take his daughter, have my way with her, and then send him body parts every week. I'll peel her skin off until she's an anatomy chart. Fuck! I can't wait to get my hands on her.'

His cold, gritted delivery stirs up doubt. Is he serious? I don't think he has a chance in hell to pull this off. Does he honestly think that Jessica Ward wouldn't be protected now that they know he is out? Val and his cronies will be dispatched in no time. This is pure fantasy, and I try my best to not laugh. I'll go along. Maybe I can get some answers out of him?

'How do you know she's a part of what her father does in there?'

'Do I give a shit if she is or she isn't?' he says, venomously. 'I don't have proof, but I'm sure he's responsible for my father's death. That's no way for a person like my father to die. He gave to the poor. He was a good man to his community, and a hit man kills him while he is sick and recovering?'

'I thought he died from complications from surgery.'

'It's a *fucking* lie! A total cover-up. My guys were there.'

What he probably means is, my guys were on the scene and couldn't do their job. 'Are you sure about this?'

'I'm sure. It's pathetic. If I ever find the man responsible, he'll be sorry he ever crossed a Baresi. But I'll look into it later. I have scores to settle, starting with the doctors.'

Coming here was a mistake, and a stupid one at that. What if Mike or Louis were to stroll through the door and finger me as his father's killer? Valentino would kill me in a heartbeat, even if I saved their new boss's life. Did I actually expect him to help me in any way? He can't even help himself.

The nonsense Valentino spouts begs to be ridiculed. As coked-up as he is, how can he not be completely oblivious to his father's reputation? He was known as Baresi the Butcher when he was a soldier. He sold drugs to anybody who could afford them. He used violence and intimidation on those who stood in his way. That should all be forgotten because he gave some proceeds of crime to charity? Sure, he must have been a saint.

No, this feud won't end until Valentino dies at the hands of professional mercenaries who could kill him any time they wanted to. Charles and Vincenzo were so adamant that he was nothing of the threat that his father posed.

He claims I am pathetic for killing his father. Pathetic is the destroyed and delusional man in front of me. From his behaviour, I should regret ever taking the assignment in the first place, saving an ungrateful piece of shit like Valentino, and ruining my reputation by not saving myself first. It's depressing witnessing him in his drug-den office, plotting revenge that will get him nowhere except in his own coffin.

Perhaps I should be easier on Valentino? After all, he was holed up in a prison and tortured. No normal person wouldn't be affected by what he went through.

'One week from now, we'll be taking *precious* little Jessie from the front door of Mercy Hospital and into a van.' His eyes light up. 'Man, what I'd give to have her work here? She'd pack this shithole on looks alone. Smoke all my hoes out of the water. Wouldn't need to dance either. Just keep balance on a pole…Yeah…I'm starting to like the sound of this. I'll just drug up the bitch like they drugged me and leave her on stage. Make that bitch work. Send pictures to her dear old daddy. That fucking slut!'

My moral uncertainty begins to protest. 'OK. So the plan is to take Jessie from the hospital and keep her for ransom?'

'That's it.'

'So how are you going to exact revenge with her? He'll come after you with everything he's got. And I've seen the number and type of people he has working for him. They're not run-of-the-mill heavies. These guys are trained. They've probably seen a lot of action and clocked up a lot of trigger time in the military. If you can't plan for that, then you may as well not bother. I know for a fact—'

'Don't worry,' Valentino interjects. 'I'll have places kept aside for these things. If I need to "go to the mattresses," I will. I've been in this situation before. Our war with Varetti was a longstanding battle. But our organisation was deep enough to deal with them, and it's still deep enough to take out a doctor and his daughter.'

Valentino's complete lack of thought has me offside. That he interrupted me removes the will to drum into him facts he cannot deny—

the most important of which is that his plan is completely fucked, that Charles is not interested in recapturing him (and for that matter doesn't even care about his organisation anymore), and that Varetti is in cahoots with Charles and his master plan. How deep this joint venture is…I can only guess.

But what bothers me most about Valentino is his disregard for any intelligence gathering. The all-guns-blazing approach to military tactics went out with the destruction of this country's indigenous population. When it comes to life and death and the games the Baresi family have been playing for all their lives, not finding out as much as possible about your enemy is bordering on ridiculous. He doesn't need a copy of *The Art of War* in front of him to know that.

The strained look of concern I must be projecting steers Valentino's next topic.

'For your part in helping me, I can offer you a good, hefty sum as…say how can we call this? A subcontractor?'

'Sure,' I say, completely flippant.

'Fifty thousand for a small night's work. That's if you're interested, of course.'

That sum is laughable, but I better give him a noncommittal answer. 'I'll have to think about it.'

'Sure, no problem. And how can I contact you?'

'You can't,' I say bluntly. 'Give me a meeting time for your move and I'll meet you there if I'm interested.'

'Nine p.m. Next Thursday evening. She finishes at eleven. You can meet us in the back alley. Who knows, I may just have some other work for you.'

'Maybe,' I lie. 'Until then.'

I exit the club shaking my head in disbelief. What a mess. If anyone at the agency is given a contract for Valentino's head, it would be the easiest money they would ever make.

CHAPTER TWELVE

The hangover is crushing. For the moment, I can only lie still and feel my pulse as my brain beats against my skull. It feels as if it has shrunk in size and there is simply not enough fluid to cushion it. I fear that if I turn in bed, it will only make things worse. I can only stare up at the ceiling and wait for it to pass.

Buster is sympathetic to my cause. He hasn't cried for food yet, and the squelching sound he makes grooming himself is the only way I know he is at the foot of the bed.

I want to sleep it off but can't. I am wide awake but in a trance with the inability to even move my head. I'm left to analyse last night, which I know I need to confront sometime but would rather do anything than to do it now.

Where do I start?

That my employment and source of income has been effectively terminated? Or my childish reaction to the news that has placed me in a predicament I was considering anyway, which was made worse by getting drunk, stumbling into a strip club, and going out of my way to reacquaint myself with the person I rescued but now despise?

What was talking to Valentino ever going to achieve? I already rejected the offer from Dr Ward, so why would I settle for Valentino's? His grip on any semblance of power is beyond resurrection, and I would just be one of a number of cronies who will be destroyed on his descent into ruin.

Lloyd's words were clear enough and by seeing Valentino, I violated another directive within hours of receiving it. It is stupidity personified. The stakes are too high for me to be acting so carelessly, but I keep doing it and I don't know why. It's probably as good a time as ever to pack it in and quit.

But I still have that drive…the drive to finish what I started no matter what the cost. My pride is hell-bent on vengeance, and it will spite myself if it has to. Knowing what I know, I also have the duty to stop Charles and his delusions of racial superiority. And if it's too far gone, then I'll have to settle for just his death. Who said justifications had to be either idealistic or pragmatic and not both?

I finally make an effort to get out of bed. I get up enough to stand and after only thirty seconds vertical, I rush to the bathroom to hug the porcelain.

The rest of the day is spent moping on the coach watching the news, sport, and a few TV shows while sipping on a large bottle of water. I take an afternoon nap to double the amount of sleep I had from last night.

The alarm clock reads six when I wake. But is it morning or night? Did I sleep for over twelve hours? I am either tired from oversleeping or groggy from not enough. I manage to get to the lounge room still confused as the curtains are drawn. My latest mobile phone is sitting on the coffee table, and unless it has been magically tampered with, confirms I haven't lost the day just yet.

More puzzling than what day it is, is an unread text message. There are not too many people who know this number. George is one of them, though, and he would be wise to assume that I will not hesitate to kill him for his betrayal.

But the number is not his. It's a number I don't know. He does change numbers almost as frequently as I do, but he usually informs me when he does and would've done so when I bought the satchel charges from him for my last job. The message is cryptic: 'Head down to the Mad Clowns clubhouse. Something crazy is happening.'

It only takes me a minute to connect the dots. Charles's threat to use his chemical compound. His promise to trial it on an unsuspecting but knowingly aggressive organisation. He must have picked the Mad Clown bikers. But has it succeeded? Did the most notorious bikie gang in Hillbay hold their own, or were they incapacitated and beaten to a pulp?

I need to see for myself. Will I be too late and only witness the aftermath? Either way, I need to know if Charles's threat is real or if he has hopelessly underestimated his own ability. If it is the latter, I will probably absolve myself of a great amount of guilt and put this whole stain on my career to rest.

I scrounge through the fridge and find whatever may be edible and scoff it down without hesitation. Not only am I starving, but I need some energy in reserve in case I find myself in a situation that requires it. I quickly get changed, and while doing so, consider whether to be armed for the occasion. What if it's a trap or if police search pedestrians? I better be protected, and I make sure I grab an unregistered SIG Sauer P229 from the safe in the study.

The clubhouse is only a few blocks from here, and I can probably leg it in around fifteen minutes. As I wait for the elevator to descend, I reach into my jacket pocket and realise I still have my phone with the message on it. I don't have time to go back and leave it in the apartment, as the cops could already be cleaning up what mess is left. I need to see this for myself. Keeping the phone on me is not a good move, as it may incriminate me even if I delete the text message.

I reply to the hot tip with a message of my own, 'Who the fuck is this?', and walk briskly out of the building before kicking into a lopsided jog that won't leave me out of breath after a few minutes. My still-injured quadriceps pinches in pain from stretching the healing ligaments. My calf is remarkably fine and there's only slight bruising remaining, but my thigh just won't heal quickly even after all of the rehab I've been doing. Then again, I should be thankful I still have a leg.

The streets have retreated to a lull. I pass couples heading out to dinner and the odd businessmen heading home. I have to be careful to avoid bowling over anyone I pass, especially around restaurants and their kerbside diners. It doesn't take long before I cross into the CBD's troubled area. French and Italian eateries are replaced by twenty-four-hour convenient stores and fast food chains. Graffiti and vandalism are more prevalent. A few shops have been boarded up, and charred remains of what once were buildings now house squatters.

I slow to a brisk walk. There's no point in giving away that I'm keenly interested in a tragedy. I take out the phone and notice I already have a response: 'A friend!'

It's unmistakable! It can only be George. I would never be interested in this event had it not been for Charles boasting. George gave me away, and now he wants me to know I made the wrong decision back when they had me bound and at their mercy.

The Mad Clowns' clubhouse is just one short corner away, but I don't need to turn into it to know that something is already amiss. Reflections from the surrounding windows of flashing red-and-blue lights are an easy enough giveaway that the police are at the scene.

There is a gathering of random people all looking in the direction of the clubhouse. This is good as I can hide in the crowd. Any surveillance teams interested in my movements will find it difficult to spot me, and there's little chance they'd be stupid enough to try and apprehend me once I move in.

Police barriers have already been erected to allow their investigative team and paramedics to do their jobs without being disturbed. I can't see anything from the back of this crowd. It must be at least ten deep, and I'm too far away.

Everyone seems transfixed on the police and paramedics while I excuse myself through the sea of bodies until about three rows from the front.

The scene before me is surreal. I count eight bodies, five of which have been covered over by blankets and lying on the bitumen just outside the entrance. There are pools of blood mixed with the drying rain that must have occurred in the afternoon while I slept. The only two windows to the clubhouse were smashed from the inside out as shards litter the ground. The myriad of glass bounces the light show from the emergency service vehicles onto onlookers. Only one body is identifiable by a full sleeve of rough and indiscriminate tattoos going down to his wrist. I can just make out the first two letters on the metacarpals of this man's pinkie and ring fingers of his right hand. They are a distinct 'M' and 'A.'

OK, so one guy has been killed, but that doesn't mean that they were completely overwhelmed. I try to find further evidence. One bikie is being cared for by a paramedic and strapped into a collapsible gurney. He struggles to move freely as if he is out of his mind and mumbling to the paramedic, who is constantly reassuring him. Another gang member sobs into a towel while giving a statement to the police. Three from three and I'm starting to get the picture.

It must have worked! Charles's Aggredisol has done exactly as he wished, and the two victims I can see have as unblemished skin as one could expect for bikies. None of them are close to resembling Boris at least. There's still Charles's master plan, but the problem is I will never know if or when it will be completed.

Among the casual commotion of the spectators, I hear a female voice to the left of me. 'Oh, my God, does anyone know what happened here?'

She sounds strangely familiar and as I glance over, I feel my own sense of terror seep in until my skin reacts with goose bumps everywhere. Jessica Ward is within arm's length.

A forty-something professional woman in front of her answers her query. 'I'm not quite sure, but it looks like a bikie war has just broken out. I think a rival gang just came through and smashed this place to bits.'

'That's not what happened,' a man says directly behind me. 'Bottom line is we don't know. The police won't tell us because they arrived after the fact. One thing is for sure, I haven't seen any other person carried out of that clubhouse who wasn't wearing Mad Clown clothing.'

Shit. The man's compulsion to inform makes me still. I hope Jessica doesn't address the man because if she does, she will certainly spot me. I can't move, and it's too obvious if I turn away. Just keep your eyes straight ahead and pray for the best.

'Excuse me,' she says. Shit. I'm doomed, again. Don't pay any attention. 'Excuse me.'

I still stupidly play ignorant but can hear her work her short way over to where I'm standing. I feel a warm hand on my shoulder and don't need to guess whose hand it is. The game is up, and I cannot make a quick exit or dismiss her like at her awards dinner.

'Dr Kruger?'

'Oh…hello,' I say. 'How have you been?'

'Very well,' she says, smiling.

Just her small, simple act of displaying pleasantness binds me into submitting. Her hair is down tonight and she has a small amount of makeup on for the evening. She is rugged-up in jeans and a warm, thick coat. Perhaps she was out with friends for dinner.

'Congratulations, on your award. I read about it in the *Hillbay Times*. You must be very proud of achieving such an accolade so early in your career.'

'Why thank you. I can't receive all or even most of the credit, as my father led and conducted most of the work. Hey, come to mention it, I thought I saw you at the dinner but I was mistaken. I see you've had a substantial haircut since we last met.'

She can add excellent perception to her list of good traits. I run my hand over my two millimetre cropped hair. Even I almost forgot that I wore substantially different wigs the previous two occasions we crossed paths.

'Oh, that…Yeah, a colleague suggested I have a fresh, clean look coming into spring. I have my reservations, though,' I chuckle.

'Well, I think it looks nice. So what's your take on this? Have you been here long? Do you know what happened?'

'I was just having some dinner around the corner when I saw the flashing lights and thought I should take a look. To tell you the truth, I have no idea what's going on. I think the lady said it right before, this was probably a dispute between two bikie gangs over something.' It is a convincing tale without a hint of truth.

'It seems odd that they would be doing it right in the middle of the city with people around. What if an innocent bystander was shot?'

'You'd hope it wouldn't come to that.'

If only she knew. If only she knew her father was responsible for this attack, and chums with such a detestable character as Varetti. It is inconceivable to me that she wouldn't know either fact. But her presence here and her shock at the event in front of us are sincere. I doubt she would know Varetti, now the most powerful underworld figure in this city, even if they passed each other in the Ward mansion's corridors.

Beyond my observations, I can't stop thinking that her innocence is refreshingly charming when every person I'm dealing with has blood-soaked hands. I need to be 100 percent certain though. I need to know she diverges from her father's megalomania. But how should I test this? I know the exact question to ask…

'And what about Aggredisol? I read about this wonder compound in the papers. Wouldn't the perpetrators of this crime be perfect examples of the people who would benefit from a course of treatment? Isn't this exactly what your drug is designed for?'

She shakes her head slowly. 'No. I wouldn't recommend it.'

'Why not?'

'Because it is too powerful…because I don't believe it would help any of these people with their problems, or society at large for that matter. It is *not* the be-all and end-all for this world. As you probably read, it permanently takes away someone else's freedom to act through the full range of human emotions…however violent it may be.'

It's an OK response, I guess. But this needs to go further. I have to push and play devil's advocate. 'But it would protect society. Isn't that the point of its conception? To save *those* innocent victims?'

'Even so, I still could not justify it. I think the media hasn't thought through the consequences of such an application. It isn't a quick fix solution to society's problems. Elements of freewill will be removed forever after its first and only treatment. That is something that cannot be taken lightly. A person's will is what makes them not just human, but a being in itself that has the power to act according to its own needs and wants. Taking away the freedom for violent conduct will mean that any subject will be forever vulnerable in life. These bikers would be at the mercy of a scrawny teenager.'

'So, when would you ever plan to use this treatment?'

'In only the most extreme circumstances. People diagnosed with psychopathy and similar personality disorders involving chronic and severe tendencies for violence. These people would typically have next to no chance of rehabilitation using standard methods. It's ironic really. Newspapers have been heralding this drug to solve crime by conditioning behaviour, but it is anything but. The people who would be treated would have been sentenced to a life of confinement in either a prison or a mental institution and would never be released to contribute to society anyway. So to say that Aggredisol will be the answer to the ills of this world is a gross exaggeration.'

'And what if there was a temporary solution?'

'There will *never* be one. We simply don't have the technology to numb that area of the brain without killing it.'

'Interesting.' I say, to not only a better understanding of her fascinating work, but to the important insight into her personality. She knows *nothing* about her father's extended work in this field. She is also nothing like him. There is none of Charles's anxiety or resentment through grief. Knowing that she lost her mother to such a tragic end hasn't dampened her spirit or her pursuit of happiness. It shows in the authentic warm glow of her eyes while she smiles at me. When I admire her, I can only see purity and the drive to achieve. Her joy is so infectious it coerces me to smile back. She is humble enough to recognise the shortcomings of her work, and it's inspiring to hear.

We lock eyes and for the first time in my life, I am incapable of hiding my vulnerability. It must be showing in my face and body language and I cannot stop it. Although she doesn't know, we are staring into our opposites. And for me at least, opposites attract.

I have to catch myself. The ridiculousness of even considering what I want to do is incredible. Am I that game to ask out and try and begin a relationship with the daughter of a man I was asked to and would still kill? In a different time I would pursue her to no end. She is the once-in-a-lifetime girl where everything seems perfect. But I can't. I cannot force myself to go against common sense and the absurdity of what would come if we were together. My history alone would disgust her enough to torpedo this relationship. If pressed, I wouldn't allow myself to lie. It wouldn't be fair to either of us. This realisation pains me to despair…

Even with the murmurs of the crowd, we both hear a vibrating noise coming from her hip. For some unknown reason, hospitals still prefer pagers to communicate to doctors on call, except these are now a fraction of their original size.

Jessica breaks our gaze and unclips the device from her hip to read the message. She is disappointed from what she reads. 'I have to go to work.'

'On call?'

'Unfortunately. I'm thinking about giving up emergency work for medical research…or at least scale it back. Coincidentally, I think some of my patients this evening will be the actors in our play here.'

'Hopefully they don't put up much of a fight.'

She giggles and touches my arm gently. The gesture doesn't go unnoticed and I become somewhat aroused at this ever-so-slight contact.

'If you're ever around Mercy Hospital again, please give me a call. You can also give me a call if you are not. I would love to meet up and talk about medicine…or this city's crime, or anything really.'

She reaches into her coat pocket and digs out a business card and hands it to me. I take one glance and am immediately drawn to the sets of acronyms after her name. More impressive than her educational qualifications is how wise she is beyond her years. It is surely a certainty that I'm not the only person who's been spellbound by her personality. As she moves through the crowd, a number of males within a few bodies of her path divert their attention and train it on her as she passes.

'You lucky bastard,' the man who spoke up earlier says. 'She was all over you.'

I look back at the card. As much as I want to, this is an impossibility. I cannot let desire get in the way of a duty, even if it has since been discharged. Imagine how ludicrous the situation would be if this were to progress enough for her to introduce me to her father?

Lucky bastard? Hardly. More like cursed son of a bitch.

I've had enough excitement for the evening. I give Jessica around five minutes before leaving the scene to avoid any awkwardness that may occur if we left at the same time.

There's no point in rushing back home. I have no tail following me and there is no threat.

Maybe it's the residue from my hangover, but I feel uncertain. This is all too much. The angst I've been carrying all of these years is near its natural tipping point. I know I am on the verge of a nervous breakdown. Everyone is a suspect, and everyone is a problem. And on top of all this, innocents are in the way or intertwined with this disease affecting me.

I walk one block. Something is wrong, terribly wrong, with what just transpired. Jessica isn't associated in the slightest with her father. She doesn't have the same perspective or blinded longing for revenge on a massive scale. She is above suspicion of what Charles wants to achieve, and it is probably a plausible arrangement for him to have it that way. He has access to the genetically gifted and brilliantly trained medical mind of his daughter under the auspice of good intentions for the mentally unstable. But in order to keep up this cloak, he would need to keep his security detail away. I need to go with the probability that he has to risk his daughter to keep her onside and help with his research.

In order to do this, Charles is making a fatal mistake and a grave injustice. He is leaving her to the whims of vengeful people like Valentino who, despite being incredibly incompetent and reckless, could just pull off the kidnap he has brashly conceptualised.

By the time I make it home, pent-up worry takes hold. If Valentino succeeds, whatever happens to her would be unjust collateral and I can do nothing to stop it.

I toss and turn in my sleep with these thoughts and scenarios running through my head. It's not just worry that keeps me awake. The hangover should be gone, but my head still screams with an unbearable ache. Concern pacifies the pain.

They simply won't stop. No matter what plan of attack I can think of, it is either ridiculous or fraught with danger and certain death from one party or another. If it isn't Valentino, it will be Charles's mercenaries, and once Lloyd and the agency find out that I have intervened, they will want me expunged. My conscience is throttling any logical thought. I am fucked any which way I turn. This one job seems to have no end to what can go wrong.

I could only have slept about two hours when I wake and decide it is futile to continue to try. I get up and just sit on the couch in a vegetative state.

What can I possibly do? Not just today but for the rest of my life?

I perform my usual routine. I have a coffee, take out Jessica's business card, and stare at what could have been before forcing myself to rip it to shreds and throw it away. A couple of hours later, I have an incredibly lacklustre workout. It does nothing for my headache.

Out of frustration, I fling my phone in the general direction of the couch and it accidentally clips Buster's overhanging tail as he naps, rebounds from the front of the couch and crashes onto the floorboards. Buster wakes instantly from the contact with his tail and, knowing that I am the only one to blame, stares me down with equal parts anger and fear.

'Sorry,' I say to him, surprised to find myself emotional as the solitary word peels out. 'I don't say sorry to anyone but you.'

This isn't like me. I have nothing to be crying over. I made my choices, and I need to live with their consequences no matter how dire. I knew this from the start yet I'm standing here, an emotional wreck and apologising to a cat of all things. For fuck's sake!

I go to the couch and sit beside Buster to console him and stroke him from head to rump, just the way he likes it. As a gesture of forgiveness, he starts purring after three strokes. Meanwhile, I am left to recognise that I am so monstrous that he is the only creature I can get along with, and even then only sometimes. I find myself contemplating our relationship and if I may be able to end it. Perhaps his petulant arse was never meant to have been domesticated in the first place. It's a pathetic observation from the pathetic owner that I've been. At least now he has resorted back to expelling his waste in his litter tray instead of my bed.

His recent mental unbalancing may have had something to do with my temporary incarceration. I grab a toy, a caricature of a fishing rod with a cow at the end of it, and dangle the bait to perk his tracking and hunting abilities. He takes a swipe and is too slow as I tease him and pull the cow away from his claws. I dangle the bait again and am met with a leap and Buster's two front paws clawing my hand. The sudden pain from his wild and unclipped nails makes me wince.

'You little bastard.'

Buster meows hard, as if saying the joke was on me. I reach over and pick up my phone. I unlock it, play with the menus, and flick through the incredibly few contacts saved. All people are listed by initials only. I scroll to 'CG,' which stands for Curious George. If I am bound by the agency and Lloyd to keep my head out of my own fuckup, then I can at least square my ledger with him. Lloyd even said I was on my own anyway.

I send him a simple text: 'We need to meet.'

I fetch a couple of codeine tablets for my headache and guzzle them down with a glass of water. I lie facedown on the couch and wait for the medication to kick in. I feel Buster's paws creep up on my back and stop high on my trapezius. His whiskers tickle the back of my neck as he sniffs around my hairline. He licks my short hair, intending to groom me as he does himself, and I tolerate it until the sensitivity is too much to bear. I roll over and Buster initially tries to surf my back before dropping down to the couch cushion when I am almost perpendicular.

My phone lights up with a message alert. It has to be him. I am not wrong as George responds, not from his new number but his old one: 'I think we should too. I'm caught in the middle of something tonight. Cool Room. Tomorrow. This time + 20 mins.'

Excellent. A public bar. I consult my watch. It's 2200. I have twenty-four hours to wait. There's no need for a plan or to investigate the bar either. The intention is to never enter the Cool Room at all. More important is the necessity to add the proper human countermeasures to throw off any scent that may be on my tail. I'm still that sceptical.

I will have my revenge.

I only need to lure him away from the venue and any possible witnesses. He'll come alone—he always does. I am buoyed because if he takes the bait, I will have a distinct advantage: he won't know I will be coming for him.

CHAPTER THIRTEEN

It's 2200. Time to move. Time to plug that leak.

It'll take me about twenty minutes to get there. I crane down to inspect my thigh. Even I am surprised at my recuperative abilities. Last night's hobbling run down to the Mad Clowns clubhouse has done me a world of good. I statically tense my quads to test it. Only a dull soreness remains as if just that muscle were subject to some intense weight training the day before. My calf, well, that's a medical miracle. I've come to accept that the injury is unexplainable, as it has made a full recovery.

I cannot say the same for my headache. It's as if the hangover from yesterday has lingered into a second day of pain. To be sure, I gulp down a couple of codeine tablets for good measure.

I grab my coat and the same SIG Sauer P229 I carried last night except I've screwed in a homemade silencer. I check its magazine and tuck it into the back of my jeans, underneath my coat. I take a wallet with a stolen driving license and $200, although I, of course, intend to make a clean getaway.

The half-brisk walk and jog at times to the closest subway station and into a departing train is restless but purposeful as I burn for retribution. A highly trained assassin against the king of surveillance. He has outstayed his welcome and has done himself a great disservice by selling me out. For that he will need to pay with his life.

I consider my options for a clean hit while on autopilot on the way to the Cool Room. I will wait outside for him to arrive, suggest that we need to talk in private somewhere, and when he doesn't notice, silently execute him out of prying public eyes. Simple and effective.

It is undeniable that he will be a loss. I held our professional and personal relationship dear. He was the one constant in the underworld that was impartial to a number of factions, placing himself above the rut and pettiness of allegiances. He was a terrific resource. It was great to know there was a contact able to be trusted and who could provide vital and always valuable information from a different perspective. Even Lloyd cannot fault my logic for having an independent flow of intelligence from the demographic I do most of my business for.

It is a terrible shame our relationship will be coming to an end, but this town isn't big enough for both of us.

I dart in and out of laneways to assure anonymity and the evasion of any tails.

By the time I make it to the Cool Room, I am ten minutes late and George is waiting outside, tapping his foot on the pavement.

The look on his face is a cocktail of worry and severe annoyance.

'You are fucking late,' he scowls. The tension is his voice is palpable.

'Hey, relax. Aren't we friends here?'

'Sometimes I wonder.'

This already isn't going how I expected. Being just ten minutes late shouldn't rattle someone enough to be unforgiving, especially George. Already something is not right. No matter. There's no need to deviate from the schedule. I must press forward. He can talk all he wants into a silenced pistol barrel pointing at him. It's the best lie detector I know.

'What's up your arse?' I ask.

'There's some major movements going down tonight, none of which any sane person would make, let alone allow.'

This generally happens every night. Why should I care? Perhaps, more importantly, why would George think that I should care? More evidence of guilt?

'This is not exactly news in this town. Why don't you stop them and call the police?'

'I hope you're being naïve as a joke? If not, open your fucking eyes.'

Something has him seriously spooked. He fidgets with his fingers. A sure sign of nerves from someone I have never seen nervous before. It is off-putting when a guy can fight off the mob and now melts before me with worry.

'Should we talk somewhere more private?'

I am mindful that we are standing at the entrance to the bar, with spotlights and a street lamp bathing us in light for the occasional pedestrian strolling past to remember us.

'Yes. You lead the way.'

He's a smart motherfucker, too. I grit my teeth to hide the frustrating snarl and nod. There would be no point in gunning him down in front of a licensed venue where CCTV cameras are compulsory and witnesses are plenty. Better to go somewhere quiet to subdue him.

As I dawdle and case a suitable location, he walks just behind my left shoulder, hands strategically in his front coat pockets.

We cross an intersection, and I notice a few dilapidated buildings. Perfect for a private meeting and a shootout. I spot a burnt-out terrace apartment building fortuitously next to a street lamp, which will give me just enough light to steady my aim.

I walk up to the door and kick it open. I don't bother to even turn before drawing my firearm as soon as I enter.

'Don't even think about it,' George says, as I hear the hammer of a pistol cock only inches behind my head while my gun is frustratingly at my side. He came prepared and had the drop on me. Good for him.

'You won't shoot.'

'If I do, you will only have a split second to discover your error in judgement. I'm testy at the moment, as you should already know.'

He's right. We are under the strain of working in trying times. But I am not stressed by having *his* pistol pointed at my head. 'Is there any reason for this?'

'I could say the same to you. But first, drop the weapon.'

I comply.

'Now kick it back here.'

I do as he says, back-heeling the pistol past him and towards the door.

'Do not turn around. If you turn around, I will shoot you without question for being an idiot and not following instructions.'

'OK. Answer my question.'

'Fine. I've been compromised. I'm not going to say who or why, but there's a building in chars I used to call my office. Unlike some, I confirm *without a shadow of a doubt* who ratted me out before I hunt them down and pull the trigger.'

'What makes you think that I haven't, George?'

'Because I would know if it were me.'

The confidence in his answer makes my head spin over my convictions, so much so that the codeine tablets I took begin to wear off and the sting of my headache returns as quickly as a venomous whip of a scorpion's tail. The problem is I now doubt both my ability for logical reasoning as well as George's answer. Should I be questioning how I came to this conclusion?

'What you do not understand, my dear friend, is that Hillbay's underworld tectonic plates are shifting as we speak. This is a once-in-a-generation shift that isn't just going to affect this city or the state but the entire country. There *will* be far-reaching consequences in more ways than one from what is transpiring. And I don't know about you, but I am scared shitless about it.'

'And what makes you think that? I thought you were as resilient in tough times as they come? You survived one of the biggest families in the country wanting to kill you, and they had the ability to devote a fair amount of resources to try.'

'I'll take that as a compliment. It's sad that it needs to be received at gunpoint. But I think you're underestimating the circumstances we find ourselves in. There are some organisations not even I will dare challenge. And before I tell you what is bothering the shit out of me, let me remind you that I left the business of killing a long time ago. I stopped it because I made so much more in surveillance and intel that there was no point in risking my life being a standover for a couple of underappreciating old-schoolers. You need to start thinking about the end game: the reason any of us would ever dare to consider doing this. You make enough money and you leave with your life. How much can you enjoy when you're dead?

'Lucky for me I have another revenue stream that is ridiculously lucrative. It's something you will probably never know I am involved with. And right now, that asset needs all my attention. If you want, you can contact me through the usual channels, but my price just tripled. It doubled because of what's going on and tripled because of the shit you just tried to pull. I'll put tonight down as an unhappy mistake.'

'Fine…I'm sorry I doubted you.'

I'm not interested in reasoning with him as much as this cursed headache. Just standing still is killing me. My head is throbbing uncontrollably. I wince and think I could pass out any second. I try to say something but can't and offer nothing but empty breath.

'There is a good reason why I wanted to see you this evening,' George continues. 'As a friend and with a warning. Whatever it is that has spooked you to this point, just let it go. There's no point in losing your head over something that you didn't need to risk it for. If you failed, then grieve and move on.'

'And what if I can't?'

'Then you're probably not going to see out the month.'

His words pop whatever confidence I have in my abilities like a balloon. George doesn't mince his words. And if the environment is scaring the shit out of him, then I should be running for my life.

'Have you got anything else for me?'

For once I sense George's vulnerability. He clears his throat to compose himself. Maybe it's because despite how serious his warning is, my latest question means that I've already chosen to ignore his well-informed advice.

'Well…ahem…let's see here. To start with, Valentino Baresi is one deranged motherfucker. I've never heard such crazy reports coming from his camp in my life. He's letting complete strangers into his office to smash through a few lines of coke before letting them go. He's fucking nuts. No care in the world about security. Being kidnapped must have fucked him up completely. He gets released and loses the plot in the process. If Luigi were still alive, he would have castrated him. The old man was kidnapped a couple of times in his life and never reacted that way.'

'C'mon. That's a little harsh. You don't know what he went through when he was taken.'

'Maybe. But the decimation of his family's infrastructure means there is nobody there to guide him through this mess. He has no advisors with experience and he won't take a hint from friends beneath him. Val has this delusional attitude of invincibility now. He's leaving himself wide open to anyone and everyone. He's got a raging cocaine addiction, which he doesn't even try to hide anymore. His personal office has more items to put him away than a police evidence room. Powder is everywhere, and it is common knowledge that inside the safe is every gun he has used on each of his hits. He collects them! He has the smoking guns, plural, I might add, for some of the biggest mob scalps over the years. If a straight cop ever got his snout in there, Valentino would be going straight to prison and would never see the light of day.'

'So what? Mob empires crumble. He probably had it coming.'

'Yeah, well, even so…this behaviour has unintended consequences that are going to affect people that it shouldn't.'

I prepare to hear what I know and fear. 'Like what?'

'Like that he's got it in his head that some doctor is the one who kidnapped him, not Varetti, and to get him back he's going to kill his daughter. He's a kooky, crazy son of a bitch!'

'Why would he do that?'

'Who the fuck knows? How could he possibly believe anyone but Varetti would have the motivation to be after him? This girl is as clean as the pope's sheets and as far as I know, she spends more time with children's charities than a saint. It's as shocking as it is absurd. There's no reason behind it. This is wrong on so many levels and there is nobody there to stop it. He's planning to kill her outside the hospital she works at. Gun her down like a marked man that has had it coming for years. Who the fuck would do such a thing?'

'When is he planning this?'

'Tonight.'

Fuck! Maybe Valentino's found that it is easier to kill someone than to take them hostage. Perhaps between his coke binges he was able to apply every electrode in that small brain of his to see that killing someone will have more of an effect than abducting them. Giving Charles any possibility that Jessica is recoverable in any state will bring an avalanche of a response. Something that Valentino would have no chance of fighting.

'Will you give me permission to turn around?'

'Fine.'

Slowly pivoting to face George, the slice of moonlight illuminating his face is enough to show the torment. He is distressed, and his profile sags as if greeted with the news his parents met a dreadful demise. He is on the verge of tears before he pulls himself together with a few grunts and an apology.

'When is he going to move on the hospital?'

'In thirty minutes.'

Again he flashes a destitute expression my way. Emotions begin to tweak and pull at my core. Why me and why now? Was I going to just let this happen? I should've known and taken action to preempt this madness. I could've taken Valentino's offer and nipped this in the bud from the inside. Hell, I could have warned Jessica last fucking night! Stupid me. Surely there have been others who have been killed in this long, protracted war, and I didn't bat an eyelid. If I challenge a direct order from Lloyd, I will surely be a marked man. And the daughter of a target no less. I can think of nothing more dire.

But should I do anything? *Can* I do anything?

In the end, it is a simple calculation that needs to be made. Am I finally ready to turn over a new leaf? And if so, how much am I prepared to sacrifice? My career, certainly, and maybe my life too? I cannot kid myself any longer. I've been preparing myself for an exit, but the catalyst is saving Jessica from falling into this abyss of destruction. If there is anyone that doesn't deserve this sort of end, it is her. If I represent all that is evil because I chose the career of a killer, then what she does is the polar opposite. It is the juxtaposition of our livelihoods and the antithetical melodrama that is now playing itself out.

If I am to truly change, I can start by not taking lives, but by saving them. However I put a stop to Valentino, it would spare Jessica. The paradox is unmistakable. I will need to use every conceivable skill I know to harm and destroy any person in the way just so she can continue to live. How many can I anticipate? If Valentino is planning a simple kill, there will probably be two or three including him that will need to be neutralised. So up to three lives for one? Is that transaction worth it? The trade-off in bodies is steep. But behind those numbers, the one life to be saved has the ability to save many more. Valentino and his sidekicks are surely not worth even one upstanding human being. He's meddled in the vices of life, and indulged in intimidation and murder to keep his share of a sizeable black market intact. His history warrants his pound of flesh to be withdrawn from the most vital of areas of his body.

The other outcome is there will be one more life to add to the count: mine. I'm more than prepared for my own death for this cause.

But I need to be truthful to myself as well. Infatuation has crept into my motivation. If she weren't so attractive, would I even be considering this course of action? Has her attention towards me blinded all rational thought and conjured a reason to justify risking everything? Has my discipline eroded that much that I am falling like a schoolboy falls for his first crush? The probability of our chance meetings spurred my emotions for her. For all of the times she has popped out from nowhere with wisdom and her flirtatious smile, it has been a relieving distraction. But this charade can only end badly. When I reveal that I am not a cardiologist, she will run from the deceit, or worse, if she figures out what I really do. The thought is both liberating and depressing. If I pull this off, I can never see her again. If I let Valentino get his way, nobody will see her again.

If I am going to make a stand in my life, there is no better time than now. George even said that our world will be changing in a permanent way very soon and stopping Valentino will only be the inevitable *coup de grâce*. I'm about 90 percent healed, and the only remaining annoyance is this resurfacing headache. If that can be held off just a little, the element of surprise might just be enough to at least ward off Jessica before the police arrive. But that's only if I can get there in time. That means walking by a man who has a gun pointed at my head.

'I've got to go.'

'That is a very brash request from a man who has no bargaining power at the moment. Are you forgetting who is holding the gun and who intended to kill me fifteen minutes ago?'

'Let's not go into details,' I joke. 'I believe you. You've never been wrong before…I…don't know what to say?'

'Good-bye would be a start.'

'Good-bye…and take care.'

'Fine. Just to be clear, though, leave the piece behind. I wouldn't want you to take advantage of our friendship.'

'Understood.' I head for the door. 'You were invaluable to me over the years.'

'Likewise.'

Likewise? Was that supposed to mean anything in particular other than financial gain? The comment is enough to stop me in my tracks. Screw it. There's no point in overanalysing one fucking word. I press on and pass by my weapon towards the door. It would be good to be able to use it, but it's not worth it if I'm going to be shot. I will have to improvise as I walk out and into the fresh night.

As I step out onto the street and break into a jog to nowhere, I am grateful to still be alive. My next concern is how to get to Mercy Hospital as quickly as possible. I am already a marked man in spirit, and this small act of redemption cannot in any way affect the plight of my soul. What I can start doing is try to erase some of that debt before I die at the hands of similarly condemned men led by Lloyd. The agency will come for me with everything they have.

I pick up the pace and sprint towards the direction of the hospital. It's a fruitless attempt to cover the distance even if I miraculously had an unlimited amount of anabolic endurance. The whip of a chilly breeze against my rushing face forces me to squint. With such limited vision, I quickly scrutinise every car I pass and evaluate every stationary vehicle for its accessibility to hotwire with my bare hands. Who am I kidding, though? There's simply no time for that.

Onto another main road I attempt to hail a cab, any cab, which comes my way. A few have occupants, which will do me no good. One eventually pulls over beside me. The driver winds his window down as I approach his side of the car.

'Where are you going?'

'I need to get to Mercy Hospital. It's an emergency.'

'I'm not going that way. Find another cab.'

'Typical,' I say, grabbing the handle of the driver's side door and opening it to his complete bafflement.

'You can't do th—'

I never let him finish protesting, as before he realises it, I've lifted him out of his seat and flung him towards the middle of the road. His Bluetooth headset flies from his ear, skittles away, and nestles next to a parked car's tyre on the other side of the road.

'You should buckle up next time,' I tell him.

I dash for the taxi as it creeps forward with the handbrake off. Once in, I plunder the accelerator, and the rear wheels skid momentarily before finding their grip and jerking me back into the seat. I clip my seatbelt in as soon as I get the car under complete control. I reach for the cabin camera installed in every taxi by law to prevent incidences such as these, snap it off, and toss it onto the road.

I am tense. My heart tries its best to exit my chest with assistance from my ballooning lungs. My hands shake abruptly, transferring the rumbling onto the steering wheel. The car speeds as fast as I can make it within a loose definition of safety. I brake at a set of traffic lights. Both lanes are backed up into two columns and four vehicles deep. C'mon and fucking change to green already! I don't have time for this shit. I check the lights directing the perpendicular road: green to amber. Good. I take advantage of the impending change to green, stomp the accelerator, and swerve over to the oncoming side of the road.

I race towards the intersection. The light hits green. The car on the other side facing me starts rolling forward. The male driver, with his head down, is playing with his phone before looking up in horror. He brakes sharply and slams on his horn. Luckily the cars behind him *are* paying attention. I cut back into flowing traffic and am now at the head of the pack. The move saves me from continuously beeping the cars in front and becoming frustrated behind law-abiding motorists.

I check my watch. It is 2300 and the clock on the dash says four past. I'm late and I'm around four kilometres away. I get reckless, pushing the car to one hundred and forty in a seventy zone. I don't need to check a mirror to tell that sweat is glistening from my forehead, a reaction from the risk far outweighing the reward. But I don't give a shit about the odds anymore. If I die in a car accident, it won't be for nothing. The tragedy would be if this car swerves and kills others. Great government purges, nuclear bombs, genocide, and now flying through traffic to be on time to save the daughter of a man that was going to kill me. Sure, anyone can rationalise the absurd.

The steering wheel now vibrates my hands from the torque reaching its limits. The bonnet smokes from stress. It could be the radiator spraying fluid terminally into the engine bay. Shit! I push the engine as hard as possible for the last straight and have to gently press the brakes to avoid the car spinning unpredictably out of control.

All right. Play it calm. I drive casually through the emergency entrance, dimming all lights and remaining idle. Thank God the smoke from the car is subsiding so I don't stand out too much.

The emergency entrance is free of obstructing vehicles. It is a fortunate occurrence for such a time. The outpatients building adjacent to the emergency and triage entry is even quieter. No human can been seen from the conspicuous buzz of bright fluorescent lights beaming into the foyer. Night vision is completely ruined by the contrast, making it almost impossible to see any distinction of shapes beyond the entrance.

Am I too late?

Darkness and shadows move irregularly in the distance to pique my hypersensitive attention. I squint trying to identify what is making those movements. I can see it now about forty metres in front. Three separate shapes. My powers of logic figure out the rest.

The more I concentrate, the clearer it becomes. Three figures are up against the corner of the entrance in complete darkness and lying in wait. I train my sights on them. What do I do now? I draw a blank. I could have called her if I didn't take her card out of my jacket pocket last night and destroy it. Shit! All those years of training and the impromptu situations I've been forced to fight my way out of, and now I cannot think of a single scenario that has me ending up alive. I am a mathematics professor stumped by simple arithmetic.

No firearm as well. Fuck, I could scream if it didn't give my position away! My mind ticks over until it is forced to spring into action…

Jessica's silhouette emerges from the same cavernous entry to the hospital I stepped into last month to kill the father of the man who now wants her dead. She stops under the lights just outside the doorway and burrows through her bag for her phone. She checks it, and I have a split second to admire her figure once more in perfectly fitting jeans, black coat and small heels that I hope she can run in.

Suddenly, from the blob of darkness, I see a little flash of light. A phone is ringing in silent in one of the figure's hands. The group scurries closer around to the corner of the building a bare ten metres from where Jessica stands. She is still playing with her mobile, oblivious to the violence that will soon befoul her.

Just run back inside, or anywhere for that matter! This is a train wreck unfolding in front of me. What can I possibly do? There must be a spotter in the emergency car park who is signalling the target's presence to the assailants. I glance over at the half-dozen or so parked cars. I spot him now, dumb enough to be smoking to give away his position in the driver's seat of a BMW SUV.

They are ready to pounce, and I don't think when I pound my foot on the accelerator and hope that forty metres of distance is enough to achieve a velocity with enough stopping power. The car impulsively winds itself up in first gear. The large-capacity engine does itself justice by propelling the car forward at an alarming rate. The gear change is noticeable and loud and I jerk forwards and backwards from the sudden change in force as I see the figures stop moving. Jessica, who has taken so much of my attention, is now frozen with bewilderment.

Hurtling towards the assailants, the car crosses the point of no return. Even if I break as hard as possible, I will not be able to avoid hitting the wall. Do I brace for impact or try and relax and let my joints be as loose as possible?

'Aaarrggghhhh!'

I shudder from the plastic-and-metal crunch as the front of the taxi crumples from the collision with two sets of legs and the wall behind them. So this is what it feels like to be a crash test dummy? My senses are overloaded from every direction before I pass out...

It is an overpowering and massive scream that alarms me to wake up. Where am I? Still in the car with a job to finish. That's right. Take deep breaths and get your bearings. Help yourself up.

I pull on the steering wheel with all my might, and use it as leverage like an old man would. My legs are a little wobbly, but they'll be OK. Lucky. Worst case would have been if the front console crushed them in the crash.

I flick on the headlights but don't expect them to work. They do, although in a distorted way. Both are mangled and point in extreme directions, but good enough to be able to see what carnage is in front of me.

The two figures pinned and slouched over the car are in such a stunned state that they may as well be unconscious. The third dived into the bed of flowers to avoid a similar fate and is still down. Dead? I doubt it, maybe wounded. I have to be quick. I get out as soon as I can, probably too soon, as I feel weak-kneed like a drunk.

I slap myself very hard to change that.

I set upon the man in the flower bed. He begins to wiggle and appears more alert than I first thought. I fall on top of him by accident from the will of trying to do too much without the coordination to do it successfully. He's holding a gun. I will be dead if I don't go for that first. I reach for it and as soon as my hand touches his wrist, strong resistance forces itself against the pressure I exert.

A beefy arm wraps itself around my head trying to distract me from his weapon. We struggle on the ground as he concentrates both his hands on the direction of the pistol's barrel. I am finding his massive frame a tough match. I elbow him in the face with my free arm but the glancing blow just opens up a cut on his jaw doing no damage to his desperate focus. He overpowers me, and the barrel is now pointed at me. I will certainly die without a last-gasp effort. His tries to manoeuvre his large index finger to pull the trigger. I flick a middle finger in there as well, sandwiching it between his and the trigger. We struggle on the micro-level of a finger wrestle for my fate.

I strain with all my might to avoid a bullet to the face. I yank my finger to crush his against the trigger guard. He winces a little, and I have my opportunity to have another go. With such a short distance, I open-hand punch him repeatedly on the nose, driving the heel of my hand onto his snout and then chopping at his bridge. Blood gushes, even while he lies on his back. He can't take it as his eyes water incessantly from the destruction of his nose. His incredible pain threshold finally succumbs and his grip on the gun relaxes. I manage to wrestle it from him and reverse the dire predicament, turning it on him, momentarily in a dilemma of whether to kill him for almost killing me. It dawns on me that the man whose nose and face is mangled in front of me is Big Louis, the simpleton guard outside of Luigi's hospital room. I ponder the consequences.

'This is the second time I could've killed you and the old man is not around to beg for your life.' I uncock the hammer. 'I guess I'll honour his plea one last time.'

Besides, Louis is in no state to try and kill me again. I go against my training and walk away, leaving him groaning in agony.

I creep to the damaged wall. The car made quite an impression, but it appears there's only minor structural damage. I flip the gun and hold it by the barrel and whip its butt onto the temple of the man pinned on the left with enough force to knock him out. I don't finish him off either.

I sprint around the car towards the now recognisable Valentino Baresi. He is awake and aims his pistol in my general direction but is woozy enough not to be able to get a shot off. I look at his legs. The flesh around the crush of the car resembles mincemeat sticking to an exposed bone. There's no way he will ever walk again. Blood from both gangsters seep onto the warped bonnet and gather in pools within the crevasses of the metalwork, like a lake in between mountain ranges. The red on yellow, the dark onto the light.

'*Fuck*,' is all Valentino can bellow.

I have no time to reply as I hear a gun fire behind me. I whip around to find the spotter, firing not in my direction, but at the listless figure of Jessica, who is trying ever so hard to work out what is going on. I take aim and squeeze a couple of rounds in quick succession from the Glock 34 I took off Louis. One lands on his chest while the other sways onto his shoulder. The impact flings his firearm through the night sky.

I hear a mumble behind me. Valentino is trying to make a serious effort to kill me now. I have to take care of this before he succeeds. I shoot at him. The round fired from two metres away easily hits its intended target. Valentino's bicep is caught flush and spasms the instant it's hit. He drops his firearm in incredible pain.

I don't bother to kill him out of cruelty. Fuck him; he's not worth it. I want this event to be a constant reminder that he's shouldn't have been so stupid and let things lie. He should have never thought of such a dumb idea in the first place. Instead of killing him, he will be suffering irreparably from the loss of his legs. Not even the incredible services of surgeons only minutes away can restore the mashing of flesh and shattering of bones below him. As I begin to hear the police sirens, a single thought occupies me with amusing fascination: I'm sure Valentino is a half-empty kind of guy.

CHAPTER FOURTEEN

The pleasure of Valentino's misfortune is short lived.

Jessica has made a run for it, sprinting as fast as she can for the car park. I'm surprised she didn't retreat back inside the hospital. I wouldn't have done it if I were her, because if she believes she is still being hunted, she would be confined.

Whether or not I can convince her that I saved her life is incidental to my own safety. The police are coming, and I have no means to escape. I will be trapped here and will have to hide in the hospital because running will not get me far. Emergency triage? No chance. I will be easily singled out by people inside. The outpatients' building? They will probably lock it down tight, especially after Luigi's death. The spotter's BMW? There's only one possible exit, and I will be heading towards responding police, and that's only *if* the keys are in the ignition. Too great a chance things will get ugly. No, my best chance is running away from me while I stand here wondering what to do among four bodies. I just saved Jessica's life; now is the chance for her to repay the favour whether she likes it or not.

My legs feel almost recovered as I chase after her, but the task is not as easy as I thought. She must be quite fit because it looks like she is as quick as I am, sprinting barefoot after kicking her heels away. Am I that exhausted from the car crash that I won't be able to catch her? Each foot forward is sticking to the ground like running in thick mud. It might not be enough. Should I just give up?

I can only gain small amounts of distance on her. Surrender to the police? No, it's not an option.

I have to keep trying. I will myself to run faster than I thought possible and close the gap considerably. She loses a lot of ground when navigating around corners. By the time we are in the stairwell of the car park, I have finally caught up to within arm's reach.

'Hey!' I gasp, grabbing her by the shoulder and forcefully pulling her to face me.

'Get away from me,' she screams.

I clasp my hand around her mouth as she begins to struggle. She attempts to bite me, her jaw clenching and opening rapidly, but I'm not an idiot and she cannot come anywhere close to the palm of my hand. The problem with her panicking is that she will not be easy to calm down in this state.

I push her lightly away, draw the Glock, and rest it menacingly on her forehead.

'OK. Enough of this shit,' I say, frustrated enough to give her the impression I may just pull the trigger.

'Please don't shoot!'

'If you want to live, you have to listen to me *very* carefully. You might not want to believe me, but I don't want to kill you. But the people who are now being treated by paramedics back at the hospital did. I need your cooperation to get out of here, and this can happen in three ways. You give me the keys to your car and as soon as we are in the clear, I will drop you off somewhere and you can scream to the hills that I carjacked you at gunpoint. Second, you help me get out of here by smuggling me in the backseat. The third way…well…you don't want to choose door number three. The clock is ticking, and it's ticking fast, so I will need an answer very soon. Either way, I will need your car keys.'

We hear the sirens becoming louder as she stands perplexed at my offer. She deliberates perhaps processing the events that just unfolded.

'I need your answer,' I insist.

The stress creasing her forehead intensifies at my prompt. Another couple of seconds and I will have to make the decision for her that will involve the unpleasant use of a fist.

'C'mon.' It is enough of an answer for me to be satisfied.

Together we run for her car: a silver, late model Mercedes SLK 250.

'Guess I won't be able to be smuggled in the backseat,' I joke after viewing the size of the cabin.

'I would've brought the Bentley if I had known you were coming.'

I laugh a little, perhaps at an attempt to diffuse some tension, or maybe that I know there's two Bentley sedans garaged at her estate.

'I want you to drive fast out of the car park, but safely enough that we won't be flying through the windscreen,' I say as soon as she starts the car.

'What? Why?'

'Because when they trawl through the CCTV footage of the incident, they are going to see you running away and me chasing after you. They will know I caught up to you. If we slip out of here as if nothing happened, then it *will* look like you are an accomplice, and I don't think you want that. On the other hand, if you drive out of here in a hurry, it will seem I have taken you hostage. *If* they think I've taken you hostage, it will be a lot easier to say I did instead of the truth.'

She is confused at my reasoning. 'You better drive.' It's probably for the best.

I wait for her to get out of the car first. It would be embarrassing if I jumped out and she took off without me! We quickly switch seats while the engine purrs in neutral. I get behind the wheel and as soon as her door closes with the gentle thud of expensive automotive trim, I floor the accelerator. I only have a split second to analyse the goings-on outside the outpatients building through a gap between the concrete walls on the ramps linking levels as we drive down to the ground floor, and to my freedom. Only one squad car is at the scene with its lights flashing to light up the courtyard and the few paramedics attending to Valentino. A fire truck is pulling into view as I pull the car away with force. We screech down the ramp to the exit gate and I almost consider driving through it until its automatic arm begins to rise. As soon as I come to a complete stop, I purposely spin the tyres so the noise will be loud enough to attract the attention of someone who can inform the police of our hurried exit. There are no cameras in the car park that I know of, except at the entrance and exits. But, knowing the response time of the police, once we are out of the surrounding area, they will not have a hope of catching us.

As we enter the intersection of the laneway and the main road, I scan for any signs that we may be approached by authorities, but there are no sirens or lights to warrant any immediate panic. There soon will be if we don't move.

It's a stroke of fortune. I breathe a sigh of relief and can casually drive without the fear I should be experiencing. I have no idea where to drive to except anywhere away from the hospital.

Slowly, I ease myself with this situation, I notice Jessica pretending not to recognise me as Dr Kruger. I don't push the topic either, but she must know. She's spotted me every time.

The tension in the air is palpable and I am speechless with any explanation, real or imaginable. Where do I start? With Luigi? With the award ceremony? With my life story? No, I better leave it up to her if she even wants to discuss why a cardiologist just stopped a criminal gang from killing her. If I talk, I will let on more than I should, and that's not good. It is not until I duly obey the third stoplight we come across that Jessica decides to speak.

'So what was all of that back there?' she says meekly. The pitch and inclination in her voice is a familiar one to me. One that reminds me that in situations like this, there are people such as Jessica who are thrust into a life-threatening situation for the briefest of moments and are reminded that sometimes even *their* lives are out of their control. It is the humbleness of human mortality that keeps them quiet.

There are two ways people react to being close to death. There's the silent, withdrawn archetype, which Jessica is now a disciple of, and the hysterical screamers whose surging adrenaline culminates in derangement beyond any sort of self-control. They're the people who need to be dealt with in an unkind manner.

'One of the men I trapped between the car and the wall is a man named Valentino Baresi. He recently inherited the now second biggest criminal organisation in Hillbay after his father, Luigi, was murdered at the same hospital you work at…the same hospital you just left.'

'Oh,' she says. 'I was there that night and remember the police. But why would he come after me?'

'Valentino is delusional. He likes to consume large quantities of cocaine and other illicit substances. From what I can tell, he blamed the hospital for his father's death and wanted to punish it by taking revenge out on a resident doctor.' I hope she swallows that load of bullshit because I know I wouldn't. 'I can't really say, though. That's just a theory. I've been tracking him for a while and he seems to have dipped into some sort of psychosis. He was probably out of his mind back there.' My lies seem implausible and utterly ridiculous to me.

'So then, who are you?' she asks.

Shit! A question I never thought to prepare for because I never thought this would or could pan out as it has. I strain to come up with any realistic cover. Current or ex-police? Very unlikely a police officer would think on their feet or pull off something like that. That won't wash at all. The military could do it, but the government would have no business tracking an everyday doctor from a hospital.

'I'm…ah…'

There is no remedy to this outside of telling the truth.

'Are you a hit man?'

'No…not exactly,' I say, failing unquestionably to be convincing. 'The Baresi family has been at war with Vincenzo Varetti, the *other* large criminal organisation in Hillbay. They're both vying for control of the city and the state's drug monopoly.'

'So you work for Varetti?'

'No,' I spitefully spit out. I have set aside a bullet for him as well, if I get the chance. His surprise appearance during my capture only tens of metres from where Jessica was probably sleeping still elicits a mild rage. 'I don't work for either, but sometimes I do. I work for whoever needs my skills.'

'What skills? Killing people?'

I chuckle at her simple view of things. But it's absolutely correct. The art of assassination and evasion to do it again and again and again.

'I don't think you understand. Do you think anyone can go out and kill? Those that do are the people you hear about in the paper when they are on trial for murder. There's more to it than that. You need surveillance, planning, and intelligence. You can't just take a life and expect there will be no repercussions. Someone will be trying to hunt you down for doing something this world says is the worst act you can do to another human…and anyway, these abilities help you with other jobs and careers.

Private investigations, insurance fraud, spying on a cheating husband or employees…'

I trail off because I know it's hopeless. I'm clutching at straws. My moral defence is as weak as my lies. Shitty surveillance, planning, and intelligence got me in this mess. I never should have agreed to take on her father and all of his resources. All I had was a hunch and little or no information to rely on and I went in anyway. I broke my own rules out of desperation and arrogance. So what if I was going to retire afterwards? And was I even going to follow through with that?

I kill people for money—that's it. And I've been doing it for long enough to be able to admit it. Jessica witnessed it first hand, as she sits beside me with her knees up and heels on the edge of her seat in a quiet state of shock, defensively poised in case I turn into a psychopath and she needs to fend me off. She's doesn't speak for minutes because she is sitting next to a monster. There's nothing I can say to reassure her that I'm not as we hurtle through the night in silence.

'So where are you taking me?' she says, tiptoeing around a confirmed sociopath. I couldn't be any more disappointed with myself.

'We need to ditch this car and grab a motel room for the night. In the morning, we can go our separate ways.'

'But didn't you say as soon as you are in the clear we would separate?'

'Indeed I did. But we are not in the clear just yet. You think I can just get out at the nearest corner and everything will be fine? One night of downtime should be enough just outside of the city before I can shoot on through and out of the state for a while.' I say this with the intention of doing exactly the opposite, just in case she decides to be truthful and relay this information to the cops.

'And what about the police?'

'You can tell them the truth in the morning. That I held you at gunpoint, kidnapped you in your own car, and drove us to the motel we will stay tonight. I restrained you by locking you in the bathroom, took your phone from your handbag and destroyed it so you couldn't make any calls for help. In the morning, I will run from the motel without you or your car while you sleep.'

'Good story.'

'It's the best I can think of at the moment. The part about your phone is true unfortunately. You can keep the sim card,' I say.

After ten minutes of silence, we pull into to a motel in Pine Lake. I used it once before many years ago because it has no cameras and discreet services. Jessica waits in the car while I check in at the rear of the complex with a fake ID, always mindful of the need to keep an eye on her in case she makes a break for it. She doesn't.

I park the Mercedes and wipe down any traces of my prints with a handkerchief I keep in all of my jacket pockets. Jessica hands me her phone, and I remove the sim card and crush her mobile with the heel of my shoe. The screen smashes as its electronic intestines splatter out around its metallic corpse.

'Here you go,' I tell her, giving her back her sim card. A tiny sigh of uneasiness furrows her face.

In the room, there is only a queen-sized bed and a couch that is too small for me to sleep on. The bathroom is disgusting with a mouldy cubicle and a stained sink that hasn't been cleaned in months. I close the shades carefully so I don't leave prints on them.

'I'll take the floor,' I offer.

'Sure thing,' she says, her mood lifted as she flicks the thermostat of the heater until it cannot be set any higher.

'I wish I had something to give you to help you sleep,' I say.

'You mean a depressant because I'm still racing? I guess I'll try and make do.'

I set myself up on the floor after smashing the bathroom door from the inside out to give her alibi some credence. The gauche silence that lingers between us is hard to fathom and even harder to break. My social skills have been reduced to nothing because of the events over the last couple of hours and her willingness to aid me in my escape by not running when given the opportunity. I doubt she will sleep tonight, traumatised like a young driver trying to sleep the night of their first minor car accident.

The problem I face is trust. Can I trust her not to run when I fall asleep or will I wake to a car park crawling with cops? There is only one fact to work in my favour: that I saved her life. She must have pieced together what happened by now and acknowledged what I did for her. My ledger with her has something in the black. I can only depend on this to persuade her to not make for the door or my gun while I sleep peacefully. I drift into slumber having not forgotten the impact of having your life spared by the heroics of somebody else…

I check my watch. It's 0400 almost to the second when I feel a warm touch on my leg. I am dazed and still half asleep when I sit up. I have no idea how long she's been kneeling over me.

'*Shh*, Dr Kruger,' Jessica whispers.

Where can this possibly head? It doesn't take me long to find out when she begins to massage my calves briefly before creeping up to my thighs. It gives me a powerful rise, and I harden with blood throbbing to my penis needing only a slight touch to petrify it. Jessica continues to tease me for a couple of minutes, kneading my sore quads for a few minutes before duly obliging. Instantly I get the sense she is no innocent flower the way she fondles me. She has an experienced and unexpected touch.

Jessica unzips my pants and takes them off in a hurry. She strokes my cock harder now that there is only a layer of cotton between her and me as I use one hand while groaning to play with her vagina. She stops momentarily before almost ripping my underwear off and continuing in a similar fashion.

I moan under the pressure as she bends over and takes me in her mouth, flicking her tongue on the head of my penis before throating the whole member down to my balls. She repeats the process, dripping saliva down my shaft and lubricating it into a slobbering tower of flesh before using a free hand to jerk wildly. The wet sensation is mesmerising and I have to moan louder. I hear a few popping sounds as the power of her suction reaches an auric climax.

Jessica's sighs are louder, too, as drips of her cum splash onto my shin. She is almost catatonic with sexual frustration and straddles up my body. We are pelvis-to-pelvis when she grabs my penis and uses it to rub her clit wildly. Her excitement level is euphoric, and she is about to slip me into her pussy when I lift her from her arse and push her down so she is sitting on my face. I lap at her while she begins to scream. Her clit is swollen. I work my way around her, prodding and licking her pussy and arsehole before sucking at her. She cums with a shuddering fit and screams while biting on her hand in a vain attempt to muffle her cries.

She balances herself off me and comes thumping down on my erect penis. The extreme vacillation she produces means there is not even the slightest of discomfort when she does this. She lets out another heavy sigh and settles on my pelvis before beginning to hump wildly. It doesn't take her long to cum again as she rocks back and forth, rubbing her clit against my pubis, while also running her sharp fingernails from my traps to my chest, leaving me with bittersweet numbness. She drenches sweat, and I can feel her slick, sweaty skin as I squeeze her slightly oversized tits in proportion to her incredibly fit frame.

She slaps me once behind the neck after I tilted forward to hold her, playfully but also with force. The pain is excruciating for a second, and I recoil briefly because of it. I turn her over into the missionary position and begin to thrust hard while she continues to let out hard groans, while raking my back. I intermittently swing my hips around as I thrust, and she coos in delight. Her nails become unnervingly vicious after a while, and I flip her over onto all fours and take her from behind to avoid more scratches. She does most of the work before I grab her hard around the back of her neck for control and drive myself into her. I believe she has no idea where she is from her wimps of pleasure as I reach a climax and throb cum into her. She continues to digitally rub herself, just to orgasm again fiendishly…

We are both covered in sweat on the ground, and the sheets under us are saturated and unfit for use. I pull out and she lets our mixture drip onto the floor without a hint of unease or embarrassment. I go and have a brief shower, something I should've done when we first entered the room. Jessica waits until I've finished before doing so herself, maybe out of conformity. She joins me on the bed, her arm across my pectorals before she is completely asleep and I am unfortunately wide awake.

I've wanted her since I first saw her. Not in my wildest dreams would I have had this sexual encounter, nor envisaged she would feel the same. Most unexpected was her passion as if she wanted this just as much as me. A complete and awesome surprise.

But at the same time, it makes me pitifully sad. I can't entertain the simple idea that we could ever be together. Nor could we meet up again under any circumstance. No, this can never happen again because this predicament is utterly insane. And for that I shed a solitary tear. A tear for what I've missed all my life. For the basic joy of companionship I gave up for a career. For the biggest mistake I've ever made.

I can't stay.

I check the time and wait a good half hour before sliding out from under her arm. I get dressed in the bathroom and leave the room in the subtlest of ways.

Maybe this was her way of rewarding me for saving her life.

CHAPTER FIFTEEN

It is still exceptionally cold even for the end of winter. The gentle breeze is little help as it humiliates me in my dirty clothes. I shiver while tracking back to the city centre to get home and finish the sleep I was not even halfway through at the motel.

I have a lot to think about but have a spring in my step. I didn't realise how much I missed sex. My encounter with Jessica is even more special because of my emotional investment. She is a man-eater.

It's a tragedy it can go no further. Yes, perhaps I am a fucking idiot for falling so fast, so quickly. It must be the staleness of being alone or maybe that I'm not getting any younger. I have plenty of time to fall head over heels again when this is all over…provided I stay alive.

I don't even give a shit that I completely forgot to remove incriminating evidence from the motel. The police might catch a lucky break with my fingerprints, but I don't remember touching anything they will be able to lift off well. I was careful with the doorknob—leaving fingerprints on that would be a rookie mistake. Mostly everything else I touched was too fibrous to be any good. Carpet, bedding, and pillows won't be good enough for them.

But there will be enough DNA evidence lying around if they want it. I've left plenty of hair and semen for collection. In a way, having sex with Jessica ensures she will be dissuaded from calling the police. If she does, the question of why a captive would be willing to have sex with her captor will come up. With no bruising, it would be hard to claim rape. And if she didn't say anything to the police when I was Dr Kruger, there's little chance she would rat me out now. Not after saving her from death.

Perhaps Jessica was suffering from an extreme variation of the Stockholm syndrome? This does, however, complicate my feelings towards killing her father. How can such an evil person raise such a balanced daughter?

I don't need to rationalise the course I will take with this…I can let religion do it for me: 'Children shall not be put to death for their fathers; each is to die for their own sins.'

Charles Ward, what he has done and what he will do, is evil. The way he champions racial purity is an overreaction to his wife's death, and his brilliant mind has applied itself to an exaggerated correction. It doesn't matter how delusional he is by saying he is doing right by this world. It is wrong, reprehensible, and must be stopped.

I have to make the effort to separate Charles and Jessica. I can't confuse controlled bloodlust with my admiration for his daughter, who, I'm certain, has no idea of his work. It is impossible to think that she would still be by his side if she knew why.

Thank God I am now only a block away from home. It seems like I've been walking forever. I judge it to be around forty kilometres at a brisk walking pace for seven hours. I could've stolen another car back at the motel, but that is not being smart. It would've been one more police report to draw them closer. Safest option was by foot. Public transport has cameras, and taxis have drivers who can be good witnesses. It reminds me that the police will be trying to piece everything together from the cabbie I tossed out for his vehicle. I'm not worried.

As I glance up to my apartment from the street, I have the sense something is not right. I walk through the foyer as the attendant pays me no mind while I wait for the elevator. The ride up isn't pleasant.

The elevator opens on my floor, and my anxiety turns into shock.

The door to my apartment is slightly ajar. I ready myself with Louis's Glock I still have in my possession, flick the safety off, cock the hammer, and hold it steady to pull the trigger at whoever may emerge. I may have been tired getting back, but I am wide awake now. I creep down the corridor along the left side wall to get the jump on any unsuspecting looters.

Everything is automatic from the years of training and countless operations. Don't kick the door down but use the angles the opening created first. From every possible angle, as high as the ceiling and as low as the floor, the living room is clear. It has been roughed up, that is unmistakable, but I'm not sure it isn't still in progress. I shoulder the door slowly without dropping my aim, as if a nonexistent breeze suddenly flushed through the corridor. Again, nothing except my strewn possessions. I quickly check what I couldn't before. There's a tiny chance that whoever did this is still here, so I need to clear every room. I go over the study. The safe is exposed with slight damage and everything is either missing or overturned. Checking the contents of the safe is an afterthought; it is low priority compared to my safety. I move on to the bedroom and lastly the bathroom, becoming more agitated after noticing the damage done to each room. The fire escape window is still intact, so they must have come through the front door and out the same way.

I feel violated and want to punish someone for it. But there is nobody to take a bullet.

What were they trying to find? What could I have that is of any value to a robber? I live miserly. That is how I've had to live and how I will always live. The only items of value are sentimental. A few medals and ribbons from the service I don't even keep in the safe. They're collecting dust on the top shelf of my walk-in robe in the bedroom and I couldn't care less if they disappear. Was this a message instead? Did they just want the impression they were after something?

I walk sullen laps of the apartment. What's done is done. There's no point in getting angry; that's what the last ten minutes were for. It's time to think this through.

At least one person has *obviously* broken in. Did they take anything of value? What were they looking for? If they know me, why bother overturning everything in sight if they were only after one thing? And finally, if this isn't just a random burglary, *how the fuck* did they find my home? I'll know what they were looking for by assessing the room with the most amount of action. The semidried and dirty footprints from multiple sets of footwear are scattered on the kitchen's tiles. Enough time has passed for these prints to dry, so they were here last night and not this morning. More than one person was here. I count at least four different shoes from the treads in this area alone. My guess is there were a few more if these people were smart and weren't just waiting for me. If they did their homework, they would have known roughly how many to bring. If they were searching for something, they would've brought at least two per room. They would've wanted to be in-and-out quickly. But that's one big if.

The pantry is the same as before, threadbare, and even the glassware and plates haven't been touched. From the dirt alone, there was a makeshift meeting in the kitchen. I go to the pantry. I'll need something that will stick to the prints. I grab fine Cajun spice powder and sprinkle it liberally over the tiles.

The living room resembles the result of a barroom brawl, with everything overturned or destroyed in some way. The only thing missing is the blood. The TV was destroyed thoroughly and the couch has many more boot stains on it than when I left. Why destroy a flat screen TV? It's pretty hard to hide something of value in an object so thin. Whoever smashed it up was either pissed off or wanted to make a point. They wanted to make it blatantly obvious to me that their intentions were not to rob me, but to vandalise. I head back to the kitchen where the powder has clumped in the shape of common boot treads, the hardwearing rubber soles of combat issue boots the military would hand out like candy to new recruits. The wet marks are easily distinguishable, and it seems there was a team of soldiers here.

My attention turns to one of the prints on the floor. It is nothing like the others, and the person stood alone in the centre of the room giving orders to the others. It is definitely a civilian's shoes, almost fashionable and contemporary, given the heel and the excessively long print that the top of the shoe has formed. It finishes with a large point. The wearer is keen on European footwear or an imitation. It is strange for a man to wear thousand-dollar shoes to burgle someone and enjoy the risk of being identified by wearing them.

A rustling comes from the closet by the window in the lounge room, and I instinctively narrow in on it with a raised gun. It's door is slightly ajar but enough for a human eye to take aim at me. I leap away from the line of sight to gain the upper hand on whoever is hiding. They won't be able to see me from here.

I sneak closer and remark matter-of-factly, 'I have a gun pointed directly at you. Come out slowly, or I'll fire five bullets your way, one of which will hit you, and I'll save the last for your skull.'

No answer. I am in two states of mind about my next move. The Glock isn't suppressed. Should I proceed with the threat and risk a phone call to the police from Mrs Rutherford or another neighbour? And how would that go down? It will be hard to casually explain trashing my own apartment. Or should I go closer and hope it is nothing but a draft in the room?

If it weren't my apartment, I would have already emptied my clip and no doubt blood would be oozing onto the floor. But this *is* my apartment, even if my real name isn't on the title. This is my property and my asset bought with money I've earned. If the cops didn't already come here and I shoot, I will never be able to come back.

I'll have to wear it. I step ever so slowly around the hazards of fallen books and DVDs scattered on the floor. I notice three bullet holes in the wall leading to the cupboard, around knee height. I am within a metre. I should be firing, but I can't. This will come down to who reacts the quickest. I reach for the doorknob.

I throw the door open and jam my gun at the target. But there is no target? How can there be no target? Was I hallucinating?

I startle when I hear a whimper at my feet as Buster brushes against my shins, stands on his hind legs then claws at my pants. The resultant sigh of relief could've inflated a football.

I safety the Glock and take stock for a while because I have the time. I think Buster is now on his ninth life. Someone must have shot at him in frustration and didn't care to follow it up with a kill. He certainly is rattled, though. I've never seen him scurry around this aimlessly before. He randomly peers over his shoulder at me with dilated pupils, unsure if it's safe enough to navigate through everything. I'll have to comfort him later.

I close the front door and head to the study to check the safe. My printer is destroyed, and everything else is either overturned or stolen. They certainly gave this room a thorough working over, so I am sure there was something of interest for them here.

The laptop I use for assignments is also gone. I can't tell if they knew what it was for or if it was just another item to be pawned. I'm not fussed, but Lloyd should know. The encryption will take a very long time to crack, and there are no sensitive files left on its hard drive, as they were all accessed via USB.

The quaint print that covered the safe is lying on the floor with its glass panel smashed. I have no drawers to my computer desk. They have gone as well in the whirlwind of larceny. There are wet footprints on the carpet in this room and many damp dirt marks around the safe with scuffs everywhere. The same, unique man who was commanding affairs from the living room decided it was best to lean against the wall and leave his mark by resting his foot on it. The shoe impression is now burned into my brain as clear as what is on the wall.

The safe wasn't opened, although they tried their best. There are dint marks and scratches around the door and hinges and the combination dial has had a working over as well. It is obvious someone tried to open it crudely with a screwdriver or crowbar and came unprepared; otherwise, they would have brought the right equipment, expertise, or even tried to remove the whole safe from the wall. A pitiful attempt really. The dial that I set to zero every time is now closer to ninety, and is smudged with some form of goo.

It would have been stupid of them to devote too much time to breaking in. It's only a small safe. Certainly no fool would actually think there's a fortune in a small safe simply because it's a safe. It's like breaking into a luxury car believing they all have a bar of gold bullion in the glove box. In this case though, there were some things of value. Off the top of my head, there are a few sets of passports and matching driving licenses, around $20,000 in cash, a few small, unregistered firearms, and three sets of explosives left over from the Ward hit. I didn't need them, but I bought them anyway from George.

I closely inspect the safe. There is one bullet hole in this wall as well. Perhaps shot out of frustration? The others in the living room were to scare or kill Buster, but this one appears to be a different calibre and strange in the way it has entered the plasterboard and most likely lodged itself into the solid brick wall behind. It would have been unlucky for Mrs Rutherford had this apartment not be surrounded by thick concrete in its walls, floor, and ceiling. Thick enough for privacy and to possibly even survive a blast from the safe. This room in particular would be good enough to muzzle a gunshot. The door is heavy and solid enough to mask most sounds, so only my immediate neighbours would be suspicious. The windows are double glazed and although sound can penetrate through them, it would need to be a very quiet night for anyone to notice gunfire four floors up from the street. As for light, bullet flares would be spotted more so at night, but again, an observer on the ground would have to be craning their head skyward to notice. With empty office buildings around, there is good reason nobody called the police.

After I fed Buster, I realise the problem I have now is not being able to find a good place to sleep for the afternoon. My bed has been soiled and the mattress sliced open. I have an alarming problem as well. Are these people planning on a return? They were armed and are willing to shoot at a cat and a wall…

I hear a knocking on the front door and I shudder.

Fuck. Have they come back to finish the job? Did they wait for me to come back? I think up a thousand possibilities. Cops? Lloyd with a death warrant? Even Valentino in a wheelchair? Who knows who has the resources to hunt me down? Suddenly, the headache revisits with substantial thudding pressing against my eye sockets. It quickly worsens to the point of almost passing out. My sight falters and doubles from the pain. Why now?

I take aim at the door but I'm so woozy that I have a slim chance to hit it if I pull the trigger.

Whoever is on the other side knocks again to the beat of my migraine. I trip on the step to the entrance and my firearm falls to the ground and slides to a stop at the door. There's no sympathy except for another grimacing knock.

I help myself up with great assistance from the table beside the front door. One action at a time or I will fall over like a drunk again. Stand up straight. OK, I can do that. Pick up the firearm. So far, so good. Now get ready for a battle. I lean against the door and peek through the viewer.

It's Mrs Rutherford. She stares straight at me on the other side. Although she can't see me, I'm no longer confident in the manufacturer's claim of privacy. She gazes disappointingly at me as if the door was unnecessary and invisible. This conversation could be worse than all of the flashes of dread I thought up on my way here.

I tuck the pistol into the small of my back. I have no choice but to open the door and do so just enough to poke my head out, not wanting to reveal the damage behind me.

'Oh, hello, Patrick.'

'Hello, Mrs Rutherford,' I say sheepishly.

Her face droops from disdain to concern. 'My, you look terrible!' she exclaims. 'Is whatever is causing your nosebleeds now affecting your health? Have you seen a doctor recently?'

'I'm sorry, Mrs Rutherford. I haven't been able to make a booking yet. I've had other things to attend to.'

'Well, that's the reason I am here. You see, I thought I should come and speak to you about last night…I think we have a pleasant relationship as neighbours and I can accept that sometimes you may want to have a get-together or a party, but it is simply too much to bear when the volume of your stereo was as loud as it was last night. I would have at least appreciated some warning if you ever intend to hold these "gatherings" in the future, which I hope will *not* be a regular occurrence.'

'I'm sorry, Mrs Rutherford. I didn't mean to cause such a racket, but—'

'A racket would be an understatement. If you think that neighbours could enjoy living, God forbid be able to sleep with such noise, you would be sorely mistaken. And another thing, the sort of filthy language used in those songs that were being played certainly doesn't help the situation. I tried to speak to you, but your friends were not helpful in the slightest. I'm afraid I do not approve of their attitude.'

'I apologise, sincerely, Mrs Rutherford. It was an impromptu celebration.' Although it is completely against my personality, I have to run with her perception of events. There's no point in fighting it. I can't remember the last time I invited someone over.

'Well, I accept your apology, Patrick. But I cannot approve of your friends. They have no respect for their elders, and even their fancy dress was awry for such an occasion. They could've at least dressed with some colour instead of these black coats, shirts, and pants.'

Black shirts and pants? Well, maybe this isn't a complete disaster. My 'friends' must have at least dressed for the occasion. Pros maybe? Did they know I wasn't going to come home last night? The music does explain the bullets in the walls. It would have made firing a gun less obvious and helped them disguise overturning the apartment. If they were going to turn on such loud music, shouldn't they have at least dressed in civilian clothes? Maybe, maybe not. Maybe they didn't have the time to figure it out and had a spotter observe me leaving last night to meet George and called it in to start the raid?

'Ah, yes. It was a black dress-up party, Mrs Rutherford.'

She nods. Not at my comment but almost in maternal disappointment that I couldn't keep my 'guests' under control. 'Still, there was one saving grace.'

'What would that be?'

'The only gentlemen that was out of costume was the only man with manners. In fact, he was quite handsome.'

'Oh really? Who was this man? Would you like me to see if I can make an introduction?'

'Patrick, don't play games with me. You should know this person, as you were there last night. And I certainly don't kiss and tell. Oh my, he was quite the charmer!'

She blushes. He must have made some impression on her. But I can't press her anymore without giving up the charade that I willingly threw this party. I'm exhausted and my headache is driving me insane.

There are only two suspects I can think of who would be daring enough to try this on. One is Charles Ward, or more appropriately his partner Vincenzo Varetti, to tie up an escaped loose end. The other is Lloyd. He would have come here to confiscate everything to do with the agency before eliminating me. Both could be so brazen to bring a few goons.

But how could they know my whereabouts? Have I taken far too many risks to allow this to happen? Judging from my crumbling integrity with work, it's the most plausible explanation. And now there's probably no going back. My life has been falling apart faster than I could ever imagine.

I lean against the front door for support and almost fall backwards as it flings open. It snaps Mrs Rutherford from her daydream. The look on her face turns to disgust when she assesses the damage from the party.

'Good Lord,' she mutters. 'It appears you've been hit by a bomb.'

'As you say, Mrs Rutherford, it was a pretty wild night. I'm sorry, but I really must be getting back to cleaning.'

'No doubt,' she says, still stunned.

I close the door on her and sob at the reality that I am now just as much the hunted as the hunter. What can I possibly do?

Part of me wants to flee. Run from Lloyd, Charles, Varetti, and whoever else wants my prized scalp. That would be the smartest move but will mean everything will be lost. No retirement, nothing. I would have to start again. Every single risk taken with my life over the years would have been for nothing. The other option is still to lose everything but stay and fight everyone. Pride's taken me down this ruinous path, and pride will have to take me to its end.

I grab a few codeine tablets from the medicine cabinet and scoff them down without water. I walk into every room to make sure all curtains and shades have been drawn. Then I brood.

The fear that I have been found out is crushed by the amateurism of the operation. This was a rag-and-tag job, hastily planned and even more poorly executed. I sweep through the rooms and take two exhausting hours checking all fixtures to find no malicious recording bugs or cameras. Fine. I'll be relatively safe here for now as long as I am armed. I'll clean everything up after a sleep. I grab a couple of blankets and with the Glock still in hand, I have a light sleep in the one place they hardly dirtied: my bedroom closet.

CHAPTER SIXTEEN

I wake to the taste of fur. Buster sits on my neck and his tail curls over my face. At least he's calmed down.

The codeine was astonishingly effective on my headache and I thank God I've finally found some relief. At least I've survived the afternoon. My first action is to beef up home security. I no longer feel safe in my own home. I need the assurance that, at least when I am home, there is less chance my intruders can return as easily as before.

I shower, change into new clothes, and head down to the hardware store. I purchase a door crossbar kit and take a couple of hours to install it. As crude and unsightly as it may seem, I will be able to sleep with a little more confidence than last night. Although I will never truly be secure, the extra protection may give me enough time to get armed and ready for a fight if they decide to visit again.

Cleaning the apartment gives me the opportunity to mull over the break-in with more clarity and hindsight. I'm only halfway sorting through the mess in the living room before I'm reminded of the bullet holes near the closet. I should've investigated this at the start! From the size of the holes made to the plasterboard, the bullets near the window are from a distinctly different gun to the bullet hole in the study. I shine a high-powered Maglite at each of the three holes and use pincers to wrangle one of the bullets from the concrete wall. Best guess is it's a 9 mm round that came from an automatic weapon given the pattern and spray angles. As for what gun it came from, I wouldn't have a clue. There's no need to pull the other two out. They will rest where they lie when I plaster over the holes.

More interesting is the single shot fired in the study. Damn. Even though the hole is smaller, the round is buried deep in the wall and I struggle to make it budge with the pincers. There is a small gap between the plasterboard and the concrete, which makes movement harder, but it's worth the struggle. I fetch a hammer and as gently as possible destroy the surrounding plaster to wriggle my finger through to get a stronger grip. It doesn't dislodge in the slightest. This must have been fired from a very short distance. I chip away at the wall as well but have to be cautious around the bullet to keep it as intact as possible. I fetch a pair of pliers for the job and after much exertion, I am finally able to muscle a grip on the tiny butt of the bullet. I chip around the edges again until my clasp is tight. I yank hard only for my hold to slip on the pliers and I hear the 'ting' of the projectile hitting the floor still in the gap. Shit. No bullet and a large hole in a wall. There's no point in stopping now. I get on all fours and smash into the base of the wall large enough for my hand to forage amid the plaster chips.

I pull out the offending slug and rub it with a salivated finger. It is a small bullet indeed.

I'm going to need help finding out the owner of the guns that fired these rounds. There's no way I can go through Lloyd if I suspect him, so I'm going to have to plead with Curious George for assistance.

I get on the phone and ring his last known number. He picks up, but doesn't speak.

'George? Are you there? It's your friend from last night,' I open.

'You better make it quick,' he replies. 'You're not exactly in my good books, and things are worse than they seem.'

'I'll be quick. I need you to run a trace for me. Two rounds, but I need it done as soon as possible. I need it done tonight. Can you give me a price?'

'It depends on their condition, now doesn't it? But for a start you're looking at twenty K.'

'How much is it normally?'

'About one.'

Jesus Christ! He really wants to burn me. But I'm partial to bargaining. 'Ten.'

'Fifteen or I'm hanging up.'

'Done. How do you want it?'

'My private drop box. It's still the same. Drop it off tonight and I'll get a forensic to check it. Results by tomorrow.'

'I don't have any other choice.'

'No, you don't. I'm hanging up. And just so you know, the only reason why I'm doing this is because you saved an innocent girl's life last night.'

'How'd you know it was me?'

'Just a guess.'

He doesn't even say good-bye before hanging up the phone, but I'm grateful for his help.

I bag the slugs in a clean ziplock bag. It's an expensive gamble but it just might help out. After removing $15,000 from the safe and putting it in an envelope with the evidence, I feel a pricking sensation on my neck. The nerves at the base of my head are flicking with agitation. I massage the area a little and can feel a solid and extraordinarily hard object barely protruding on top of a tiny dried scab just above my hairline. What the fuck could this be? I begin to fear the worse as I keep touching it. Tumour? Shrapnel from the service or more recently? Probably a better chance of an alien baby growing than either. I am almost in a state of panic as I rush to the bathroom. I grab the shaving mirror and adjust it to get the light and angles to reflect well enough to just get a glimpse of the scar in the bathroom mirror ahead. The lump is impossible to identify. Where could I have scratched, bumped, or otherwise hurt myself to have caused such a wound? When I can't even come remotely close to an answer, my panic is widespread and horrific.

I don't have time for this shit. I need to get this evidence to George. I prepare for an evening jog and add a small note in the envelope with the cash and fragments: 'Models?'

I take off as soon as I leave the building. If there are people tailing me, they'll need to be fast and on foot. I set myself a quick and steady pace at first. By the time I hit Freedom Park, I kick into a run through the narrow pedestrian pathways neither a car nor motorcycle could follow.

Almost all of my extra attention is worry for the lump at the top of my neck. Once I pop out of the park, I dash across the road, dump the package at the post office, and quickly turn back to run into the protective bosom of darkness and greenery. It isn't until I am almost back to the apartment when I am stunned by the too-coincidental marking of a large tree at the other end of a small public playground. The tree is marked by a chalked pink circle, with a massive one slashed across it with a thirteen next to it scrawled inside the circle.

To anybody else, it could be just a little graffiti, or maybe the work of an arborist, but to me, it is a sign that Lloyd has news and wants to meet. The message is clear: 1300 on the thirteenth of this month, which is tomorrow. The colour pink signifies location: the steps of Parliament House.

I stop momentarily to let it sink in. I just don't know how much more of this I can take. I've got to do some recon. I detour over to Parliament House and really turn my jog into a workout.

But why would he want to meet me out in the open like this? We have a few coded places to meet and he chooses this out of all of them? One we haven't used for years. If the agency plans to kill me, shouldn't they have directed Lloyd to use a more secluded spot? Freedom Park is a great spot for a sniper to hide and pick me off with little or no witnesses.

Damn it! I should've been checking our signposts with my telescope every day. I should have been doing it every morning. I have no time to plan any countermeasures.

By the time I reach Parliament House, the first thing I notice are two policemen standing relaxed at the top of the steep stairs to the closed building. In my frayed mental state, the clock is ticking to absorb as much as possible and get out. I haven't been able to watch the news or read the paper about last night's escapades at the hospital, so I have no idea if I am wanted by the police or not.

The surrounding buildings are a nightmare. There is any number of windows available to house a sniper or an eavesdropper. There are no obstructing trees, and I will be out in the open with Lloyd, probably with hundreds of workers stretching their legs away from their offices and on their way to a respite of lunch. Sadly for me, the mass of people will not be comforting enough.

I turn towards the policemen, who are chatting away about last night's football game. My attention quickly shifts between them to the large and regal entrance to the Parliament's foyer and its sitting houses where politicians abuse their opponents on a daily basis. This meeting is just another gauntlet I will have to run.

The long hand of my watch unwinds slowly over a silver baton. I am fifteen minutes late for my appointment with Lloyd. For the first time since he became my handler, I will be, and planned to be, late. My only hope out of this is to survive. If I am not shot dead, I will surrender my employment with the agency, unequivocally, on the spot. No good has come from my last mission, none but the scurrilous evasion of anonymity and the abandonment of any decent work practices I've acquired and mastered over the years. Ever since I accepted this assignment, my personal rules have been broken and the protocol that has kept me successful and alive has fallen away. Before I fell asleep last night on the floor of my bedroom closet again, I berated myself over my indiscretions. Cursed myself for everything I've done wrong that led up to this moment. Curious George is 100 percent right: the end game is survival, and I'm acting like it doesn't matter.

I have to assume the agency knows everything. At the top of their grievances, they would know it was me who worked Valentino and his cohorts, that I rescued Jessica and broke a top directive to mothball myself until further orders. That should be punishable, and their punishments are swift and capital. So of course my apprehension of a well-aimed sniper's bullet is as real as it is grave. I need to protect myself even if I have to be wild and erratic to do so.

I can see Lloyd in the distance at the bottom of the steps of Parliament House. Is there a bullet waiting for me if he gives a discrete signal? If there is, it would be a cowardly way to go.

Out of every party that would love to see me dead, it is the agency that would have the shortest odds of succeeding. The difference is a country mile. I am far more afraid of them than anyone else, and the meeting ahead will only heighten my weariness.

Their moves are as unpredictable as the wind. I remember Lloyd's warning the first time we paired up. He said only the board can pass judgement on the fate of a contractor. The process goes through some deliberation, but most of the time, they will pay another contractor to extinguish one of their own. It's easy to see the benefit of the dog-eat-dog scenario. They tie up a loose end and set an example for the contractor taking on the assignment. Well, whoever it is, they better be ready.

I walk through the double doors of the Parliament's foyer and down the busy steps, approaching Lloyd from behind. I am just one in a sea of bodies. I blend in well sporting a clean, pressed suit. He would've thought I'd be waiting for him, or I'd be approaching from the subway station in the other direction.

I grasp his shoulder. 'Let's go for a walk,' I say, spinning him around and walking him up the stairs, my arm around his shoulder as if he is an old-time friend.

'I was about to leave,' Lloyd complains with discomfort as I hurry him up. His disabling limp slows him down. 'What are we doing?'

He speaks with such a calm tone. He was ready for this. He is aware of my jaded behaviour and expected it.

'We're going on a tour of Parliament House. That's why you called me here, isn't it? I've never been.'

'Very funny. But we have a lot to discuss.' We are halfway up the stairs when he asks, 'Can I at least tie my shoe lace?'

I glance down to find that it is indeed undone. Sneaky bastard.

'You can do it up when we get inside. I've got a firm hold on you in case you trip.'

'Oh, thanks.'

Lloyd doesn't protest or do anything odd on our way in. I finally let him go into the foyer before we both are herded into separate lines and through metal detectors. Lloyd isn't dumb enough to pack any firearms but is still scrutinised by a handheld scanner. It goes off from the metal in his artificial knee. He is waved on by the inspector and we start walking through the wide corridors. I am a lot calmer by making it here alive. I can even take the time to admire some archived documentation and photos of the city and state. Lloyd camouflages steaming irritation by persisting with good-natured banter.

'You look like shit, Aaron,' he says.

'I haven't been getting much sleep lately.'

'That's to be expected. Concerned you were set up to be erased?'

'Maybe.'

'Hmmm. I'm not surprised. The board can get tough at times when people do the wrong things and ignore instructions. They like to correct them. To set things right. As you know, contractors are only warned once when they sign up. You have to understand we're not talking about just money. We're talking about lives and a network of reputations. Reputations in society, with special stakeholders, and within institutions of power…like this building.'

'What about the reputations of the people that work for the agency?' I say as an afterthought.

'Of course there is always that problem. We don't profess to uphold the law. That's the police's mandate. This is just business. And we take our business more seriously than anyone else. Each client has their own motive, and we assess those with the utmost care. You know we don't accept work over a small grudge or squabble, and there are very good reasons for that. It's too much risk and bound to create problems. Those requests are far more easily swayed by guilt, and guilt is a powerful and much more dangerous emotion than people realise. It can cause a lot of hassles, especially for us, and more problems than it's worth. But you already know this.'

'Is that a personal assumption, or an assumption I'm supposed to have found out in my line of work?'

'C'mon, Aaron. We know you went against orders and saved Jessica Ward. You must have your reasons, of course, but none that I can think of. I can only imagine it was your conscience getting the better of you. I've always known you to do things by the book and take orders as given. But who am I to say you can't think for yourself? The only problem is when you do something against the wishes of a person or persons more powerful than you. Then you're in trouble.'

The moment of truth. 'Well, then. Am I?' I snap back, maliciously and impatiently.

Lloyd chuckles. 'In this case? No, you're not. And I'm just as shocked as you are about it. Saving her could've been a highly lucrative contract to someone if they had known in time and offered their services.'

I heave in relief. But can I believe him? If I walk out the front entrance, will I be able to make it home? I may as well press this further.

'So they've resorted to going around and scrounging for business?' I bark.

'Sometimes. As just a simple cog in the machine, I can tell you they don't take sides. Playing politics is not good for business. All they do is give people the opportunity to make a play, provided there are no conflicts of interest.'

'Like what?'

'Use your head, Aaron,' he challenges. 'Say having two contractors on a competing mission trying to take each other out. That is not a good situation to be in. And once again, I'll repeat, you were lucky they didn't have someone for the job.'

Lloyd's string of logic doesn't sit well. Surely they couldn't have organised a buyer, let alone an operative, to save Jessica from Valentino in such a short time? Surely they couldn't find people prepared for such a high-risk, no-notice assignment? Could they? I can only use myself as a benchmark because I know no other contractors. My previously overly cautious, fastidious approach to work might not be the norm. Maybe the agency has more than enough expendable assets lying around on their books that are willing to put their hand up on short notice. But I've never felt they were ever in that sort of a game. Good people are hard to find and even harder to keep. Protecting their assets should be their highest priority.

'Then what about the leak?' I ask.

'There's been a full investigation. And when I mean full, it was extensive and complete. I've had my life examined to an uncomfortable degree to the extent that everything I do on a day-to-day basis was magnified and analysed. My relationships with associates and relatives were also tested. That was of course, part of my arrangements with the board so I can't complain. Needless to say, they found a hole, nothing to do with me, and have since plugged it. A handler had connections with ex-army personnel, hired by Charles Ward, and was able to access the server and certain files beyond our firewall capabilities with the help of a hacker. Your case was compromised. It is terribly difficult to explain without being fully briefed on the matter. Our servers have now been redesigned and rerouted. Security systems have been overhauled and upgraded very quickly that handlers have been having trouble coping with the new procedures, so I'm told. Computers are a funny thing. I once heard a great truism: "In order to have a safe computer, you'd need to bury it," or something like that. As long as computers are connected to others, they are not safe. Now, the mainframe has been completely disconnected from the rest of the servers. To access sensitive information you need to physically walk into a very secure room with the right access level. Simply put, it won't happen again. It *can't* happen again.'

His assurance, as genuine as it appears, still doesn't gain my trust. 'So what's next?'

'Now's the good news,' Lloyd suggests with a smirk. 'You are back in with full compensation for your last assignment. They've even thrown in a kicker as a bonus. Two hundred thousand. You like that? We're just getting sign-off now, and it will be transferred to your account within thirty days. You also get some holiday pay as well, seeing as you'll need some bench time. How does six months sound? Then your status will be upgraded to available and we'll find some work for you. That is, of course, if you will be staying on?'

I shut off from the news. The greyscale portrait of Parliament House in front of me is exquisitely painted, and I concentrate on the perfect shading as a distraction to hide my astonishment. I want to yell in celebration but can't. I've been miserable for far too long to experience this sort of joy. It leaves me with the feeling of a new dawn slowly peeking from a pitch-dark horizon. I'm almost back to square one. Everything is right again except the break-in, which I don't dare tell Lloyd. Maybe it was the agency all along? Maybe they wanted to investigate and make sure I was in the clear? I probably shouldn't try and rock the boat on this. With such a large payout, I'm in the clear and don't need to worry about making ends meet anymore. I am again at the crossroads in life and pondering my next move.

Can I start a new life? Do I even want to go back? I've been protesting to myself for a long time now that I wanted out. Then why is it so hard for me to make that decision? What can I possibly do with my life outside the work I've been doing all of these years? Be a bartender? Drive a taxi until I die? Go and get a PhD? I realise I'm still young, but maybe the window for a drastic career change has already shut. I have specialised skills that are not easily transferable to 'real-life' occupations. Where can my skill sets be of use to anyone but the fine art of human destruction? Would I be able to handle reintegrating into a society I generally loathe because of the work I do? I'm optimistic that I can at least make an effort.

'I'll have to think about it,' I say, not averting my gaze and finding myself bound again with an internal struggle.

Does the agency deserve me back? The best thing to come out of this is the relief of being vindicated in this whole affair. But what if a breach happens again? I know, I know. I shouldn't be so worried.

Do I deserve to live life like a normal member of society? Or am I the lucky one who has seen the dark side of human nature, the taboo side that nobody dares to discuss but sometimes thinks about? Inhabitants of large cities like Hillbay are prone to having their individual identities marginalised. People get lost in the masses and it inhibits their interactions with others. I am perfectly fine with that. Lost in a mass of people has been how I've wanted to live. But for others, it causes anxiety and fear. Fear of leading an insignificant life. With the way Hillbay is shaping with a quasi-fascist assault of political correctness, more and more people seek blame for their misfortunes on others. People are growing up without discipline and are becoming prone to harming others more than I ever could.

No wonder violent crime is so high—weekend assaults, nightclub stabbings, and daytime muggings like my ill-fated friend in the park earlier this month. Aggressiveness and the need for men to dominate in a way that promotes fear, I will never fully understand.

Maybe I'm the lucky one in all of this? Maybe I'm one of only a handful of people that feel so disconnected from a decaying society that my isolation is not greeted with despair, but with a calm satisfaction that I don't need to put up with spats of violence and the tantrums. I don't need to confront them, the type of people whose pride entraps them when a small bicker turns into idle threats that end with a barrage of hazy punches. The way Valentino would react in a drugged-up rage at something trivial.

At least the people I've killed died knowing they did something wrong for it to happen. I saw it in their eyes, just like Luigi Baresi's confession, that they knew it was their time and finally recognised their own moral servitude to embrace their fate. The comparison of Luigi to his son is night and day. Luigi, the man who earned his fortune even if it was through criminal acts and Valentino, the spoilt son who will squander it all before being killed by another gangster more tempestuous, hungry, and ruthless.

My latest interaction with him will most likely teach him nothing, because he is unwilling to learn, reflect, and piece together happenings in his life to find out why things have gone the way they have. If people can't see the present for what they have become, how can they plan their future?

Lloyd waits for me to answer a question I never heard him ask.

'Sorry. What was that?'

'What I asked is, are you having second thoughts about retirement?'

'I haven't decided. I always think that if you're very good at something, why bother changing if you're successful?' I lie.

'Sure. You should stay on. The board would be glad to keep you. Sometimes we don't know how good an arrangement is until we give it up.'

I linger on his words, like an examiner tries to find fault with a student's thesis.

'Can I ask you one last thing?'

'Sure.'

I move over to a window that drapes the corridor with afternoon light. 'I need you to tell me what this is.'

I bend over and point to the lump on the back of my neck. He takes his time analysing it, comparing it to his own cranium while prodding and squeezing at the offending item. I begin to worry.

'I have no idea what that is…perhaps you should go to a doctor about it if you're that concerned. Could be a tumour for all I know? Or maybe you knocked yourself on the back of the head?'

'I'm get it checked out straight after this…so I best be off. I'm pretty tired and I have to think about things.' The only truth I reveal is that I am, still, exhausted.

'Fair enough. You know how to contact me when you make up your mind.'

I depart without a good-bye. My mind is contaminated by a smog of disbelief. I feel redeemed by my employers but sense there is still something wrong. Why the substantial change of heart? My dressing-down in the park was as dire a scolding as I could have received. To be accepted back into the fold after my guilt-edged heroics has me at a complete loss to explain.

I slip out of the back of the building and sprint to the nearest subway station to get lost in the crowd. I am still apprehensive, not just with the meeting, but with any possible deceptive epilogue. I'm sure there's been at least one contractor terminated shortly after being assured they were in the clear. Not me though. My cautious self is back to its best.

As I wait with other commuters, I believe this is a turn of mass good fortune. I will be making an appointment to see a doctor for this lump, just not today. Maybe Lloyd is right, maybe it is just a lump? I don't think it could have turned out any better, given the circumstances.

CHAPTER SEVENTEEN

My good mood wanes quickly enough. Even on the crowded city streets I feel I am being watched. I am even more distressed when I reach my building. There is far too much random activity around for my liking. A painter up a ladder, a construction crew at a sewer opening, a mass of foot traffic, and people leering about makes me restless. I don't want to go home. The flip side of hiding in a crowd is that surveillance can be just as easy a gig when there are this many bodies to blend with. I resort to staring down as many faces as I can to find out if there are any amateurs in the midst. When there are none to be found, my heart sinks. Every tradesman and every idiot on a bench could be an operative! The people from last night perhaps? Maybe I underestimated their professionalism after all? Or maybe one is a contractor from the agency to take me out because he didn't get a chance earlier today? My eyes dart from faces to footwear and anything in between to find that one out-of-character mistake to confirm my fears. Nothing. It frazzles me enough for my headache to return. I keep getting these damn headaches.

Calm down. I've already been compromised once. There's not much I can do to stop it, so it doesn't matter if I go up to my apartment. They'll already know, because they know where I live. They could be camping in a room across the street, laughing at my behaviour as if I'm a confused rat in a maze, knowing the piece of cheese at the end has been electrified. I should act normally, head upstairs, and get armed again. I sit on a bench opposite my building and take the time to calm down. I let about ten minutes pass before entering the building's lobby and, when nobody is looking, head through a side door and up the emergency stairwell.

I approach the fourth floor with incredible caution. I peek out to see the corridor is clear. My front door at the end is as it should be: closed. When I unlock the door and open it, the heavy push is comforting, and there are no explosive surprises or a swarm of armed men with itchy trigger fingers. A paranoid reality I must deal with for the foreseeable future.

Once inside, I do another check to ensure all curtains are drawn so nobody can see in before switching on a light. Buster emerges from my bedroom with wispy eyes and stretches his hind legs on the way to greet me. I switch on the kettle while he snakes around my legs, brushing his scent onto my calves, marking me as his property. His neediness for affection is unexpected and pleasant.

I fetch some milk from the fridge while he continues to weave under my feet. It's acts like these that make me think he is finally coming around to enjoy human interactions. I prepare myself a mug with some sugar and coffee as he purrs loudly with satisfaction.

I bend over to attend to his desire for a pat while waiting for the kettle to boil. As the back of my hand touches the soft fur on the top of his head, a shock of pain gushes from my neck and disperses along my nervous system with enough force to knock me to the ground and send Buster frightfully skidding away.

It's a searing electrical sting.

As I try to stand, the damaged nerves tick again. I crash to the floor.

I lay prostrate on the tiles until the pain dies. In an almost sympathetic gesture, Buster comes back and licks one of my eyebrows. I don't dare move. I simply can't. Buster cleans me with intent, licking the hair against its natural flow. It feels like hours as I wait for him to remove his paw from over my eye and any risk along with it. My depth perception was at the mercy of a stray cat. I would be amused if I didn't think he was capable.

I struggle but manage to turn onto my side. I need to know where the pain is coming from. I finger the muscles in my neck to not only see if they respond to touch, but to pinpoint the problem.

I know and easily locate the culprit, and I fear it is more sinister than a tumour. I run my fingers around my head to that lump. Lloyd was no fucking help. It feels as if the swelling has subsided but left something more horrifying: a hard, alien bulge.

What could this possibly be? There's no way this could be something human. No human body could grow something this uniform from a bump. I need this out and now! I want to break something out of anger if I could only get up. I don't know if I can even step out of this apartment, let alone go and see a doctor.

It takes roughly an hour to get to the point where I can prepare to stand. I down another three codeine tablets and gradually make my way over to the couch, take a seat and rest, until I have enough strength to walk. Aside from thinking about the pain, I plan what to do next. Whatever it is, it will be drastic.

I head to the medicine cabinet and reach for the antiseptic liquid to partner an old, barely consumed bottle of J&B Scotch. I crop my hair to one millimetre in length with clippers in the bathroom. The regrowth from the time of the Luigi Baresi hit floats to the ground. I stare at the reflection in the mirror, at my hair, and am reminded of the routine. It was an essential part of what I did before I left on a job. A one-millimetre shave is always preferred unless I go out on a paramilitary suicide missions like my last job, then it doesn't matter at all. Generally, the shorter the better because hair and the DNA it contains is just as incriminating as fingerprints.

I pour myself a glass of scotch and drop a fresh, double-edged safety razor blade in the shallow, old-fashioned glass. I wait for the alcohol to sterilise the razor and am left with the sombre silence of motivating myself for the excruciating self-administration I'm about to perform. There's no other way, and there's no turning back. It's the same nervous energy right before I first jumped out of a Blackhawk into a hot zone: terrifying. If I can survive that and everything after, I can survive a little self-mutilation.

I adjust my shaving mirror behind me again so I can see the back of my head clearly in the mirror ahead. I trace the lump carefully with a red marker. It is not hard to outline, and the circle I draw appears larger than I anticipated. I take the blade from the liquid and while holding it, slam down the alcohol for good measure. A lively three large gulps of a better-than-average blend. I wait until it kicks in. It doesn't take long before it is overwhelming. The initial reaction makes my head sway a little as the warm sensation falls and disperses quickly, cell by cell, emanating through my body as the scotch flows down my oesophagus.

It takes a while to prepare myself for the first cut. My hand is poised at the base of my head as I control my breathing down to a calm and soothing rhythm to steady myself.

I pierce my skin with a corner of the blade and grimace as it enters seamlessly. My face contorts in pain. Maybe this is a bad idea? I can stop now if I want to. No. I have to persevere and finish this. Blood pours down my naked back and drips to my underwear. Before I gently start pulling the blade up, I grab a towel and shove it in my mouth. I bite hard as the horrific discomfort becomes unbearable. Drops of liquid I know is my blood splashes on my calves after soaking through my underwear.

The razor touches the object, pushing it slightly forward. Oh, my God! Whatever it is, it isn't human. It's not supposed to be there. Nothing like this can be organically grown. There's absolutely no way in hell this is a tumour.

My reflection in the mirror shows a frightened, whimpering face as tears pool at the pain. I have to keep going as my shaky hand threatens to cramp. I am halfway there as the razor contours over the glistening lump. I may pass out from shock, but the numbing effect of trauma gives me as much of a second wind as I could hope for.

Continuing with the blade, I reach the end of the red line I previously marked, which is now covered with blood. I carefully remove the blade. It is both relieving and revolting. The fine sheet of metal remaining between my fingertips is a mess. Blood drips from it onto the floor to join the rest of the pond. I can't feel sorry for myself. I need to be quick or risk passing out and dying from losing too much blood.

I stick a finger in the slit and feel the slickness of the object. It feels metallic.

My phone rings, and I spring with enough surprised distress that it almost lifts me off the ground. It can only be Curious George, but I can't answer his call at the moment. I'll have to let it go and ring him back. As I poke, nudge, and dig into the top of my spine, the ringing becomes acutely excruciating, running tandem to the physical stress and my anguished grunting. The ringing. It's driving me mad. More tears are shed.

My thumb goes in next, snaking its way to pincer the object. I bend over now, not needing the mirrors anymore, and guess I'm ahead in the race against critical blood loss. That prediction comes undone when I notice it cascading on both sides of my face and collecting mostly at the tip of my nose before dripping consistently into the plugged sink.

The drops start to splatter as I shudder and continue to murmur loudly underneath the towel. The vacillation of plasma and the steely, unbelievable touch of the object make it impossible to get a firm grip.

The phone finally stops. I have to hurriedly collect my thoughts and devise a new course of action. I try and knock the object free with a knuckle, but it only sharpens the agony. It's far too late to go back and not have anything to show for it. My stubbornness could lead to a worse outcome. Passing out and not stemming the flow of blood will result in going into shock and most likely death. Harsh measures must be taken quickly to divert a lethal reality.

I put my thumb and index finger back in. The rest of my fingers, although not in the wound, criss-cross the two that are, as I again bend over and pull from such an obscure angle that it is hard to generate sufficient strength.

The object shifts a little and the movement gives me more determination to see it through. I push the flaps around the lump so the object sticks out of my head. From there I grip it with my whole hand, taking a little time to get a strong hold. I pull, and it is not until I give it a little twist that it finally breaks off and comes out. I become woozy from complete exhaustion but have to fight myself to stay awake and tend to the wound I created.

I drop the object into the sink and don't bother to see what it is before grabbing a handful of cotton wool and dousing it with antiseptic liquid and applying the large, saturated ball onto the wound. There is no way of escaping the pain, but infection is just as much of a worry. I carefully apply a fresh bandage and wrap it around my forehead before even thinking of resting. There's a good chance I might need a prescription of antibiotics, but now I have an excuse to ask for it.

The complete fatigue I endure reminds me of coming home after escaping for my life. It is the last thought I have before collapsing on my makeshift bed in the closet, only able to feel the small terrestrial fluff of

Buster's coat as he comforts me by curling up against my aching body. I manage to flop a hand onto his soft side. The delicate texture of his fur is soothing as I pass out.

It seems like only a few seconds after I close my eyes and fall into a light stir when the phone trills with the annoyance of an alarm. I check my bedside clock across the room, next to the bed I wish I were resting in, and note I slept for at most half an hour. I better answer it. My mobile is hard to reach because I'm so tired. It's only at my feet.

'This better be good news,' I mutter to whoever is down the line.

'It's the news you paid good money for,' Curious George replies dully.

'I guess I shouldn't hang up the phone then?'

'Only if you want to waste your cash.'

I gather that he is still pissed at me for pulling a gun on him. I don't blame him. Our once friendly relationship may never be the same, at least not in the immediate future.

'What did your forensic friend come up with?'

'Well, my *friend* came up with something that doesn't make any sense. The first slug is a nine mill. Standard issue really. Nothing to write home about except that it was fired from the H&K MP5SD series of silenced weapons that are not as easy to come by—'

'How does he know it was from a MP5SD and not a detachable silencer?' I say, cutting him off.

George chuckles. 'He thought you might ask that. And he gave me the answer. Although those silenced models are detachable, they slow down the bullet enough to be subsonic, hence the need for submachine guns in the first place. Slowing down a bullet that much has its fair share of problems, the largest of which is the significant decrease in stopping power. You're going to need more bullets if there's a chance they can't even pass through basic body armour. He wasn't one hundred percent certain, but he *is* sure because the slug you gave was that much intact that they must've used the factory stock. Which leads me to what I was going to say before about those guns. They're pretty unique.'

'Which means the person that fired the weapon probably didn't belong to any regular armed forces,' I say, completing his thought. 'It also must have been a burst-fire shot.'

'You're good, but it was pretty damn obvious. Most groups, be it police, special ops, or even the army, wouldn't generally pick up these weapons. What's the point? If they are going in to use force, they'll cordon off the building or street or whatever and let the bullets fly when needed. I can only guess, but really the only tactical operations that would need them would be a major op, overseas, on someone else's soil that would need to take out a few targets in the one place and not wake the locals.'

'Quick in, quick out. No need to bother the neighbours,' I joke, turning off the tap and becoming less interested in his findings.

As George waffles a bit more about the guns, I get up and head over to the bathroom sink. With my free hand, I pull the plug to drain the mixture of blood, alcohol, and antiseptic and turn on the cold faucet. I can hear George talk but don't pay any attention when I realise what's left is a nightmare. I freeze, immobilised and horrified.

My hack job has yielded a small, metallic ball that teases me by willing itself to drift down the drain as the water runs. It dances in the hole, almost floating, with the cross of steel covering the drain protecting it from being lost to me and on its way down to a stormwater pipe that leads into the sea.

I hesitate to pick it up, as if it will electrocute me. I pad it gently with a finger and it zaps me with current. It burns my nerves all the way up to my shoulder but is not enough to floor me. What the fuck? This is what caused me such pain! I fetch a rubber glove from the kitchen to insulate myself from any further shocks. I touch it again with a gloved hand and when I get no response, I pick it up and inspect it. What *is* this? There is simply no way to explain what it is or how it ended up in my body.

It is a shiny, polished metal ball whose texture is too perfect for it to be a chunk of shrapnel. The confusion causes me to lower the phone and with it, Curious George's paid-for particulars.

I turn the orb over and discover the only anomaly that separates what I hold in my hand with what would appear to be a large, perfect solidified drop of solder. It is a constant, flashing, tiny LED.

My thoughts are clear on only what I'm holding between my fingers. The dull post-operative pain in my head diverts elsewhere, along with the grasp I have on the phone as it slides from my hand and crashes on the floor. The crack snaps me to attention like a drill instructor screaming on a military parade. I scoop up the phone.

'Are you there?'

'What is going on over there?'

'Nothing…I, eh, had the phone on my shoulder and it slipped. Sorry.'

'Yeah, cool. OK. So what I was about to tell you is even more crazy about the second bullet you gave me.'

'Oh, yeah. And what's that?'

'My source doesn't believe that bullet could come from the same scene. It's out of place. Nobody in their right mind would use it in any military or police operation. He said that gun would have sentimental value to its owner.'

'Why is that?'

'Because it's a sports gun,' he declares. 'That's why. That slug is a shitty little twenty-two calibre. From a semiauto Beretta 75.'

I can't believe it. I need it confirmed. 'Can you please repeat that?'

'It's from a Beretta 75. There is no reason a Beretta, especially one that was designed for use on a shooting range, should be anywhere near, let alone in the same room as, an MP5SD. To make it stranger, they don't even make them anymore. It's fucking ludicrous.'

I let the craziness sink in. There's nobody else who would own or even carry such a weapon. It confirms one insane proposition: it was Vincenzo himself who had been in this apartment. The new and undisputed king of the underworld. The man who is now the most dominant criminal force in Hillbay, and who could make a strong claim for the rest of the country. It's unmistakable. He was the man running the show. He was the guy wearing the hideously exaggerated footwear, setting himself apart from the rest who were Charles Ward's men in more appropriate combat boots.

But why would he want to risk being identified? Maybe he doesn't give a shit. He certainly was a cocky son of a bitch when we met. It still doesn't explain why they needed to raid my home, or how they know where I live. What could I possibly have of interest to a man who could have anything he wants?

Even in my fragile state, I realise this won't stop. Charles and Vincenzo will do anything they can to take me out. I've been had. They know where I live. They have the power to hunt me down. I doubt more than ever that they were looking for anything. No, they were sending a message. They want me to know they know how to find me and have the power to do what they want. There's no point in running either; they'll find me, eventually.

There's only one way out. I have to take out Vincenzo and move on to his partner in crime, and I have to go against the agency to do it.

Fuck the agency! They got me into this mess. I should be entitled to get myself out of it. The last thing they need are rumours flying around that they're not secure.

It is not about it being personal, or even unfinished business. I will not be able to let this go knowing he was here and can track me down. They have the reach to be able to find me. If they got to the agency's files before, they will do it again. They have the police in their pockets and probably judges as well. Until this is finished, I won't be able to trust anyone, including the man on the other end of the line. Perhaps this phone call is being traced or bugged, on his end or mine. That's OK by me. I will no longer be using this phone after this call anyway.

Questions tick over on the likelihood of Curious George's involvement in this given his sordid history with Varetti. Is it possible he could be playing me? Why would he give away Varetti's gun if he did? Or maybe Varetti wants me to know and George is a neutral conduit?

I have to question this logic. Maybe Varetti wants me to think it was him? Or maybe he wants me to *know* it was him? How else could he force me out of hiding to ambush me?

More questions pop in my head than I have time to answer. It is as if all of the people I know are smiling and nodding and giving me the information I want to hear: Lloyd and the agency, Curious George and even Charles Ward. Except the moment I turn they all conspire against me. The information they feed me jiggles me to act for them like a marionette.

George is right. I should've made certain I knew who was fucking me over before gunning for them. And now I know.

And now I know what has to be done.

'George, I need you to do one last thing for me. Can you do that?'

'Sure. What do you have in mind?'

'I want you to put the word out with Varetti's people.'

'Yeah? What?'

'I want you to tell Varetti's people that in three night's time, he will no longer be their employer.'

I wait for a reaction, and it seems an age before Curious George shouts down the end of the line: '*Have you lost your fucking mind? What the fuck are you talking about?*'

But I am above his yelling: 'I am going to kill Vincenzo Varetti this Saturday night. You got that?'

'Why would you do something as stupid as going for the most untouchable man in Hillbay?'

'Because I can. And I want him to know I'm coming.' I give George some time to comprehend the situation. 'Do you need any money to make this happen?'

It takes him a while before answering. 'Fucking don't worry about it. You'll be dead before I get paid.'

That's what I'm counting on…

'Thanks, George. For all of your help over the years. I'm sorry it had to end like this.'

'Consider it a parting gift for all of the work you've given me,' he says, half-sincere, half-pissed off as he hangs up the phone.

CHAPTER EIGHTEEN

For the first time since the Baresi mark, I was able to get the most blissful night's sleep, even though it was still in the cramped closet. It was incredibly deep and even better, a migraine-free slumber.

I check my watch to find I slept a solid twelve hours. Not bad, except that my biological clock is so out of whack that it's 0400. Still, I'm rested enough to begin preparing. I thought long and hard about how I can isolate Varetti from his helpers.

I know I have to take my chances and a little luck needs to swing my way. I'm due for some after this fiasco. My disgust towards Charles Ward and his work has abated for the moment, replaced by a professional and calculating grudge against Varetti. One target at a time. Divide and conquer.

The safe is cleaned out and I take stock of every last piece of equipment I own. Most importantly, I prep a trusty Glock 22C with a homemade disposal silencer I cooked up months ago. I confirm the silencer fits down the barrel and preload two spare magazines. I put all of the other firearms back in the safe but remove a Ka-Bar knife.

I search for Buster in all the favourite places he likes to curl up. I eventually find him in the corner of a windowsill, preening himself meticulously as only a spoilt cat can. He continually laps his front paw before it circles around his ears and face.

What can I possibly do with my homely companion? I'm reluctant over the choices. There's a chance we will never see each other again, and it saddens me more that I may be abandoning him when he's finally settling in. My home has been a palace compared to his previous life as a stray. I am in despair when I realise my friendship with him is currently stronger than any relationship I have with a human.

It's as if our lonely lives were comparable before twisting together to form a cordial partnership that turned into mutual affection. It's as close to an intense emotional apex as I've experienced in years, setting aside infatuation.

I prepare to disturb him while he grooms. If only he could understand.

I scoop up his little body and surprisingly, he doesn't fight me. Instead, he uses my arm to balance himself. He's so relaxed he forgets to spring his claws out to advise me it is not in my best interest to be so affectionate. I flip him so I cradle him like a baby, and he enjoys it, squinting with content.

'C'mon,' I whisper.

His complete submission makes it harder to go through with what is necessary. He stretches an arm out and places it on my chin. At that moment I choke and feel like crying into his furry belly. I am shocked at my reaction. I never thought it could ever be this hard with a pet.

I walk him over to the front door to place him in the cat cage I bought a year ago but only now have the need to use. As soon as he descends, the resistance starts. He claws hard at my shoulder, but I am too strong for him and unpin his claws from my T-shirt. Even with such a large cage, he isn't pleased with being contained and attempts to jump out but only makes it as far as my waiting wrists.

Buster meows loudly when I finally close the hatch, and despite having plenty of room and the ability to see in all directions through the thin metal caging, his immediate reaction is to urinate. I laugh with forgiveness and anguish when I would normally be annoyed. But there is nothing to be gained by being angry at something that is expected. I replace the towel in the cage and let out a tear while doing so as he tries to escape again. His desperation is as if he were being taken away to be put down.

I quickly change into jeans and a dark grey sweater while packing all I'll need into a black kit bag. I leave the light on and sneak out on my belly into the empty corridor so nobody can see me through the open curtains from the street. I push Buster's cage and the kitbag along in front of me and only get up once I've closed the front door.

I stop outside Mrs Rutherford's apartment. Should I knock and speak to her or not? It's still quite early for a senior citizen to be awake. I better not. Sooner or later, Buster will wake her up for me. I lay an envelope on the cage addressed to her. In it is $5,000 and a note to apologise again for the ruckus the other night and to ask that she takes care of Buster for a few months while I'm gone. The money is to help with any expenses she might incur. Of course she will think it is too much. But if I don't return, it may be too little. Most likely, it will go straight into her daughter's hands and be spent on an illegally good time. Hopefully Buster will be able to convince her to allow him to stay.

'It's all up to you,' I tell him.

I stroke his head by poking a finger through the wires and despite Buster appearing less than appreciative with his incarceration he still has enough love to raise his rump in the air. As I leave I turn to see him settling into a particularly warming fold of the towel in his cage. I stupidly wave a silent good-bye while waiting for the elevator to part us, perhaps forever. As soon as the door closes, I cringe with emotion.

The elevator takes me to the basement and I make my way to a lone vehicle covered by a silver car cover. I whip off the cover to find my dark blue Ford sedan in the same condition it was since I last drove it four years ago. I place my equipment bag in the backseat, pop the boot and grab the portable jump starter kit. After inflating the tyres to forty-five psi, I top up the water in the radiator and jump start the engine. It kicks over well, and while it runs I inspect the oil gauge, deciding it doesn't need adjusting.

I jump in, pull out of the parking bay, and reach for the glove box for a cap just in case there is someone watching the vehicle entrance. The side and rear windows have the darkest possible legal tint. I navigate slowly around the basement car park, up the ramp and out onto the quiet street. Although it is 0600—people are just beginning to rise for a fresh spring morning—I am more than awake and focussed on the job at hand.

Everything seems as it should as I turn onto the sparsely populated main road. Driving a few slow concentric circles to see if there are any tails, I head over to a nearby supermarket to pick up supplies. I buy a couple of large bottles of water, some protein drinks, a few granola bars, a couple of bags of biscuits, as well as both daily newspapers, and a couple of current affair periodicals.

I drive back to the apartment block and park on the other side of the road after the clearway hours have just finished at half past nine. I reach for my windscreen cover on the backseat and lay it over the dashboard, shielding any view one might have inside the cabin. I unbuckle my seat belt and climb over the central console into the back and start skimming the paper. Reading cannot keep all of my attention. I have to be conscientious of the cars and vans parking across the road and those going into the basement car park of my apartment building. I grab my binoculars, just to be ready, and settle down for a long wait.

Stakeouts are among the worst part of any operation I can think of. The job is extremely boring, and I can't fathom how private investigators cope. The normal routine is parking in one spot and having to be on the lookout for activity. It isn't my idea of a good time.

Perhaps the worst aspect is the need to be constantly aware. I find myself only half-reading the newspaper and not absorbing any information about the latest drunken brawl in the city. I can only allow myself short bursts of reading. The victim's injuries were a broken arm and probable permanent brain damage. I fold the broadsheet and toss it away, fed up with not only with my own ill-discipline, but also by the story and the disintegration of any cohesion of this community I live in—drunken and drug-affected fools running around seeking a way to prove they exist.

I keep my attention on the building and people walking in and out, and say a little prayer that my play will reap me success.

Twelve hours later I am still in the car, restless and ready to give up. One large bottle of water has been filled with urine over the course of the day. I lift up the passenger floor mat to reveal a cork-plugged hole in the ground I drilled when I first bought the car for situations like this. I pull the cork out and pour my waste carefully through the hole, where it will trickle to the gutter. I glimpse over to my apartment with its light still on and nobody in sight.

Eventually an inconspicuously large van, about the size of a bus, turns into the vehicle entrance of the apartment block while a blacked-out, midnight-blue Maserati creeps slowly towards the front of the building. Finally I am rewarded. Holy shit…this is it!

The Maserati double parks. A couple of heavyset goons step out with bulges under their arm. Nearly a full minute later, the short but powerful figure with his full head of silver hair steps out in a grey suit, white shirt, and black coat. It is the unmistakable figure of Varetti, even down to his shoes: the incriminating, outlandish footwear he wore last time he was in my apartment. The tactical team must be exiting the van storming up to the fourth floor with their MP5SDs.

I can afford to smile because I can push Varetti's buttons enough to get him to act how I want. Sometimes it only takes a threat to lure someone out of hiding. Thank you, Curious George, wherever you are.

Varetti would naturally be scared or angry, as any rational person should be, when told someone is out to kill him. Maybe he thought it wasn't going to be me, but I had to take that chance. He knew I would want to get back at Charles and him for our encounter at the Ward compound. Whether he wanted to plant the evidence in my apartment or Curious George tipped him off in connection with the gun is incidental. My threat worked like a charm. He would either be holed up and fear a hit that was never going to come, flee the state and country—which I doubt his ego would let him do—or rightly so, take the confrontation to me and finish it personally. Setting a definitive date would force him to make a decision. And for me, he made the right one.

But Varetti doesn't enter the building. He stands outside, head up at the fourth floor while prepping a cigarette. It seems he is more content to let his men clean out the apartment instead of leading the assault. Damn. This was not expected. I thought he would want to kill me personally. I have to improvise about what to do next. The situation has become dynamic, and I have to assume those two men who are flanking him will have their suspicions aroused when they realise I am not where I should be. One of them is already suspicious of the parked cars, holding his gaze longingly at me despite not being able to see me through the tinted car windows, unless he has godly x-ray vision. He chats out of the corner of his mouth to Varetti before passing me over and continuing his examination.

I could be in trouble. If they somehow know I am here and decide to fire at the car, it will be shooting fish in a barrel. I have no means of escape, except to fire first.

Together, all three of them train their vision in my direction. It heightens my anxiety. Was I seen leaving the building by a spotter who noticed I parked and *never* got out of the car? It's a ludicrous theory, because they could've investigated, surrounded the car, and shot at it until there's nothing left.

But all three systematically glance up again as Varetti checks his phone. Why the confusion? What could he possibly be waiting for? And then it dawns on me. The cause of my awful headaches and the reason why they could track me back to my apartment: it was the metallic orb! They were using it to monitor my whereabouts. I was a human beacon! All this time I had thought it was skill and tradecraft. No, it was something far easier. They must have implanted it while I was held captive without me knowing. Another one of Dr Ward's sick experiments? What's more effective than an ankle collar when this is under a person's skin?

The confusion before me is as clear as it is comical. Varetti has access to track me from Charles Ward. But what is stopping him at the moment? Is there another tracker somewhere on my body that wasn't so discoverable? I pat myself down uselessly to check with a similar panic as if there is a deadly insect crawling under my clothes. No way. No fucking way am I still bugged.

I glance up to my fourth-floor windows, its open curtains and can see no movement.

The three of them stare at me menacingly. Varetti begins to scowl. I can see the soldiers in the room now, in column formation, guns poised and shouldered before one of them quickly draws the sheer curtains to block any clear view from the street. It was an important five seconds to witness. At least they have the brains to try and keep it discreet. But unfortunately for them, I know where they all are. They leave the light on, and their shadows against the thin curtains cast distorted human shapes. I would have considered it sloppy work if I hadn't pulled the heavier drapes off last night and thrown them in the cupboard.

'Things might be getting out of hand,' I mumble, as Varetti and his mob fidget with their weapons.

I go into my kit bag and pull out the silenced Glock and a remote detonator. The three remaining explosive charges kept in the safe were planted in the kitchen behind the knife rack, wedged in between a couple of cushions on the couch and one in the open safe, next to the metal ball I had removed last night. All of them had been crudely wrapped with nails, tines from the end of forks, and any other small, metallic object that has the capacity to tear through human flesh when an explosion is set off next to it.

Varetti plucks out a two-way radio from his pocket. He listens intently, all the while glaring in my direction. He doesn't scream, but he mutters a couple of words into the speaker before beginning to walk towards me.

It's now or never.

I look up one more time at my apartment to see shadows dance across the windows. I don't hesitate to arm and activate the detonators. I have a minuscule moment to mourn the cosiness of a home I had such a fondness for before the charges explode.

The apartment lights up as the windows are blown out with an almighty roar created from the tearing force of three separate explosions in a confined area. I don't see any traces of blood or bodies, but I know there will be when the police come to inspect the damage. Glass rains onto the street before smoke bellows out, along with debris.

It comes as no surprise to me, but Varetti and his two goons are thrown onto the street from the blast. He will at least be paying to get the Maserati fixed as warped and unidentifiable bits of metal and brick land on his car, dinting the perfect body and paintwork.

It doesn't deter Varetti for long. His determination to confront me is unwavering, and he robotically picks himself up from the asphalt and marches over to me, not even taking the time to assess what has happened to his men. I open the door behind me and roll backwards onto the footpath clumsily. It is effective enough to protect myself from Varetti, who has now drawn his Baretta and fires wildly in my direction, not caring about the safety of a couple of bystanders on the footpath.

I stagger to the front of my car behind the more solid cover of engine parts. I poke up and fire off a quick, silenced round at one of Varetti's guards gathering himself against the Maserati. The small, suppressed click of the gun obscures the effect of the bullet. I know it hits him as he arches his back in agony before slouching over the bonnet. His priority now should be to keep breathing.

I don't have time to admire my marksmanship when Varetti fires again. The bullet dints the front-side panel of my car. I can't believe he's trying to kill me with that piece of shit Beretta 75! I pop out of cover and fire again, this time at Varetti. My aim is true, and I hit his right thigh. He screams and falls down on the median strip.

The job's not over by a long shot. What about the third guy I haven't been able to keep an eye on? Where did he go? He must be behind the Maserati. My head is still exposed as I wait for him to make a move. He bobs up from behind his boss's car and whips out a silenced MAC 10. I duck again because I don't want to witness him firing and catch a bullet to the skull! He begins to fire at me in shorts bursts. I can tell from the metal-on-metal clang the bullets make on my car that he is pretty accurate. I move over to the back of the vehicle to give myself a positional advantage. I peer from the rear of the vehicle instead of over the boot to find he has also taken cover somewhere. This guy at least knows what he's doing. I can respect his professionalism even though I have to kill him. I try and think up a move that will flush him out. I need to hurry as well. Sirens cannot be too far off.

The stalemate lasts for about a minute. I'm fresh out of ideas. As each second passes, I get more and more fed up. I'll be left here for the police to catch me. Is that what I want? Anger begins to overwhelm my thoughts very quickly until I am furious. I never wanted to be in this situation in the fucking first place. If I give up now, I may as well be dead! Get moving, now! It's me or them. There's no need to play fair.

Rallying myself, I feel hardened, which inspires acts of cruelty.

Fuck trying to live by any type of code with these people. They're animals who cannot be reasoned with. Why did I bother from the beginning? There's no point in trying to limit collateral damage—that much is clear. There's no better example than witnessing the destruction of my home. I let the fact that I can never come back to this place sink in to fuel my seething wrath.

'Give up, dickhead,' I yell over at him, secretly hoping he understands English. 'Look what I've done to your boss. Look what I've done to his men. You think you can survive a shootout with me?' My brash and uncharacteristic attitude convinces even myself. I wonder how he is feeling? 'Did you like the fireworks, pal? I can smell some of your cooked friends from here.'

'Don't listen to him, Lenny,' Varetti cries. 'You have to kill him.'

I peek over again and still cannot find him. But perhaps I can force his hand in surrendering. I only take a second to aim and let off another round. A large, boisterous cry of pain is heard between us as Varetti cops a second bullet to his leg.

'Can you hear that, Lenny?' I shout, making sure he'll hear me. 'Can you see how much pain your boss is in at the moment? It's entirely your fault! I'm giving you five seconds to come out or the next bullet is going in his head. You see how good my aim is. You know I won't miss him from here. You got that? In his *fucking* head! Then you won't be getting another pay cheque from that Italian prick. In fact, you'll be out of a job, so you won't need to be trying to kill me. It's up to you.'

I pause a few moments to let it sink in amid the sobs from Varetti. He mutters an inaudible response that only exacerbates the dire situation.

'Five!'

Nothing.

'Four!' I yell, rechecking my pistol by adding a fresh magazine.

'Three!' More sounds, this time snippets of Italian from the median strip.

'TWO!' I shout, propping myself up and getting ready behind the car to accomplish my coup de grâce. 'Lenny-boy, prepare to be the cause of a lot of grief to crooks associated with this arsehole! When they find out about it, they'll be gunning for the guy that could've saved his boss instead of killing him.'

'OK! OK!' I hear from the other side of the street.

His surrender doesn't provide any relief to my fierce, menacing demeanour. It only makes my job that much easier.

I can see Lenny emerging from a car two over from Varetti's Maserati with his arms up and the offending MAC 10 in his right hand. His walk is slow and tentative. I take aim but don't pull the trigger and stand still knowing I can take him down before he could ever drop the submachine gun and fire off a burst of .45-inch ammo. His eyes tell me he knows that too.

'Put the gun down,' I command.

'Shoot him!' Varetti yells.

'You try and you'll get one in the face. It's *that* simple.'

Even from the distance of tens of metres, I know his mind is switching between two poles of thought. One is following the orders of his boss and his duty, and the other is the rational side of surrendering but to the fate of an unpredictable person who can kill him anyway. He is at a crossroad and needs to choose a path before I have to make the decision for him.

'*Shoot* him!' Varetti screams again.

Sirens can be heard in the distance, speeding us along to a resolution and breaking the stalemate. The tension is beginning to haemorrhage my will to be involved any longer.

I pull the trigger. I've crossed a line. It is the line that separates me from the shadow of myself. That self was up until now viewing the world with resolute optimism despite working as an agent whose clients are the complete opposite. The side that readily resisted considering humans egotistical and exploitive even if, from time-to-time, they nurtured the desire to kill others. I accepted the inherent contradiction of doing heinous acts for others, but as long as it was the occasional *anomaly*, I was fine with it and dismissed it as the very brief guilt-edged low of human activity.

But now, within the split second between the expelling of the cartridge and the calamitous effect it will have on the skull, brain, and life of its next solid contact, my outlook on the world has changed forever. The bullet mirrors the destruction it will cause for the man it will find. No more can I stand by wishfully thinking. I see now the occasional low is not a sharp point but a trough. We are inherently wired for not merely survival and self-interest, but have also picked up the insidious need to dominate and hold over others the power of will. What for? For petty status and to revel in a stranger's humiliation.

It's as if a number of worlds are colliding within my psyche. However, one thing is constant. I felt no emotion when that bullet left my gun, or even when it hit Lenny squarely on the forehead, piercing his skin, skull, and softer frontal lobe. To me, though, I didn't just destroy another human. I destroyed any hope I may have had for salvation for what I've ever done.

My sin is being the same, although I hadn't realised it until now.

Lenny keeps his balance and mystifyingly holds his arms up momentarily before they collapse in front of him, shifting his momentum forward and causing him to crumble in a heap. My psychological pain doesn't abate. Why should it?

He hasn't even finished falling when I turn to Varetti, still lying on the blood stained concrete, with the expression of defeat I've seen so many times in my life, the last of which on a person he would never want to be associated with: Luigi Baresi.

I don't need to point a gun at him, although I do. He is not fit to hold any firearm let alone the gun he used to get himself into trouble. I don't have much time before the police, ambulance, and fire brigade get here.

'Any last wishes?' I ask.

'Fuck you!' he spits.

'Do you want me to leave you here for the police to explain why you've got a gun at your side and why there is a squad of burnt men on the fourth floor of that building and two dead men over there?'

'They won't do a thing to me. I'll be patched up and sent along my merry way and this will all be swept under the rug. Don't believe me? Just wait and see.'

'You think I'm a fucking idiot? You use my services to kill others and make me destroy my home. Do you actually expect me to let you live?'

'I'm not the only one who is playing you like a fiddle. There are others closer than you think.'

'I know. And I'm going to kill them as well. You're messing with someone who you cannot control. I cannot be swayed by money or prestige or any other worldly thing you can dream up that you think I might want. I'm not going to stop until you and Charles and anyone else who fucked me over are all dead. I'm not going to stop until this is finished and either they or I…have perished.'

Varetti laughs likes he knows something so vital to me but would rather die than reveal what I want to know. For that, I shoot him in his outstretched hand, the one propping him up and formerly holding his Beretta 75, which lies just twenty centimetres from it. I am now his puppet master as he scrunches his wrinkled and leathery face into a grimace.

'Funny now, isn't it?' I joke.

But he quickly brightens up to my astonishment. 'You stupid fuck. You think you can stop this? You think you can stop a government?'

'I've done it before.'

'Well, you'll be doing your country a huge disservice if you do.'

'Then me and my country will be even.'

Varetti sighs in defeat as if reasoning with a child. He will not be able to sway me from my bloodlust.

I fire again, hitting him in the stomach and inflicting more pain. He squirms as he screams. I tuck the Glock in my jeans and reach for his Beretta.

'You want to be patriotic?' I rhetorically ask. 'Then you won't mind being a victim of your own pride. Open your mouth.'

He turns to me with his teeth clenched in defiance. I deliver a short punch with the butt of the Beretta, caving his front teeth in. I pinch his nose and pry his mouth open, forcing the barrel in. When he realises he cannot escape, he bites down hard on the barrel grating his gums and cracked stumps of teeth on the cylindrical steel.

'I'm going to enjoy this,' I remark before pulling the trigger and seeing a spurt of blood spray from behind his now lifeless body. I kick his body down to the ground.

I quickly pull out a cloth and wipe down the gun. The police will not be able to lift any other evidence from this crime scene.

The sirens are louder as I run to my car and rev the engine. I pull out and drive over the median strip only a couple of metres from Varetti's body and in the other direction of the oncoming emergency services.

There will be witnesses; that's a certainty. They were staring through the windows of the surrounding buildings and cowering. They *will* tell what they've seen to the police and truly jeopardise my ability to live in this city. The police will find a connection to the incident at Mercy Hospital when I saved Jessica and a state-wide manhunt will be on for every cop and decent citizen to help catch the murderous bastard that I am. I won't have any defence for this either. If I get caught, it will be the quickest trial ever held. Self-defence and one good Samaritan act is a little hard to justify to a jury when there are numerous body parts lying around in my former living room and an old, injured man with his brains splattered on the street next to his own gun.

There's also the problem of suddenly exploding a fully paid-for apartment that I cannot claim insurance on. Years in the army were spent to save up the money to buy the loft under an assumed identity and I've blown it up. I had the dream: a piece of real estate with small upkeep and enough savings to live off when times are tough. Now it's all gone.

These thoughts occupy my mind as I drive at the speed limit towards The Hills and away from the police arriving at the scene of destruction, mayhem, and murder I used to call home.

CHAPTER NINETEEN

It takes me a while to get over destroying my home and my life. All that effort choosing the place I thought I would live for the rest of my life, furnishing it, and making it mine is gone in an explosive instant.

I knew when I got into this game that I would have to be open to making such a sacrifice if a situation like this was to come. I just never thought it would actually happen.

But it had to happen.

I thought I would easily deal with it when planning my counter-offensive. It was the only way of neutralising a number of enemies at once. The little bug I pulled from the back of my head was the ace in the hole I needed to attract them like moths to a flame even if I didn't know exactly what it was. With the reinforced concrete walls, floor, and ceiling, it meant as long as the explosives weren't picked up and moved, my neighbours wouldn't have been at risk.

I worry just as much about Buster. Surely Mrs Rutherford would have picked him up and taken him in? The blast wouldn't have made any significant damage to her apartment except giving them both a terrible fright.

But losing my home is the least of my worries. I'll be on the run for the rest of my life from every law enforcement agency in the country and, more importantly, Lloyd and the agency. If I didn't cross the line before, I have now. I have no doubt they will have me erased from their collective memories. Their reputation will be severely damaged, if not in tatters, from my actions.

But I've come this far; it's time to finish it. I may have been paid for the hit already, but it doesn't unbind me from my desire to kill Charles Ward. He probably knows about the fireworks and the death of his underworld ally, and I hope he is cowering in fear or for his sake, fleeing the city as quickly as he can, abandoning his experiments and repenting a life and career misled. If he doesn't and I find him, the pain I will inflict will be ghastly.

It is an emotional breakthrough. To want to kill somebody as badly as I do right now gives me the sensation that I feel alive and worthy and lucky to be able to try. And there's good reason I've never felt like this before. All through life I've had to suppress my feelings to stave off a nervous breakdown. Only this time the trauma is far more personal, and so are the consequences.

But I am not even halfway there when morality strikes. Where does Jessica fit into this? How can I be so condemning of a father when I so desperately respect his daughter? It's true she shouldn't be punished for his crimes but if I kill him, and he justly must die, won't I be punishing her anyway? And what will happen if she is there with him when we meet? What if she begs for his life?

If this goes according to plan, she will be in the same parentless boat as me. The only difference is that she got to know hers. But maybe that's worse. I am completely indifferent to my parents because I never knew them. They could've died in a car accident or completely abandoned me and are still alive. I just don't know. And if I don't know, I cannot judge them for being good or bad. So I don't. They are indifferent, and that's good enough for me. If I had the time again to accept Charles's offer with everything that has happened since, I may have said yes. But I can't entertain the possibility of rewriting regrets out of convenience. The path I've chosen, chose me.

Jessica's situation is worse than mine. She knew both her parents and will have to grieve for the loss of her paternal bond. My only hope is she finds out what sort of inhumanity her father has strayed to and accepts that this is wrong.

The road winds its way through the suburbs before the climb to The Hills and the even steeper climb beyond. I look out for police but find none. There is no congestion and better still not a cop in sight. I expected at least one roadblock or a checkpoint to sprout on my way out of Hillbay. Somehow, I'm disappointed.

The streets become tree-lined with magnificent skeletons, bare of any greenery. They should be budding soon and providing shade for the summer months ahead.

I park the car in the exact same place as last time. I can only hope that the backing property hasn't bolstered their security.

I go to my bag one last time, remove the silenced Glock, consolidate my ammo into one magazine, and equip the sheathed Ka-Bar knife. I linger in my seat with uncertainty. I may not have the opportunity to return to the car and restart my life. All of my possessions have been reduced to the gun in my hand and the clothes on my back. I leave all of my documents back in the bag: the counterfeit passports with driving licenses, a couple of AMEX cards that would be useful for one quick transaction before getting rejected, and my personal ATM cards for cash in various savings accounts under different names.

If I don't make it out alive, the police will find these identities baffling, but they might just piece together my true identity as one of the aliases.

I lock the car and leave a single key to the vehicle on the rear tyre facing the road. Tucking the Glock into the back of my pants, I navigate carefully around the property in front. I leap with purpose over the solid brick front wall and run around to the rear fence. The lights are on in the mansion and the middle-aged owners fail to notice me. They are, instead, keenly attuned to the massive flat screen TV hanging on their living room wall. Their familiar backyard is easily negotiated, as large as it is. The owners should really think about investing in a guard dog.

I approach the wall to the Ward's estate with apprehension. This is the last time I will set foot on this property and there will be only two ways I'll leave: on my own two feet or in a body bag. Either way there will be closure. If Charles has fled, he won't be back.

The small guard tower is unoccupied and silent with eerie abandonment. I look out for anything that might need lethal attention. When it is clear, I scale the large oak tree I previously used for cover and it takes me a while to realise it is not just the tower that is vacant, but the rest of the grounds lack human activity. There is only the dull light of the rear building where Valentino and I were kept that is generating any interest aside from the mansion beyond. Could they have sent them all? Or is this an ambush?

I cannot hide my indecision and impatience. It is hard to keep control when I have a cloud of retribution hanging over me. I wait for half an hour knowing every second I stall is potentially a second conceded to Charles if he runs and to the police if they have been brought in to protect him. Eventually my inaction will be my downfall, so I hop out from the branches. I jump down and take a run up and clear the wall I previously stumbled in exasperation, with little effort.

I duck inside the rear building to find it has been cleared out completely. There is nobody manning the supervisor's dock. I run through the corridor of cells and peek through all of them to see nothing but the stained remnants of the vicious experiments Charles and his cohorts had the audacity to perform. The odd bloodstains are a lasting reminder and appear to have been hurriedly washed over with bleach and ammonium. Any test subjects must have been otherwise moved or disposed of. I shudder when I pass the cell I had been held in. The tingle of reminisced fear solidifies my resolve to maintain a vicious edge.

Did Charles do it? Did he succeed with his final agent? How many victims could there have possibly been? It's something I should've asked Luigi Baresi. I should have heeded his warning. How many experiments had been performed? How many people were plucked off the street to come to a terrifying end here? Only Charles would know the answer.

Back at the supervisor's desk, I bluntly kick a door until the lock gives way and splinters from the wood. I am careful up the staircase, popping around corners while aiming my Glock, but I needn't be. This building is as deserted as the grounds outside. On the second floor, I turn on the lights. As soon as they flicker on, the seriousness of the moment catches me. This is worse than I could have ever imagined.

The lab is a severe contravention of the Hippocratic Oath. It holds a collection of human body parts too numerous to believe. There are limbs, torsi, and heads of men, women, children, and infants stored in containers. Eyes from severed heads bulge in preserving fluid to speak for the souls they once belonged to. They appear sad and destitute, as if to say their bodies had been taken against their will. Was this where I was going to end up, too?

I find no consistency with the body parts. They belong to people from different races and they have been separated from their bodies in various ways. I don't need to be a forensic scientist to be able to tell the sets of arms in front of me have been sliced, ripped, charred, and some burnt at the fingers and shoulders as if they were conducting ordinance testing. My heart sinks with sorrow and without any plausible explanation for why they can muster this kind of torture on such a grand scale.

I reel from the sight enough to close the door out of melancholy from witnessing such an abomination. I've come across enough destruction of human flesh over the years, but never in such a civilised and process-driven way. The closest I can remember was when I was operating in troubled nations during spiteful civil wars, but it was never so organised.

I want to vomit but can't.

Trudging back downstairs, it is difficult to pull myself out from feeling traumatised. What is the point of being here? Aren't I already too late to do anything? If Charles is working for the government and the government intends to support his work to ensure they have a tactical weapon to plunder any opposing force or population, how can one man stop what has probably already been finished? I think about the recurring nightmares of Fitzgerald and my other brothers-in-arms I've lost over the years in the service. Shouldn't I be supportive of what the military wanted? If it were available during my time, wouldn't it have saved the lives of people like Fitzgerald? We could have all been happily unemployed and never needed to have chosen a career that would eventually kill us.

The back of my head begins to itch and I am rough when I scratch it, causing me a pain I should be trying to avoid. The wound is a memento of a device designed to control, placed by the same man who is working to save people like me. It's a reminder that he will truly stop at nothing. He shouldn't be allowed to do this. Nobody will stop him if I don't try. And if I don't succeed, who knows what he could think up next.

I realise I am gnashing my teeth at the thought of Charles getting away with his master plan. If not for the sake of his future victims, I have my own reasons. Even if it is already over and I kill him, and take as many people down as possible, then at least I have done something right to redress the balance.

I scurry down the steps and out of the building to find the stillness of the night paining me in a way I cannot describe. The previous time I jumped the wall to save Valentino, it was an intense experience, but now on my second visit, I expected some sort of showdown to take place, or at least some resistance. There is no déjà vu, but unexpected and unwanted ease as the opulent mansion looms before me.

I leg the cobbled path and manicured lawn all the way to the edge of the mansion. I am blind as to what armed personnel lurk or what cameras I need to hide from. Maybe I've already been spotted. The possibility vanishes when moments pass and no security burst out of the mansion to greet me. I am in the clear.

But instead of making my entrance on the ground floor from the patio, I notice a sturdy steel drain pipe behind me and only five metres away. I pull it to make certain it can hold my weight and inch my way up with care. I am in line with the second floor and its massive balcony when I leap from the pipe towards the edge of the balcony's railing and grab a hold of a balustrade. Thankfully the thick wrought iron is strong enough to support my weight. I pull myself over with ease and compose myself to expect anything when I enter through the doors and into Charles's home.

With my weapon out and its safety off, I carefully push down on the lever and am lucky the door is unlocked. The massive hallway is overwhelming. If there are cameras nestled in nooks pointing to my position, the game could well be over.

But I wait three minutes for a violent response. None is forthcoming, and the closed doors to bedrooms and studies and any other superfluous room one might need from a gargantuan property pose a feeling of entrapment. If I had the time, I would check them all and clear each one of any undesirables. But this would generate unnecessary noise on the parquet floors and take time I cannot spare.

I creep my way down to the room at the end with its door closed and a strip of light peeking underneath. It's the only room with its lights on. It must be the main study. With each tentative step I take, my attention diverts from my destination.

What grips me beyond any concern for my safety are the large glass enclosures spaced perfectly along the hallway. I stop at each one, as I am close enough to make out their contents and read their inscriptions with the scarce light. Encased in glass is the history of warfare comprised of peculiar antique weaponry from among the ages, complete with its description and the significance of its technological innovation in human cruelty. There is an early adze with its stone head in the shape of a crude axe attached to an antler horn sleeve. Across from it is a gold ceremonial dagger from Sumeria beside an Assyrian bow and arrows. After a collection of Egyptian short swords, there is a Greek hoplite spear with a Corinthian helmet opposite a Roman gladius decorated with a gold-and-silver scabbard. After Viking axes, a Chinese mace is eloquently decorated with an Ottoman Gurz facing a Japanese katana and a beautiful Aikuchi. There are European staff weapons for maiming. A Halberd and Bardiche with a vicious Morning Star have me in awe, and I am only halfway to the study.

I fail to appreciate Charles's interest in military warfare, as even his ethos of racial purity is curtailed by his respect for a different culture's weaponry. Primitive Aztec weapons and Indian and Sri Lankan Talwars and scimitars precede stilettos and other Renaissance assassin's tools before muskets and firearms are the last weapons before I reach the study door. The exhibition of death tells me more about Charles's beliefs. Did he ever care about *saving* human lives? Did he ever set out to cure them and take their best interests to heart? Or did he always hold a morbid fascination with death? Did these artefacts motivate him to design his ultimate creation, or was the death of his wife the final spur?

Standing just outside the door, I have no way of telling what is beyond the mahogany separating me from the unknown. Without the safety of up-to-date intel on where Charles is and any other relevant facts, I would usually retreat to think this through.

But I don't, and not even checking to see if it is locked, I follow through with a powerful front kick near the lever that destroys the door. It swings wildly on its hinges, and I almost expect it to come off completely, but it doesn't.

Charles is seated, on the phone and waiting as if he expected me. I am surprised that he is relaxed even after the eruption of noise. He is behind a grand desk with large bookcases from floor to ceiling with voluminous medical journals on each side. The room is noticeably hotter than in the hallway. The air is stale and stuffy, and reminds me of that fateful night Fitzgerald and I sat tracking our mark before he died.

'I'll have to call you back,' he says calmly to the person on the other end before hanging up. He gives himself a measured moment before he speaks. 'I'd like to say I'm surprised to see you.'

'Tell me why I shouldn't blow your head off right now,' I say with calmed fury.

'Because if you decide to go down that route, you'll find yourself being pursued by so many *more* parties out to hunt you down and kill you that you won't make it two blocks from here. It's a shame that you've been able to thwart my efforts thus far and not realised the clear and thoroughly magnanimous accomplishments already achieved.' He tenses and a strain of anger in his voice is detectable. 'We are on the verge of creating something great. This will change the world as we know it. Public spending on the military will be next to zero and will be better spent on greater concerns. And to have that all *fucked up* by a little, petulant renegade bent on revenge, who is completely out of his league and without the whole facts, is *ridiculous!*'

Even with a gun loaded, cocked, and aimed at him by someone bound to pull the trigger, he has the nerve to build up rage and let fly with it. I have to confirm that *I* am holding the weapon. But he is adamant on continuing, all the while increasing his anger and shouting.

'Can you imagine a world without the need for a standing military? A country as great as ours that can achieve the best possible outcome for the world and stop violence completely? The ramifications are so numerous and so beneficial that it can save this world from itself. If this had been introduced years ago, products like you would never have been conceived. We wouldn't have needed your services, and it would've saved the military from unnecessary deaths and the need to experience the horror of war. But you want to *fuck* it all up.'

'Last time I checked, people don't deserve to be tortured. You think you are above the responsibilities of a doctor to his patients. But they weren't even your patients. They were bought from a gangster. He gave up the junkies hooked on his product to be experimented on when they ran out of money. Well, that's finished now because your partner in crime has holes in him that can't be fixed and your private force is in little pieces,' I seethe.

'Varetti was going to get his!' Charles exclaims. 'When I finished perfecting the formula, he was going to be disposed of when his services were no longer required. Hell, we were probably going to use your services. The only reason he was engaged was because our government didn't want to get their hands dirty. They've been burned too many times before.'

Charles subsides into a calm that unbalances me. Why is he not afraid that I will kill him? Does his narcissism extend so far that he thinks he's invincible? I give away my unease with a squint of suspicion.

'It doesn't matter. It all ends here,' I declare.

'Is that really what you believe?' he sighs.

'Well, I am holding the gun and about to fire a bullet at you. Unless it's made of chocolate, I don't think you will survive it.'

Charles smiles to let on that he is in charge. But his smug expression holds just a tiny amount of doubt.

I hear footsteps behind me in the hallway. They are heavy and distinct. I don't care at first until I realise they are uneven. They are uneven enough to distinguish that their owner has come across a misfortune. The horror I feel is indisputable as I catch my breath from the reality of knowing whose imbalanced gait it is. The *clop-clip* and pause before another *clop-clip* of wooden soles on the hardwood floor fills me with enough dread to want to confirm what I already know and have to face.

The sounds stop, giving me the cue to turn and see Lloyd casually leaning against the doorway. His smirk predestines my downfall.

'You *fucking* bastard,' I mutter, perplexed as ever as to why he is here. I've been wrong all along. Curious George was *not* the man who sold me out. It was my own handler. His demeanour puts me into an internal rage I cannot express because he is aiming a pistol at me.

'Surprised to see me?'

'Why? Why are you caught up with this dickhead? Are you as twisted as him?'

Lloyd blurts out with a laugh. 'No…not at all. My reasons are far simpler. I can't say I am against the good doctor. He is an innovator and a groundbreaker in his field. All he is trying to do is make the world a safer place.'

He lowers his weapon to his side and as soon as he does, I raise mine, aiming it at his bloated head.

'Put the gun down,' he says, calmly.

'How do you know I won't shoot?'

'Because being your handler, I can smooth this whole mess over and make you whole. You'll be able to work again, even for the same fee as before despite being *tarnished*.' I am offended at his gesture. 'You know you weren't the only contractor at the agency that had an almost perfect record,' he spits with disdain.

But he doesn't need to continue for me to know where this is going. 'So let me guess. You're that jealous of my success that you had to purposely go out and sabotage me?'

'Not exactly. Why would I sabotage you when I get a nice cut from your contracts? No. I wanted total control. Enough to forge contract papers for the last two jobs and see you scamper off like a good errand boy and kill the people we wanted you to kill. Before your perfection had swept the board off their feet, it is hard to believe that *I* was the best they had ever seen. I had an unblemished record of high-profile kills. *I* commanded record fees. And then…then I got capped in the knee while on a consulting mission.

'I was advising one General Luis Lopez. Do you remember him? Because I cannot forget. It was a Dragunov sniper's bullet to be exact. A bullet that hit him, exited, splintered, and deflected a piece of shrapnel into my knee, shattering the patella and ending my career in an instant.

'My career was cut short. After I recovered, I promised myself I would hunt down whoever did this and end his life. When I gained access to your military file, I had to take the chance and investigate further to see if you were my man. Do you know how much money I spent bribing up the chain of command to get my hands on your operational record? I almost went broke. I've been keeping up with your charade of identities for a long time now…'

The revelation is stunning. Was the government hedging their bets on a communist? They must have. There's no reason for him to lie. Otherwise, he was unknowingly baiting the general to us, and he was used, as were we up on that rooftop. But *he* was more expendable than me.

I thought I would've recognised and remembered Lloyd on that rooftop with Fitzgerald. I guess I was more interested in the target. The years haven't been kind to Lloyd. Apart from the general in that hotel room, I can remember that all of the men in the room were fit and able-bodied. But I feel no remorse that a grown man cannot forgive someone when he chose to play the game. He took on those risks, and the risks were high. He fails to see he should be grateful for surviving, even if I helped him into retirement from active service. He shouldn't have wasted his time and money to avenge unlucky happenings. Instead, he should have been angry with his superiors.

'But first we had to take a guarantee,' he says, tapping the back of his head.

'So you bugged me. Thought it would've been a little smaller than that?' I goad.

'You're an imbecile!' Charles exclaims. 'That wasn't just a bug. If it were, you wouldn't have known, just like the other one. No, it was something greater. It could've incapacitated you anytime and anywhere with a push of a button. It would send a small electrical pulse through your spine, knocking you out in an instant.'

That must've been what caused me to fall just before I cut it out. 'Well, you should've thought about making it smaller, dickhead.'

'A prototype. The next one will be better.'

'There won't be a next one.'

'You really are that naïve to understand this is a fight you shouldn't have picked. You're probably curious as to why I can be so calm with you holding that gun in your hand, pointing it at Lloyd and itching to pull the trigger.' Charles read my mind as he grins. 'For the past few minutes you've been here, I've been pumping gas into the room—the airborne-perfected agent of Aggredisol—that will have surely taken effect to make you harmless enough that you cannot possibly pull that trigger in anger. By now the chemical airborne agent would've coursed through your bloodstream via your lungs and then up to your brain, where it desensitises your emotional output for violence and destruction. We can still have a heated argument, but you *cannot* and *will not* pull that trigger.'

Charles's comments force me to stop and think. If he is right, I am doomed.

'Now all that's left to do is for Charles to press the distress button on his desk for the handful of gasmask-wearing soldiers left to come and take you away to be disposed of,' Lloyd says.

I am truly fucked. And I have nowhere to go. Another trap! Perspiration trickles down my face. No wonder they are so relaxed.

I start running through every possible scenario. What if this is just a trick? A clever little scam from Charles and Lloyd to steer them from the inevitable. What if there is no gas? What if it is one big lie and I die by not testing the simplest of hypotheses?

I raise my gun at Lloyd and pull the trigger. The bullet zips through the thick air and into his forehead, piercing his skull. The flash of blood I expected to see littering the doorframe doesn't come as he slumps to the ground, and only then does vital fluid and brain matter seep out. When he drops I realise there is no exit wound. The bullet rattled inside his skull tearing up his brain matter.

Instantly, I picture myself on the run. I just shot my handler and I have no evidence to justify it. The agency will be after me with everything they have to bring restore order. Their current greatest asset has gone crazy and needs to be put down.

Charles gushes from my unexpected capability. I turn to witness a wide-eyed state of shock on his face.

'How? Why?' he cries in disbelief. 'That gas has been tested on terrorists, criminals, and all kinds of violent humans.'

I realise what sets me apart from his experiments and from everyone else. 'You forgot the most important element a person with my experience needs to be successful. You need to be comfortable enough to believe what you do is just a job; that's all. You need to be able to detach yourself from your emotions. Rage, hate, and spite are not needed to kill another human.'

He shakes his head. Over time my emotions have gently imploded with every kill and every death—that part of my psyche, where emotional rage for revenge has been whittled away into annihilation. Even I am surprised I can kill for my own survival without thinking or feeling. I am…a psychopath.

I never knew I was that much of a monster.

Charles is close to tears. Even if he pushes the distress button under his desk to call the guards, they will be too late. He falls with resignation into his expensive executive leather chair.

I set upon him.

'We could've been on the verge of world peace.'

'Taking someone's will to fight is not world peace,' I retort.

But Charles's impotent sigh, as if scolded by a teacher, is a faint admission that his ends cannot justify his means by killing the innocent.

His downward stare is interrupted by the sound of my Glock's metal slide on his polished, wooden desk. I place the gun on the table, only because I know he wants to have another chance of saving himself. I walk beyond the desk to the extravagant bookcase against the wall, silently removing the Ka-Bar knife from its sheath under my jumper.

I hear the gun lift from the desk but before Charles can turn, I cup his mouth with my left hand and draw him violently towards me, forcing him to drop the gun.

'The one responsible for this madness needs to be dealt with,' I whisper.

Ignoring his desperate, muffled cries, I plunge the knife horizontally into the side of his neck. His cries turn to whimpers from the pain. His eyes roll into his head as he begins to lose consciousness. I saw forward and effortlessly sever his windpipe and carotid arteries. Nothing can save Charles from his quick descent into the afterlife.

I feel nothing. Absolutely nothing. It is the complete antithesis to how I felt during the drive over here. After being able to kill Lloyd because of his betrayal, I know even if I have the anger to murder, I can stifle that desire as if it is just another contract. I wonder about Charles and his inability to do the same. He picked up the gun from his desk. Did he not try and turn it on me and pull the trigger? Was his own invention going to stop him? Is he wearing some sort of filter that would stop its effects? I will never know.

As his body drops, I hear a bang. A searing pain strikes the right side of my abdomen.

I look down. A gunshot wound?

I finger the bullet hole in my side, just below my rib. The pain wakes me a little as I dip into shock. Who could possibly be left to inflict this sort of harm?

Could it be Valentino? Could he have pieced together the puzzle that I murdered his father and made it out here? Surely he isn't that smart. The balance of power has tipped again in his direction tonight. Hillbay's underworld is now his.

A second bullet explodes and shaves a piece of my bicep before entering my chest. My laboured breathing means the bullet is ravaging my lungs and causing great internal bleeding. It saps enough energy from me that I have to drop the bloodied knife.

I sway, drunk with pain, and lose my balance. Was Charles able to press the distress button?

I think I purposely collapse on my left knee, although I'm not sure if it wasn't pure luck, just so I can see my assailant. The agency? Curious George? Lloyd coming back from the dead? I have so many theories to entertain I can almost smile.

As I fall beside Charles, my eyes widen at the sight of my shooter.

It all makes perfect sense now. The person behind the door when I was captured. The one Charles was talking to. It wasn't Lloyd, or even Varetti. It was someone who has just as much motivation as Charles himself. My killer has the same, if not more, reason for revenge and to apply her brilliant mind to his project: his daughter.

I have to wonder. Was it all planned? Did they use rubber bullets to clip my calf when I was at their mercy on the wall during my escape? They couldn't have been that bad a shot. The smack behind the ear during sex? She's a man-eater; I should have realised. I should have seen it coming. Was the slap a test to see how good her surgery skills were? Was my escape all planned, too? Maybe even luring Varetti to hunt me down when I had the bug out? All schemed by a doctor just as brilliant and as sick as her father.

It all makes sense. The text message to go to the Mad Clowns clubhouse…Our first meeting…She was there to check up on me before I took out Luigi…I was her insurance policy against Valentino she cashed in. There are too many coincidences.

It is something I will take to my resting place…That Jessica, who I first thought was so innocent, was far more dangerous than she ever appeared.

ABOUT THE AUTHOR

Alexander Lycur is the proud author of *The Mark*, his debut novel, available on Amazon as a paperback or as a Kindle title.